Maggie sat with h... ease her tension, to think, but even after ..... recuperation her head still ached uncomfortably, a constant reminder that the ordeal she'd been through had taken everything out of her. And now worry kept her off balance. Opportunity to search for the arrest warrant or for her gun hadn't presented itself. With each passing hour she became more certain Will must have found them and knew exactly who she was. So why didn't he pack up and leave?

An open book in her hands, she tried to ignore him working at his potbellied stove. She didn't want to notice the little things about him: eyes that twinkled when he allowed himself to smile, or his hands, large and capable, when they cut up potatoes, when they tended the fire, when they checked her ankle each day and rewrapped it. It took Herculean effort to remember those same hands had stabbed a pretty young girl to death.

Maggie leaned against the back of the chair with a sigh, uncomfortably aware of the strange sense of uneasiness growing between them. There was something damnably compelling about him, and she couldn't ignore it.

She swallowed and tried again to read, but it was no use. "What are you cooking over there? It looks like enough to feed an army."

He turned, and his eyes flashed with tension as though aware she'd been watching him. His expression softened. "I've got six hungry dogs outside. Sled dogs expend a lot of energy, so they need a lot of food. I try to get a week's worth of cooking done all at once."

She rested back against the pillows on the chair, and he turned back to his cooking. After a while the images around her began to blur, and her eyelids grew heavy. If she closed her eyes and emptied her mind for a minute or two, she'd better be able to deal with him, with her plight. Her eyes blinked, once, twice, and then they stayed closed.

Vaguely she remembered him lifting her. On the edge of sleep she breathed in his scent—the wood smoke, the meat he was cooking—as he carried her to his bed. She forgot all about searching his cabin for her gun and the warrant. He laid a blanket over her, and she thought she mumbled, "Thanks," but wasn't sure.

A Cry From the Cold

Ann Merritt

~~~

Highland Press Publishing

A Cry From the Cold

For information, please contact
Highland Press Publishing,
PO Box 2292, High Springs, FL 32655.
www.highlandpress.org

ISBN: 978-0-9833960-1-7

HIGHLAND PRESS PUBLISHING

Circles of Gold

To my family—my wonderful husband, Mac,
My sons, Bobby & Scott—I'm so proud of you.
My beautiful daughters-in-law, Beth & Stephanie
My grandchildren, Allie, Caroline, Sarah, Parker, & Will—each
one special in his own way.

Patty Howell, Senior Editor

Chapter One

Inside the log cabin a dog growled, low and menacing. Seated at his worktable, Will Connor stopped drawing and cocked his head, listening to the wind moan across the mountain, a lonesome sound. Gradually, he became aware of another noise coming with the wind—one unexpected and unwanted.

It grew louder. Moments passed, and he was certain; the drone belonged to a single-engine airplane. The plane flew low over the frozen Yukon River between the mountain ridges, like it was looking for a place to land. A chill ran down Will's spine. The nearest town, Circle City, was over a hundred miles away. If the plane was flying mail from Fairbanks to Circle City, it was way off course.

He stood, forgetting the sketches piled on his lap. They tumbled onto his Husky's back. Hilde shook, scattering them on the floor. Will leaned across the table and rubbed the ice-crusted glass of the cabin's solitary window. He strained to see out.

After a moment he straightened and raked four fingers through hair that hung long and ragged over the collar of his flannel shirt.

On a clear day, Will loved flying over Alaska's spectacular mountain ranges, rivers, and lakes, and miles upon miles of barren tundra. But only a greenhorn or a fool would take to the air when the skies were socked in with snow-laden clouds—a fool or someone hell-bent on a mission.

The drone of the plane's engine receded. Will held his breath. When the pilot circled back, he balled his fingers, refraining from slamming a fist onto the table.

Hilde joined the she-wolf Lucy in front of the door. Will glanced at the dogs, and relaxed his mouth. These two dogs were his only family. Both his 'girls' growled, low and worryingly.

He waved a hand at the dogs, "Quiet, you two," and returned his gaze to the window. "Let me listen." But he'd already heard too much. Even after all these years of living in secret, his stomach knotted with fear. A former U.S. Navy Air Corps pilot, he was now an Alaskan adventurer, a bush pilot, and he ferried people from village to village, on safaris, often flying where no one else would go, usually carrying a load of mail.

"Damn," he hissed between tight lips.

He grabbed his fur-lined parka from behind the door and his field glasses from a coffee table littered with sketches and books, then unbolted the door. A blast of arctic air slammed his face, and he shut the door, guessing the outside temperature must be closing in on -15°. The wind made it feel colder.

Wistfully, he glanced around for the beaver-skin hat he'd made—the one he'd misplaced yesterday. He gave up, and slipped on a pair of calf-high boots without lacing them, then lifted his hood over his head and hurried outside.

He kept close to the house, skirting the eaves-high stack of wood, and searched the sky for the aircraft. The plane was coming from downriver and the engine sounded rough. Something might be wrong with it, but he couldn't be sure.

With binoculars he spotted the plane when it popped out between the clouds for a few seconds, a red spot maybe a mile away. He examined it, looking for landing skis before it disappeared again in the snow and clouds. If the pilot intended to land here, he'd have to set down on the frozen river or along a short stretch of bank free of trees. The river was best. And skis were essential.

Because of the low clouds, he didn't think he saw any skis. So whoever the pilot was couldn't be planning on landing. He breathed easier. Maybe some over-zealous fool making a reconnaissance flight, or who'd lost his way, but even a fool should have skis on his plane.

If Will's cabin had been spotted, he could pack up and be out of here in less than half an hour. Not what he wanted to do, but he'd done it before. He'd learned not to become too attached anywhere. But he did like this place.

Here, everyone knew him as Will Connor. Not a bad name, just not his real name.

Lured by a better view, he laced his boots and trekked up the mountainside where, in places, snow mounded up to his thighs. Halfway to the ridge, he crouched low beside a tall spruce and searched the sky. The wind moaned through the trees, bending their tops. Every now and then a clump of snow fell on his head and reminded him of his misplaced hat.

From the ridge, he could barely make out his cabin. Only the thin smoke stream twisting its way through the treetops gave evidence someone lived inside, that and the cleaned window and trampled path to the front door. How had the pilot spotted it unless he had first-hand knowledge of where to look? The question made him swallow uncomfortably. Even his carefully chosen friends didn't know his secret.

The plane was hidden in the clouds. Will followed the sound as it faded into the distance. When he no longer heard it, his mouth set into a grim smile. Maybe his luck still held. Maybe.

For thirteen years he'd been living on borrowed time. One day his luck would run out, and he would die. Was today that day? Squatted beneath a Sitka spruce, where he couldn't be spotted from above, he watched and listened. Even under the trees the wind was strong. It pushed the hood from his head and tugged his scarf, slapping it against him with a snap. The dogs moved through the deep snow with accustomed ease, tails wagging, noses close to the ground. Occasionally, one would lift her head to the sound in the sky.

Over his left shoulder, Will heard the plane's engine again, rougher than before and coming steadily down river toward him. It flew even lower this time, certainly looking for a place to land. Binoculars weren't necessary to pick up the plane's bright red color, then the landing skis. With a hiss he clamped his jaw and looked away. The uneven engine sound, coughing almost, drew his attention back to the small aircraft. It flew much too close to the side of the mountain for safety, like the wind was having its way with it.

Suddenly, the plane's engine quit. Will wasn't sure he'd heard right. Through the snowflakes the faint outline of the plane moving downriver was visible, but up front where there should have been the humming of the engine, he heard only the howling of the wind. Will's stomach churned with the fear he knew must be surging through the pilot's veins. Perhaps the carburetor had iced over or a fuel line had frozen. Not that it mattered what caused the failure. It had failed and unless the pilot got that engine started in the next second or two, the plane was going down.

Instinctively, Will searched the ground ahead of the plane where it could set down on the river, but the pilot made a fatal error when he overshot the thin strip along the banks where the river was wide and flat and mostly frozen. Where Will had landed. But even knowing the place as well as he did, it wasn't an easy landing.

Where the plane now flew, the riverbanks were almost nonexistent, far too narrow for a plane to land. Choosing to land farther downstream wasn't an option. At that point the river was riddled with fallen trees that under the snow undulated in sharp rises and falls that would wreak havoc to the belly of any plane, skis or not. The slopes on either side of the river were a possibility. On the west side of the mountain, where Will had built his cabin, the angle rose too steeply even for a dogsled to maneuver, not to mention for a plane to land; but on the east side, for a short stretch the grade was more gradual. If the pilot threaded through the many trees on the far bank, he might survive the landing. But with the wind throwing the biplane toward the steep side of the mountain, Will didn't like the odds.

Rising to his full six-foot three-inches, Will felt the pilot's helplessness deep in his gut. His fingers twitched in vain for a phantom joystick to bring the plane under control. He reached for the imagined ignition then balled his hands into tight fists at his sides. Alaska was a harsh and inhospitable place to live, even more so to fly in.

He waited with the knowledge that if by some miracle, the wind and the limited visibility failed to drive the occupants of the plane into the mountainside and certain death, the icy cold awaited them on the ground—waiting to kill.

Will had witnessed death in the Alaskan wilds. Even before he came here, he'd been a part of a death. The memory of when he'd run from Chicago shivered through his mind like an unexpected slap in the face. He shook his head, annoyed he'd drifted there, and pressed the heels of his hands against his temples, hard. The memory came anyway, the bewildering confusion, the absolute fear. It shuddered through him like an electrical shock, only cold and chilling, like the wind that gusted across his mountain. The icy chill seeped deep into the marrow of his soul. He'd been out in the cold for almost half his life.

Out of sight, he knew the plane was going to crash. He breathed hard in anticipation of the impact. Still, the distant snapping of treetops and branches accompanied by the screech of tortured metal, didn't stop the shudder that ran through him. He doubled over. "Jesus . . ."

After a few moments, he straightened and headed for the cabin. The plane had gone down somewhere upriver, toward Circle City. From the sound of it, the craft couldn't have gotten too far. Then again, snow, clouds, and mountains distorted sound.

The most likely scenario was that the impact had slammed the pilot and anyone else into the instrument panel, killing them instantly. If the pilot had managed to make it ten miles downriver where the trees were thinner, there was a slim chance of survival. A couple of landing places were closer to Circle City. But the plane probably hadn't gotten that far.

Will walked toward his cabin, deep in thought. He didn't own a satellite phone, never wanted one, never wanted the contact, but for emergencies he had a two-way radio. Unfortunately, it was busted. Only his friend Gene Pryor knew his frequency, and Gene only used it in the summertime when Will was needed in Fairbanks to fly clients. Radio reception here was fickle, at best. Even if it had worked, his gut told him not to make contact with Fairbanks.

Hilde came up beside him, nuzzling his hand as if she sensed his unease. Either the plane was miles off course or the pilot had learned where he was hiding and had come to arrest him. Prudently, he should assume the occupants were looking for him and remain in the relative warmth of his cabin.

He had to make a choice. Go out into the teeth of the blizzard to the crash site and rescue any survivors and in so doing expose himself, or forget he'd witnessed the crash and let Alaska's winter take care of them.

The cabin was dark and still inside. He entered, leaving his dogs outside. Hand still on the latch, he arched his head back until it touched the thick pine of the door. He rubbed a tight muscle in his neck and clenched his jaw.

If he had any chance of rescuing anyone, there was no time to waste. He needed his ax and some rope for maneuvering down a cliff if necessary, and warm blankets. And he needed to find his fur hat.

His backpack was mostly packed—he kept it that way, knowing he might have to move on at any time. He took the pack from a large storage box and lifted his snowshoes from the wall peg beside the door. He decided the sled would be more trouble than it was worth. Unless he missed his guess, he'd have to cross the river, and though the thick ice would hold the sled, the incline on his side of the mountain was too steep for the dogs to pull it.

He eyed a small army surplus tent. No. If he had to stay the night, he'd sleep in the shelter of the downed plane, but he hoped it didn't come to that. The temperature would drop to between twenty-five or thirty below zero. Thinking how cold it would be, he added his down sleeping bag to the load. Then he looked for his hat, and found it on his drawing table under some drawings. He hefted the pack, judged it to weigh a comfortable seventy pounds, and headed for the door. At the threshold he looked back at his place. Small and isolated, it was snug and warm. A hiding place that kept the authorities from finding him, he'd hate to give it up.

Shouldering his pack, he picked up his rifle, and stepped into the cold. Outside, he strapped on his snowshoes then glanced up into the bleak, low-hung sky and whistled for his dogs. He dreaded the search.

Chapter Two

The black-tie fundraiser was still in full swing shortly after eleven when Senator Hilton Raine took his leave. Entering his car, he instructed his chauffeur to head to "The Bell and Whistle," a bar in the heart of the city. At the door, the senator was recognized and ushered to a table where several politicians who'd attended the same fundraiser were seated. Moments later the senator was served a dirty martini. He took a swallow and leaned back, relaxing for the first time that evening.

Shortly after two a.m., Hilton's chauffeur pulled up in front of a three-storied Victorian residence in a fashionable neighborhood outside Washington, D.C.

Fourteen years earlier, Hilton's first wife, Mary, selected the large brick house, expecting that their four children would join them there at the end of the spring term. It was not to be. A few months after closing on the house, his oldest daughter was tragically murdered in Hilton's family home in Chicago. The scandal propelled the congressman into the limelight and boosted his sagging campaign for the U.S. Senate to a landslide win.

He'd intended to move his three surviving teenage children to Washington, but when Mary pled that the upheaval would be difficult for everyone, especially her, he'd rethought the issue. Mary's frail health deteriorated frighteningly with the considerable stress of losing her adored daughter. The easiest course was to let Mary stay in Chicago to oversee the children's upbringing when Hilton's senatorial duties kept him in D.C. The children agreed, and Rutland Manor, the antebellum mansion overlooking beautiful Lake Michigan continued to be the place Hilton called home.

"Watch your step, Sir. The snow's made the walkway slick."

Hilton noticed the snow for the first time. Far from sober, clutching the goblet he'd pilfered from the bar, Hilton accepted his chauffeur's hand and allowed the short young man to assist him up the brick steps. He fumbled in his pocket for his keys then handed them to the chauffeur. Newly employed, the chauffeur looked to be just a kid. Hilton couldn't remember the young man's name and didn't care enough to ask.

Hilton had second thoughts about going directly to bed and headed for his study. He helped himself to a nightcap from his stash kept out-of-sight behind a panel and fell asleep in his leather recliner.

The grandfather clock chiming woke him some time later, or was it the telephone? Whatever, he was too inebriated to care. The noise stopped, and he staggered up to bed.

Shortly after eight, the telephone woke him. He glanced at the clock and jerked upright. The sudden movement brought a rush of pain to his head. He closed his eyes, rubbing his forehead. "Celia! Answer that damn phone, will you?"

Celia was his third wife. They'd been married two years, together a year before that while divorcing wife number two. Mary died within a year after their daughter's murder, and Hilton had wanted someone to warm his bed and look after his children. Wife number two, the independently wealthy ex-wife of a powerful business entrepreneur, had been a big mistake. She'd warmed his bed all right, and the bed of several others. She'd not cared an iota about his children.

Celia, from a prominent Philadelphia family that had made their money in railroads, was fifteen years Hilton's junior. Her face was angular and plain, but he'd married her because of her money and pedigree.

He reached for the phone. It stopped ringing, but he picked it up anyway. The line was dead. He cursed his wife for letting him oversleep, then remembered he'd sent her to their Palm Springs home so he could charm the new senator from Arkansas, a petite blonde who'd been assigned to the Armed Services Committee. He'd pulled strings to sit beside her at the fundraiser.

Still irrationally angry with his wife, he stood and stumbled to the bathroom. The Arkansas junior senator hadn't been charmed. In fact the evening had gone poorly. He'd made a strategic blunder not allowing his wife to attend with him. He turned on the shower, warmed it, and stepped inside.

While toweling off, he glanced at the photos on the dresser. His youngest son Matt, dressed in a Dartmouth rugby shirt, smiled broadly at the camera, while Paul, slightly taller than his brother and looking stern, stood with his arm draped over Matt's shoulder. He'd opted for Yale. In a separate frame, Libby's delicate features stared out at him, a teddy bear she'd won at a carnival in her arms and a broad smile spreading her thin lips. Still living in his Chicago home, she'd taken up residence in the garage apartment where his parents once resided. He touched a finger to the image of his youngest daughter's pale face. Of all his children, Libby was the one who loved him the most.

Suddenly remembering Matt's phone call last week, Hilton frowned. Matt was going out of town for a couple of weeks, possibly longer, and hoped when he returned he'd have good news to report. When Hilton probed about the nature of his sudden departure, Matt had been secretive but excited, like he was hatching some sort of plan to his father's liking. Hilton could only think of one thing that would get his son so excited— the capture of his sister's murderer. But after all these years, he didn't have much hope of finding Jamie Donovan.

Back in the bathroom, Hilton wiped the steam from the mirror, took a moment to admire the wealth of white hair that contrasted handsomely with his bronzed skin. Thanks to his Florida home and a sunlamp, his skin retained its tan throughout the year.

He shaved and dressed quickly, choosing a dark blue suit and blue tie with white fleur-de-lis to go with his starched white shirt. A large portrait of Celia hung over the bed. Dressed in a short-sleeved yellow evening gown, the artist had softened the hard angles of her face, given volume to her dark hair, and enhanced her thin figure. But he was already tiring of her. She was spoiled, wanted children—a subject they'd failed to discuss before their nuptials—and held a tight rein on her money.

Hilton hurried outside to his chauffeured car, and heard the phone ringing. He hesitated, decided it was for his wife, and got inside the car. Hopefully, he'd be only twenty minutes late for his breakfast meeting.

* * * *

With no sun, Will guessed it was close to noon. This far north, the November sky didn't light things up very long. He had two, maybe three hours before nightfall.

By the time he'd made the downhill trek to the river's edge, he was sweating. To prevent dehydration, he stopped to drink from the goatskin pouch. Worn beneath his parka, body heat kept the water from freezing. Cupping a hand over his eyes, he scanned the horizon. Visibility hadn't improved with the wind driving the snow in fits and starts.

He hiked south along the river where he thought the plane had gone down. Deep snow made walking rough. Several times he stumbled on crusted crevices of ice and blown debris. Wind and snow assaulted his face. A scarf covered his mouth and nose, but he wished he'd brought goggles. Numbness quickly set into his feet and fingers. He rubbed his hands together, but could do nothing about his feet.

Every few miles he stopped and drank. He saw no sight of the plane or of the trees that had caused the pre-crash racket, but he was afraid to leave the riverbed. Surely the pilot would have followed it, looking for a safe place to land.

This time of year the average plane crashed or was forced down by the weather, resulting in deaths one hundred times more than planes flying in the contiguous states. Snowstorms and gales created havoc. Will knew the risks. He'd been forced down several times, once sustaining a few broken bones.

The yellow Piper "Super Cub" Will flew had been crashed by its former owner. The pilot narrowly escaped with his life, and was anxious to sell. The price had been cheap, but it took Will over a year to save enough money to purchase the new 150 hp Lycoming engine and other parts he needed to put her in working order. He'd christened her *Everhawk*.

She was a "no frills" flying ship with basic navigational tools, including a compass and an "iffy" radio, and a heater that rarely worked. He seldom flew in winter, and then only when conditions were good. Even in summer, landing was an adventure. Prudently, last month he bedded his plane down for the winter, securing it in relative obscurity outside Fairbanks. He made his return trip from Fairbanks with supplies by sled.

No aviation school taught how to fly *in* snow. However, all pilots were required to be proficient and certified in Visual

Flight Rules or VFR and know weather minimums. Many planes carried emergency locator transmitters (ELT), but from personal experience Will knew even if you had ELT, in Alaska it rarely worked as intended, since only sixty-percent of Alaska was covered by radar.

When the red plane didn't arrive at its scheduled destination someone would come looking, but he doubted anyone would come until the gale-force winds and snow let up, which could be several days or longer. If the plane's occupants were dead, he'd return to his cabin, pack up his sled, and be long gone before anyone came.

He pushed aside thoughts the occupants had targeted him and were heading to his cabin. Instead, he concentrated on crossing the river.

Just as daylight faded, his dogs located the site about 200 yards up the mountainside. Despite the snow coating, the red made it visible though if he hadn't been looking, he might have missed it. Another few hours and the plane would be entirely hidden from view. The Cessna 150 lay half on its side with a wing wrapped up on a tree. A relatively viceless plane, its light weight, large wing area, and low-crosswind capability made it sensitive to turbulence, which could account for why the pilot was unable to maneuver out of the river valley winds. Then again, Will compressed his lips into a hard line, something *had* caused the engine to fail.

He didn't see any indications of life. After calling out with no response, he removed his snowshoes to climb the steep slope. Both wings were badly mangled and the skis were crushed, but amazingly the metal fuselage remained pretty much in tact. A good sign someone might have survived, but the closer he got, the more his stomach began to quiver. Something was disturbingly familiar about the Cessna.

A hundred yards away, he stopped and gave the wreck a long look. *Hell*, he groaned. A branch had slammed through the cockpit, a branch thick enough to shear through the windshield like a guillotine. He walked the last steps knowing death would greet him.

He tried the door handle—jammed. He cleared the snow from a spot on the door's window, looked through with his flashlight, and found what he expected. Two people, either unconscious or dead.

Even with his ax it took a long time to wrench the door open. He leaned inside. The pilot, coated in snow and sprawled against the instrument panel with his seat restraint still attached, had a broken neck. Will lifted the dead pilot's head by his frozen hair and stared into his face.

Jack Ricks. "Hell," he hissed. *Damn it, buddy, you knew better than to fly in these conditions.* Will cupped both hands over his face and sagged to his knees. Of all people, an experienced pilot like Jack Ricks should have known the winds between those two peaks could sabotage his plane. He knew to turn back at the first sign of the storm. What made him take the chance? Too many pilots over-trusted their skills. Was that the case here? Too often the mistake was a fatal one. It only took one small thing, and a plane could go down. Jack knew that.

Will scrubbed the back of his hand over his burning eyes. Jack, a partner in Will's air transport company, was one of the few people he called friend. An error of judgment by a greenhorn pilot unfamiliar with winter flying conditions, Will could understand, but Jack had flown in Alaska as long as he had—longer. Jack Ricks and their partner Gene Pryor had flown with Will in Desert Storm when they'd dreamed together of the airline company they'd start in Alaska at the war's end. Jack knew about Alaska's sudden and unpredictable storms, the sheering winds, the lack of visibility, and certainly Jack knew the limitations of his Cessna like Will knew every nut and bolt of his Super Cub.

Had his equipment failed, disorienting him, even before the engine quit? Whatever had caused the plane to go down, it had cost Jack Ricks his life. Will stared at Jack's face, so white and still in death, and thought of Jack's wife who was expecting their second child. Will lifted his jaw and railed to the Heavens, pounding his fist on the twisted fuselage that had become Jack's tomb. Anguish depleted, he shrugged out of his bulky pack, dropped it to the snow, and crawled over Jack's body to determine if his passenger had suffered the same fate.

Will clasped the other man's wrist and found no pulse.

He lifted the dead man's head, and stared into sightless eyes. Suddenly, as though some unknown hand struck a blow to his chest, he couldn't breathe. Detective Matthew Raine of the Chicago Police Department, not the pudgy kid Will had once known, but a grown man—a cop. For several stunned moments Will gaped at Matt's lifeless body, feeling his own heartbeat race in his chest.

They'd found him.

He swore and squeezed his eyes shut. In his mind's eye Ellen rose before him, his Ellen, the love of his life. The image of her reclining on the sofa with the corsage of white roses he'd sent her pinned onto her pink party dress couldn't be banished. Nor could he cast out the sight of the blood, *her* blood splattered everywhere. Horror rose from his gut like putrid bile and washed through him like it had that night, like it did in the nightmares that had plagued his nights ever since. He gagged and reeled backward, clasping his hands behind his neck, pressing his forearms against the sudden pounding in his head.

Not that he believed Hilton Raine would ever give up the search, but seeing Matt here in what Will thought was his safe haven was proof that Hilton's long tentacles reached even to the remote wilderness of Alaska. All the more stunning, because so many years had passed—thirteen long, damn years he'd been running from them.

A part of him wanted to pound Matt Raine's dead body into a bloody pulp, and a part wanted to shake the life back into him so he could ask him why. Why? Why?

The pressures of years of running and hiding roiled inside him like boiling lava, building until he thought he might erupt. He quaked from the rush of his torment. One day they'd catch him and it would be all over. No more running, no more betrayals to endure, no more lost love to mourn.

God! How, after all these years, had they tracked him down? Shaking his head, he slowly pulled himself back from the abyss of memory. How had he given himself away?

Once, a long time ago, he'd considered Matt and his older brother Paul friends. Not now. Now he couldn't say he was sorry to see him dead. With an anguished groan, and still shaking he shoved himself away from Matt's body.

Since Matt was here, others couldn't be far behind. Over the years since he'd run from Chicago, he'd followed the lives of Ellen's father and her siblings as much as he could. They were a prosperous and powerful family often written up in the news and on the Internet. Hilton was an important senator whose name recently had been mentioned as a possible vice-presidential candidate.

Matt's sister Libby was occasionally mentioned in the gossip columns, too, when attending some social affair or touring this country or that with her father or her brother, Paul, a well-known defense lawyer for the Hollywood rich and famous.

Matt might have caused the wound inside Will to break open again, but, he reminded himself with solemn resolve, he wasn't a naïve boy any longer. When Senator Raine faced him this time, and sooner or later he would, he wouldn't be facing a seventeen-year-old kid—he would be facing a man.

Will checked the pockets of the dead men for identification papers. Both carried wallets. After confirming Matt's ID, he stuffed the papers of both men into his parka's pocket and replaced the wallets. Nothing he could do for either of them now. He'd leave the bodies in the plane until the weather let up.

As he crawled backward to exit the plane, the beam of his flashlight bounced off something on the cockpit floor. Closer inspection revealed a gun wedged up under the seat. Will picked it up. Was it Matt's or Jack's? Both had plausible reasons for carrying. Checking, he found it loaded.

If the authorities weren't at his cabin ahead of him, he'd try to contact Gene Pryor on his two-way radio so Gene could let Nancy know what happened to her husband. Gene wouldn't betray Will, nor would have Jack, though admittedly, seeing Jack with Matt Raine and so close to his place gave him pause. Then he remembered the busted radio, and his plan to pick up a part during his next trip to Circle City.

Will examined the gun again in the waning light, then stuffed it and the bullets into a pocket of his pack. Had Jack gone off course with Matt's gun pointed at his head? It would explain why Jack might ignore the worrisome weather conditions. Or had the crash simply been a matter of engine failure?

When weather permitted, Will would come back for his friend's body. The risk was one he'd have to take. Soon as Jack's body was delivered to a place where Gene could pick it up, Will would have to move on to begin another life. How depressing! He was tired of running.

At the cockpit doorway, Will stopped and looked back. One of the seats had been removed from the four-seater Cessna. Maybe Jack had taken it out to accommodate the mail he was transporting. Perhaps Matt had had other ideas that Jack didn't know about. The point was moot. They'd discovered Will's whereabouts and he couldn't risk staying at his cabin. He shined his flashlight over the duffels of mail, a couple boxes, and other paraphernalia shaken loose in the crash and piled against the seats, confirming Jack's destination.

A low groaning jerked his head toward the rear of the plane. Will searched the dark interior, but found nothing. *Still and soundless as death.* He exited the plane. It must have been the wind he heard. He was sorry two men had died, but truthfully he felt a measure of relief about Matt. Who else knew Matt's plans? *Probably the whole Chicago PD, and Hilton Raine, too,* he scoffed, his mouth tight.

For now, the bodies would be safe. And at the rate the snow was coming down, he figured the plane would be invisible soon, unless the winds kept the fuselage swept. Either way, once the snow quit, the skies would be full of search planes. Maybe a search party would find Jack before Will returned for his friend's body.

What difference did it make now? Either way, Will had to move on. Hopefully the authorities wouldn't find his plane where he'd wintered it before he could get there. But to travel across Alaska's wilderness in winter looking for a place to hole up until he could get to his plane wasn't a pleasant thought. But he'd do what it took to survive.

He was shouldering his pack when he heard the sound again. Barely audible over the wind, he couldn't be sure he'd heard it at all. He shot a glance at his dogs to see if they'd picked up on an animal nearby then fixed his gaze on the plane. Slowly, he let the pack slip from his back and fished out the flashlight. He opened the plane's door.

"Help me . . ."

The entreaty was weak, but Will had no doubt someone was still alive. The two men he'd checked were certainly dead.

Perhaps someone had been riding in the back with that jumble of mail and equipment and was now hidden from view.

He wedged his way through the door over Jack's body. The flashlight offered limited visibility in the black interior of the cockpit.

"Hello. Anyone in here?"

"Here . . ."

Swinging the flashlight, he saw a hand reach out from behind a duffle. At first that was all he could see. He crawled halfway into the plane and took the hand into his. "Hello there."

Through the thickness of the wool glove, he found the hand to be surprisingly small. *A child?* He directed the light down to the face. Not a child, a woman, her face awash in blood. At the sight of all that blood, he sagged back to his heels, and for one hellish instant, he thought he was seeing Ellen all over again.

"Sweet Jesus . . ." he breathed and rubbed his hand over his mouth.

Chapter Three

Covered with a thin, moth-eaten wool blanket, woefully inadequate to keep a person warm in these temperatures, she lay on the floor behind the seats. Her parka hood had slipped to her shoulders exposing soft red hair and a nasty cut on her forehead, oozing a lot of blood. Her skin was deathly white, and her blue-tinged lips bled where her teeth had bitten through.

Everything inside the fuselage was snow coated. The tree limb had ripped off most of the windshield, and the wind blowing through the gaping hole was filling the plane with snow and stinging cold.

Will figured she was already halfway frozen to death. She needed to be warmed in a hurry. Unfortunately a fire was out of the question. The smell of spilled fuel was powerful and a spark might explode the plane. He'd definitely have to forgo a fire.

Clamping his jaw tight, he crawled close to her, and placed his free hand against her face, turning her head until she looked into his eyes. "Where're you hurt?"

"Cold . . ." Her teeth chattered so he could hear them.

She blocked the light with her hand. When he moved the beam from her face and set the flashlight between his thighs so it illuminated the ceiling and him, her eyes grew wide. No mistaking it, she recognized him and was aware her ex-husband was looking for him. Suddenly the gaze she riveted on him was full of fear.

She shook her head free from his touch with obvious pain, and for a few moments stared at him through frightened eyes, breathing in and out through her nose like she were taking her last breaths. Visibly shaken, she didn't say anything. He'd be frightened as hell, too, if he'd been a woman as badly injured as she appeared to be and come face-to-face with someone on the FBI's Most Wanted list.

"The men . . ." the woman sobbed. "They don't answer me. Please . . ." Her words sounded thick and slurred as though she were having trouble forming them.

Four years ago Will had seen wedding photos of Matt and his bride in Chicago papers. This woman looked like the one who'd been standing at Matt's side in her wedding finery. Several articles had mentioned Matt's bride was a cop. The following year another article announced the divorce. But she was still a cop, and without a doubt she'd traveled to Alaska with her former husband to arrest Will. His mouth tightened and he reined in his emotions. No doubt she struggled to get hold of her own.

The slurred speech, nausea, and weakness, she was close to hypothermia, but he could attribute the same symptoms to loss of blood. The cut on her forehead screamed for immediate attention. The coat pulled up around her neck looked to be saturated from the free-flowing blood.

"That cut on your forehead is nasty." The gentleness of his next words surprised him, and probably her, if she'd guessed his identity. "We'll take care of that first, but please, where else do you hurt? I have to get you warm. Before I can, these wet clothes have to come off. I don't want to move you before I know if any bones are broken."

"The others . . ." she started again. "Can you help them f-first, please?"

He glanced at the two corpses. "There's nothing I can do. Both men are dead."

A strange sound issued from her throat, something between a cry and a sob. She quickly turned away, but not before he saw a fresh wave of tears run down her already tear-stained cheeks.

While he removed a sheepskin parka from Matt's corpse, not an easy chore from a frozen stiff body, which testified how cold it was, she probed the debris beside her, coming up with something black—her purse. He couldn't see it clearly in the shadows, and for a second he grew still. Was she going to draw a gun from the bag and shoot him on the spot? A cop would be well armed on a mission such as this. But she just clutched the handbag to her breast. He went back to removing Matt's jacket.

"Sit up a bit so I can put this jacket around you."

She tried, but was too weak. Without his support she would have fallen back to the floor. After laying the jacket over her, he pulled off Jack's gloves and shoved them under his jacket to warm up. He removed his own gloves and hers, and despite her resistance, he gently rubbed her fingers between his. Except on a dead man, he'd never felt such cold skin.

Carefully, he slipped her wool gloves back on, then retrieved Matt's fur-lined ones from inside his parka and added those. When he continued to hold her hands, she looked surprised and a little less frightened. Her mouth drew into a straight line, and she turned away. He didn't care what she thought of him, but he wanted to know who'd killed Ellen—with his knife, no less—and why. And what happened to the Rutland Diamonds that disappeared the night Ellen was murdered? Could she answer these questions?

Suddenly she jerked her hands free of his, and he gave her a long look.

As for this frightened woman, he'd just as soon leave her to freeze and get the hell out of here. It was no boon to him if she made it safely back to Chicago. She'd just bear witness he was alive.

He glanced around for something to stem the bleeding on her forehead. Nothing caught his eye, so he used his knife to rip off a piece of Jack's shirt, filled it with snow from the floor, and placed it against the cut.

"Hold this here." On his hands and knees he backed slowly to the door.

"W-where . . . you g-going?"

He swallowed the urge to smile. *She's afraid of me, but more afraid of being left alone.* He couldn't fault her. Under the same circumstances, he would be, too. "I'll be right back. I need to get something to bandage your head. I won't leave you. You'll be able to see me. Keep holding that snow on your forehead. It'll help stop the bleeding and lessen the ache. Then I've got to put in a few stitches."

Tears leaked slowly from her eyes, and he thought she was ashamed of them for she turned her head away. He slid into the thigh-high snow and searched his pack for the supplies he needed.

Hopefully, the woman could walk. If not, he'd have to block the snow from coming in or they'd both freeze to death by morning. Whether she made it out alive or not wasn't his problem, but he knew it was, she was. Unfortunately, if she couldn't walk out on her own, he'd have to stay, and it would be a helluva cold night with only the thin shell of the plane to keep away this storm.

* * * *

The man who'd murdered his high school sweetheart crawled into the plane and sagged back on his heels then pushed back the hood of his parka, revealing a hat made from some animal skin and a frown on his grizzled face. Wordlessly, he looked at her. Maggie tried to focus on him, but her brain was fuzzy, her vision blurry, and it hurt her head to concentrate.

No doubt this man looked like the murderer. And how many men lived in this remote area? She stared at his hard mouth and his dark eyes to reconcile the scars and changes with the photos she'd seen of the man she and Matt had come to arrest. Though this hard-looking man bore little resemblance to the gangly seventeen-year-old-youth pictured on the wanted poster, with each passing second her certainty grew that this was indeed Jamie Donovan, the fugitive wanted for murdering Ellen Raine.

Now her life could depend on him thinking she and Matt were merely hitching a ride with the mail service to Circle City for a day of sightseeing and not trying to land near his cabin and take him into custody. If he guessed why she'd come to this remote region of Alaska, what possible reason would he have to keep her alive?

Had he recognized Matt after thirteen years? Matt had just been a skinny kid of thirteen then. She recognized Jamie solely from an old photo, so there was a good chance he recognized Matt.

The thought sent a wave of near panic flooding through her. Breathless, shaky, and frightened, Maggie's police training told her that maintaining her composure was imperative. With great effort, she clamped shut her jaw and notched up her chin to meet the tough look he directed at her. She must be very careful.

If she died here, she'd likely not be found until spring, when the snow thawed. Someone out for an adventure in a canoe or kayak would see the red plane and stop to investigate, or maybe pass by and mention it casually in a conversation after he returned home.

What a silly fool she'd been to insist on coming to Alaska. She'd let her animosity toward Matt's newest girlfriend, the reporter from the *Chicago Sun Times* who'd made the trip with them and was safe and sound in Fairbanks, get the best of her. Plain and simple, though she'd not been Matt's wife for a number of years, she was still jealous of the pretty brunette who fawned over Matt as though he were Brad Pitt. But for the life of her, she didn't know why. Certainly she didn't love Matt, hadn't for years, and long before the marriage busted up she'd grown sick and tired of his affairs.

When the pilot said he had to limit the passengers to Matt and one other in order to accommodate the large load of mail, she'd pulled rank as a Chicago PD detective and insisted on going. Now look where her asinine pettiness had landed her.

Matt had never made a secret of his fixation to find Ellen's killer. Before Maggie had married him he'd shown her the wanted poster he always carried and talked of that grizzly night his father found Ellen's badly beaten body. Prior to meeting Matt, unless she'd lived on the moon, she'd seen photos of Jamie—the Montgomery Preparatory Academy student wanted for murdering his sweetheart.

Photos and stories from the time he'd been found at St. Mary's orphanage to his fight with Senator Raine were plastered across every newspaper, and headlined by every TV news broadcast. His persona had been analyzed and dissected ad nauseam by psychiatrist and hack psychologist alike. His juvie police record of street fights before he entered Montgomery Prep had been studied with a microscope. From what he ate and drank the night of the murder to the psychological injury done him as an orphan, everyone had an opinion.

Widely noted was the irony that Jamie's attendance at the exclusive and costly private school where he'd met Ellen Raine was made possible by the scholarship sponsored by Congressman Hilton Raine. Currently, every news item about

Maggie's ex-father-in-law, Senator Raine, contained at least one paragraph about the tragic murder of his beautiful and popular daughter at her brother's graduation party.

Maggie shivered, fighting overwhelming depression and fatigue. She wished she'd worn the extra thermal underwear and wool pants she'd left in her suitcase. Inwardly, she groaned at the painful numbness in her back and legs, and tried to rise. It was no use. She was too cold, too weak, and her legs and head throbbed with equal ferocity. What would happen if she just went to sleep? *You'll turn into a frozen corpse just like Matt—.*

"This is going to sting." His words interrupted her wandering mind. "I've got to clean this cut before I try to close it." From a crude first-aid kit he drew out a packet, extracted a gauze swap, and dabbed her forehead. Whatever the gauze was saturated with stung like crazy. Despite her best efforts she flinched.

"Now I'm going to put in a few stitches. The cut's partly in your scalp so it won't show much, but when you get back, you can have a doctor fix it up right for you."

Was he trying to reassure her? She couldn't reconcile that after what he'd done to Ellen.

Maggie clamped her jaw tight against the expected pain, yet when he jabbed the needle into her forehead, her body jerked. She squeezed her eyes shut, stifling a cry and a wave of nausea.

The pain settled into a persistent hammering in her head, and when she opened her eyes again, he was wiping the blood from her face with snow and a rag. Despite the frown creasing his brow, concern darkened his eyes.

"Stitches are all in." He rubbed his forefinger and thumb over the grizzle of beard on his chin and seemed to come to a decision. "Now we've got to get you out of those wet clothes."

Undressing in subzero temperatures in front of a murderer was the last thing she was going to do willingly. He anticipated her protest, put his hand up, and shined the flashlight to the floor beside her.

"Look. See that? It's ice. Your overcoat is drenched, or rather *was* drenched. Now it's frozen to the plane's floor and probably to your skin. I found half a dozen smashed water bottles under some boxes. They must've gotten crushed in the crash, and water ran under you—that's why you're having trouble getting up."

At that moment the wind raged against the hull of the plane, and it suddenly rocked and shifted.

Maggie braced herself. "What was t-that? Are we about to roll down the mountainside?"

"I hope not. The plane's wedged between some trees pretty good. I can't see it going anywhere, but I'll check. If we have to stay the night, I'll shore it up to keep it from pitching. Right now the first order of business is to get you warm. You need to understand if you want to survive, there's no place for modesty here. In temperatures like these, hypothermia is a real possibility. You're probably well on your way to it. So, which one of these duffels has your clothes?"

"N-none of them. I'm af-fraid there's n-no bag for me. We were supposed to b-be back in Fairbanks by nightfall . . ." Maggie stopped, her thoughts jumbled. Had she told him she was going to Circle City for the night as she'd planned to say? If so, how would she explain not having any luggage?

Suddenly she remembered her fight with Matt that morning, and regret filled her so strongly her voice caught. "M-my companion had b-business in Circle City. We expected t-to return to Fairbanks by nightfall." She swallowed the lump in her throat and looked away, shivering from the cold and from regret. "When we t-took off this m-m-morning, the sky was clear. The weather report didn't s-say anything about snow."

"Weather reports are often unreliable here." He turned and began taking the clothing—jackets, shirts, long johns—from the corpses. "These clothes will have to do."

Horrified, she attempted to lever herself to her elbows to protest, winced, and lay back in a wave of dizziness.

"The clothing isn't doing either of them any good." Had he read her thoughts? "You're going to need something dry to wear. Remove your jacket and anything that's wet right down to your underwear, including anything that's wet from all the blood gathered round your neck. And hurry about it. If you need help, I'll be happy to oblige, but the wet and frozen clothing needs to be gone immediately. And we need a little more room in here." He lifted one stiff body, stripped down to skin and drawers, onto his shoulder and began to back from the plane.

"No, oh, n-no, you can't p-put them out there . . . please . . . they'll . . ." Her words died when she couldn't think of a single logical reason the dead men needed to stay in the cramped plane. Almost immediately he gave her a reason.

"The dogs will keep the wolves away."

"Wolves?" she gasped under her breath.

Either he didn't hear or ignored her, for he didn't speak again. He carried the naked bodies out of the plane. Then taking some tools from a package he found inside a panel beside the door, he went to work on the seat bolts. With a vicious yank he jerked them from their moorings, then set the cushions beside her and tossed the metal frames outside.

When she didn't move to undress, he lifted an eyebrow. "What are you waiting for? Take off those clothes. I'm not playing games, sweetheart. It may surprise you, but you're not the first naked woman I've seen. If you'd rather, I'll gladly take them off you myself. In case you're refusing altogether, think of frostbite on that back of yours that's been lying on ice for hours. Let me assure you, these temperatures aren't what you're used to in the lower forty-eight, and they're dropping fast."

She stared at him in indecision. Had he forced himself on Ellen to get her pregnant and move up in society? For some reason she couldn't make herself believe that of him. The many high school classmates, interviewed after the killing, had only good things to say about him. According to the testimony she'd read, he was as popular as Hilton's daughter and universally admired for his athletic abilities. So what had made him take such a drastic turn?

She sighed, wishing to God she'd never met him, that she'd never left her comfortable home in Chicago. He looked away, not seeming to care what she did, took out an army knife, and tore strips from a pair of long johns taken from one of the men.

After a few moments of waiting for her to begin disrobing, he put the strips aside and sat back on his haunches. "If you'd prefer not to get undressed, that's fine with me. I'll just leave you to your own devices." He rose on all fours and backed toward the door.

She gave him an aggravated little smirk. But he had scared her. She clamped her teeth together, took off her gloves, and placed them on the closest duffel. Under Jamie Donovan's watchful eye, she shivered violently as she attempted to free her arms from her coat, frozen to the floor of the plane. Wordlessly, he leaned to ease the jacket from under her, adjusting her position so she was no longer directly over the puddle of ice but on the cushions he'd stripped from the seats. Shaking, it took her a long time to unbutton her ski sweater, and he took over that chore, too.

When she was ready, he helped remove the sweater from her arms and then ease the turtleneck jersey, the neck soaked with blood, carefully over her head so as not to dislodge the bandage. Down to her silk camisole, skirt, and panties, the frigid air washed over her like a tub of ice water. She could hardly breathe for the sting of the cold.

"Leave your skirt on." He rubbed her arms and back vigorously which felt wonderful. "It isn't wet, but better get the stocking off if I'm to check your leg. Any place else I need to look?"

"No, j-just th-the ankle." Sliding the tights past her hips and buttocks, she tried to roll them off her leg, but was assailed by a bout of dizziness that triggered the nausea again. She reeled backward, but his hand on the small of her back kept her from hitting the floor.

"Take a deep breath." He covered her shoulders with the moth-eaten Army blanket that did little to hold back the cold.

She breathed deeply and the frigid air settled in her lungs like shards of ice. He slipped Matt's thermal top over her head then surprised her by pulling her close against his chest . . . he was so warm . . . and she allowed him to hold her until the nausea passed and only the pain remained. When he laid her back on the cushions, he removed her tights. She had no will to stop him. His hands ran over her knees and calves, pulling the stockings from one foot then the other. The touch of this murderer's hands on her in such a tender way unnerved her.

As though sharing her thoughts he hesitated, and then he challenged her with a smile, a smile full of amusement and a sense of decorum. It softened the chiseled planes of his face and took some of the cold from his eyes. "I don't usually get under a lady's skirts until I've at least introduced myself. I'm Will Connor."

She recognized it instantly. One of the names cited beneath the newspaper photo that had arrived on her desk. Maggie turned from the penetrating gaze he directed at her. Will Connor was listed as a partner in the airline company they'd hired, where Matt's current amour, the newspaper reporter, was waiting for him and for her story. But the name on the wanted poster wasn't Will Connor. The name on the poster was James Donovan. 'Jamie' her husband had called him. The poster had a photo, too—a skinny seventeen-year-old kid, standing with his arm looped around Matt's sister, Ellen. Ellen's image had been cut from the photo on the wanted poster, but Maggie had seen the original.

His gaze on her, his hands on her leg, he asked. "And you are?" Creases emphasized the chilly smile directed at her. He had even, white teeth, and keen intelligence glowed from his eyes.

"Margaret. Maggie—Maggie Kilpatrick." She gave him her maiden name and wiped a crooked finger over her lips, ashamed of her fear.

She lay back down and her gaze swept over the inside of the plane, trying to take in everything—anything that might help her escape, survive—and came to rest on the backpack he'd left in the snow outside the plane. In the waning light it was barely visible through the door. Could she steal the backpack? It must contain some survival equipment. Could she carry the pack? Even if she could, which way was his cabin? Where would she go? Night was closing in, but even if it were broad daylight, she had only the vaguest idea where Circle City was. Bottom line, she was injured, making immediate escape moot.

She groped along the frozen fuselage for her purse. It contained her gun. Not that she wanted to shoot him. The notion of knocking him unconscious and making a run for it was a far more reasonable choice. In her present condition she was pretty certain she couldn't stand on her own two feet, much less render this powerfully built man unconscious, then trek through a blizzard. She could try and spray him with the pepper spray in the side pocket of her purse, but he hadn't escaped the massive police dragnet by being a fool, and surely he would notice her fumbling around to find the spray. Even if she did manage to spray him, how long would he be incapacitated? What would prevent him from shooting her as she tried to run, *if* she could run? She wasn't entirely sure she could even walk.

Insistent pounding in her head made her thoughts jumbled and fuzzy. She pressed a hand against her temples. Thinking clearly proved a difficult chore. Although she was a detective like Matt, unlike him, her days were spent behind a desk, pouring over evidence, trying to solve crimes with the tidbits of information others gathered. Never before had she come face-to-face with a killer.

Dear God, she was cold. A gust of wind drove through the door he'd left open behind him, and a branch scraped along the fuselage, scaring her, making her more cold, more afraid. Her body convulsed with uncontrollable shivering, and she pulled the blanket up over her chin and mouth. What was he planning to do to her?

Exhaustion overcame her, like a wolf in sheep's clothing, all soft and urging her toward sleep. Suddenly, she no longer had the will to fight to stay awake. She blinked and saw that he was staring at her, his eyes dark, his mouth stern like she'd disappointed him somehow.

From far away she heard his curse, then his voice. "Damn it, Maggie Kilpatrick, don't cave on me. Help me get the rest of these dry clothes back on you now. Come on, sweetheart. Time is of the essence here."

She lifted her hand to comply, but her fingers were too cold, the muscles too weakened. *I'm not going to make it.*

* * * *

Gene Pryor accepted the frosty bottle of beer from his wife and sank into the soft leather sofa they'd recently bought. He took a deep swig, wiped the back of his hand over his mouth, then reached for the remote. Brier followed him, sitting on the couch's arm. Snow fell outside the windows behind her; the sky dark and gloomy.

Gene had been at the office of Alaska Bush Air Transport Company most of the day— the company he, Will Connor, Jim Foley, and Jack Ricks started seven years ago. When the weather rolled in, he'd canceled his scheduled safari, finished the paperwork, and left for home, knowing he wouldn't take to the air until the weather improved. Jack had flown out before the weather turned bad, heading for Circle City with a load of mail. He assumed Jack, becoming aware of the worsening weather, would either make arrangements to stay in Circle City or turn back. Gene couldn't rest until he got word Jack was safe somewhere.

When Brier put her hand on his shoulder without saying anything, the beer curdled in his stomach. He pushed his wet hair back from his face and looked up at his wife.

"What?"

"Nancy called while you were in the shower and begged off coming for supper."

"Why? Jack staying in Circle City, or is the baby coming?"

Brier shook her head, and her mouth wobbled. Gene's jaw tightened. Nancy's baby coming three weeks early wouldn't cause his wife to tear up. He set his mouth, not wanting to ask and hear his worries given credence, but needing to. "What then?"

"There's been no word from Jack. No one can raise him on the radio. Circle City said he never arrived there." A tear broke loose and rolled down her cheek. Immediately she scrubbed it with the edge of her apron. She was thinking of him, that it might have been him, his plane that was missing and presumed down.

Unable to meet her eyes, he looked out the window at the storm. He took her hand and brought it to his mouth. "Let's not jump to conclusions, honey. Jack's an excellent pilot. If he ran into problems, it's likely he's taking care of them. We'll probably hear from him at any minute, at least by morning." Did he believe his own words? His stomach roiled with the same sickening feeling he'd had when a couple of hours after Jack had taken off, the storm that had been predicted to come through tomorrow had showed up a day early. Soon as he'd heard, he'd tried to reach Jack on the radio, tried throughout the afternoon, but the radio was either malfunctioning or the mountains were blocking the reception, or . . . he refused to let his thoughts go there.

"Jack had a couple with him." He raked his hand through his hair. "They wanted to see the sights, so he took the scenic route over the mountains before he dropped off the mail." Even taking that into consideration, Jack should have been to Circle City and back hours ago. They both knew that.

Gene sipped his beer, swallowed, pushed himself to his feet, and moved to the window. Brier came with him. He put his arm around her slender waist and pulled her against him. "Why don't you call and persuade Nancy and Jenny to come for supper anyway? They can stay the night." He kept his tone light. "Erika will be upset if Jenny doesn't come, and it'll be better for Nancy to have company. Meanwhile, I'll head on back to the office and see if there's anything I can do."

Brier grabbed his arm and held him. "I know you love Will and Jack like brothers, but don't even think of going after Jack. Don't. I mean it. It would be suicide to fly in weather like this."

"I agree."

"You've got a wife and two kids, Gene. Don't try and be a hero. I know you, and I don't want to have them bring you back in a body bag."

She was as stressed out as he was. He looked at the uncompromising set of her jaw, at her eyes welled with tears again, and at her kissable lips. He tipped up her jaw and kissed her hard, pulling himself away before he got sidetracked. "I'm not arguing with you, honey. I just need to be there in case there's something I can do."

"Nancy will want to stay at her house in case Jack calls."

"Yes, of course. Well then, pack up dinner and the kids and go over there. She'll need company tonight. Just let me know where you are."

And while you're gone I'll try and radio Will. He needed the place to himself to make that call. Gene had forgone college for the Police Academy and come up through the ranks of law enforcement for a few years before joining the Navy where he briefly worked in Naval Intelligence, found the work tedious, and needled his superior officers until he got transferred into the Naval Air Force. The career change was a perfect fit, and he'd been flying ever since. While in pilot training, he'd met Will Connor, admired his huge talents, and they'd become fast friends. Soon as obligations to the Naval Air Force were fulfilled, the love of flying had carried both men to Alaska and the adventures of flying in the wilderness. His wife was right about Will and Jack. They were as close to him as brothers could be without sharing the same bloodline.

Not even his wife knew he could reach Will after he retreated to his mountain to hibernate for the winter.

Chapter Four

Disturbed by her apathy, Will shook her. "Talk to me Maggie."

Nothing. She was drifting off. There was no way to tell if she were bleeding internally. If she were, if a lung or some other vital organ were punctured, he figured she was a goner. All he could do was try not to hurt her or dislodge any more bones, try not to injure her more, and try to ignore those perfectly shaped breasts that were brushing against his wrists and hands at every turn in his efforts to get her clothed.

As he worked to pull a second thermal shirt down around her torso, she cried out, a soft whimper that caught in his gut. Every time he moved her, she groaned. Was she hurt in places he didn't know about? He wanted to curse the fates that had led him to this place, to this woman. She had the body a man dreamed of curling around at night, eyes that were wide and as frightened as a child about to be whipped. No, he didn't like the effect Maggie Kilpatrick—or whatever the hell her name was—was having on him. He didn't like it at all.

"Maggie!" Will took her shoulders in both hands and gave her another little shake. It was more important not to let her fall asleep. Not yet. "Don't you dare go to sleep." She'd only been exposed to the cold for a minute or two, but after all she'd been through, hypothermia could happen fast. "Wake up, sweetheart!"

Her eyes fluttered open.

"That's better, baby, stay with me." Lethargy had settled into her eyes, and like a heavy blanket was suffocating her.

"I'm so c-cold . . ." Her whisper drifted off.

"I know you are, sweetheart, and I'm going to get you warm just as soon as I can." Will dressed her in Matt's lined-wool shirt on top of the thermal shirts then a fleece from Jack over that, followed by Matt's sheepskin parka. He worked fast, trying

37

not to hurt her too much, but the clothes were cold, and she wasn't shaking enough to generate her own heat. Her legs were still exposed, the right one he suspected was in need of a splint, and she wouldn't warm up properly until he got her completely covered and got the warmth started.

He considered building a shelter away from the plane then getting a fire started, but he didn't dare move her, not yet. Besides, it would take too long, and as freezing as the fuselage was it was better than any shelter he could build in short order. But he was losing her. He had to get her warm, and fast. Only one way he could think of to do that.

He wrapped both her legs in the wool blanket, tucking the ends under her, and on elbows and knees crawled up and drew her into his arms, opened his parka, and enveloped her. Careful not to put any weight on the damaged ankle, he swung his leg over her thigh to bring her closer to his warmth.

Even half dead, she squirmed in protest. Will placed a hand on her cheek and moved her head so he could look into her eyes. "Hold still, sweetheart. I'm not planning to rape you. You've begun to babble, and I'm worried about hypothermia."

* * * *

As offices on Capitol Hill went, Hilton Raine's wasn't a particularly large one, but no expense had been spared in appointing it to create an atmosphere of power and wealth. Rich wood paneled walls, built-in bookshelves filled with law books and a few first editions. An oil painting of the senator, looking stern and omnipotent, prominently hanging behind a plush, burgundy leather sofa.

However, the focal point of the room was the mahogany desk in front of a large bay window with a view of the Lincoln Memorial. The desk, built on specifications set down by Hilton, was overly large. A photo of his sons taken last summer when the three had gone hunting Big Horn sheep in the Canadian Rockies was framed on a shelf between some books. Beside that was a photo he particularly loved of his daughter Libby, laughing in her high school graduation robes.

Though someone had cracked the window, the room smelled strongly of stale smoke. Cigar clamped between his teeth, coffee cup in hand, Hilton stood, surveying his office.

His secretary entered, carrying several slips of paper. "You've had several calls, sir. And I've set up that appointment with Senator Dewberry you wanted for three this afternoon."

"Put the calls on my desk." Hilton waved her off and strode to the window, peering into the drab sunlight filtering through the clouds. Last night's snow hadn't stuck but left the sidewalks covered in dirty slush. All but a few brown leaves had fallen from the oak across the street, its limbs black webs against the sky's bleak gray.

Behind him, Hilton heard Jane place the messages on his desk then retreat. Before she reached the door, her step slowed and stopped. He pictured her tucking her short brown hair behind her ears, a nervous habit.

"What is it, Jane?"

"Excuse me, Senator, but I think you should know that one gentleman called three times. Apparently he had your home number, too, because he said he tried unsuccessfully to reach you there. He said it was vital he speak with you as soon as you came in."

Hilton tensed. He could think of several reasons why someone might want to get in touch with him urgently. None good.

"The switchboard said his first call came at around 6:00 a.m. I spoke with the caller myself at seven and then again about fifteen minutes ago. He was phoning from Alaska, but declined to leave a message."

Hilton swung around. "Alaska! Alaska's four hours earlier than D.C. That would mean he called at two in the morning his time." The first shivers of alarm ran through him. "Matt's supposed to be in Alaska. You're sure the call wasn't from Matt?"

"Your son's name wasn't mentioned. Would you like me to ring the number for you?"

He nodded and sank heavily into the plush leather desk chair, a wave of foreboding suddenly making him weak. He rocked the chair back, then back and forth, and drummed his fingers over his thigh, impatient for his secretary to reach the caller. He looked around the office, and his gaze settled on a framed photograph of his oldest daughter, Ellen, taken on a ski trip the winter of her junior year of high school. He unlocked the bottom drawer of his desk and pulled out a copy of a wanted poster. His rocking stopped. Wanted for murder, the poster read. The picture on the poster had been taken thirteen years earlier, several months before his daughter was murdered. The face that stared out at him was that of a seventeen-year-old kid. Hilton's eyes narrowed with malice then grew wide with hope. Had Matt captured Donovan?

"Sir, I have Deputy Sheriff Douglas of the Fairbanks Police Department on the line."

Hilton cleared his throat and picked up the phone. "Senator Raine speaking."

The line crackled. "Good morning, Senator. Deputy Sheriff Douglas here. Can you hear me all right?" The man's voice sounded not only as though it were coming from deep in a well, but nervous.

"The connection's not the best, but I can hear you fine. What's on your mind?"

"I'm sorry to bother you," the man hesitated, "but I thought you should know that your son's plane is overdue."

"What do you mean 'overdue'?"

"The pilot, Jack Ricks, flew out of Fairbanks early yesterday morning on his weekly run to Circle City to drop off mail. He was supposed to return to Fairbanks before dark. It's my understanding that your son and a woman were passengers on that plane."

"You're sure about that—my son was on that particular plane?"

"Yes, sir, your son *and* a woman who I believe is also a detective from the Chicago PD. I have a man right here who helped them load up the mail. And a woman by the name of Vera Phillips who says she writes for the newspaper in your area verifies that the two of them were on board. Shortly after the plane took off unexpected weather came in. Sometimes weather can do that out here, comes up fast and catches you not looking. Wind's the worst, but this time it's wind and snow. When that happens, you want to get your plane down soon as you can before it gets worse. Trouble is, it's hard to find a place to set down in the mountains between here 'n Circle City. "

"You try radioing them?"

"Yes, sir, soon as we saw bad weather was coming we radioed right off. Several of us have tried to reach him since, and we've kept trying all through the night, Senator, but so far we haven't gotten a response. I assure you that doesn't necessarily mean anything—could be he's just out of radio range. Flying between mountains like he was doing, a radio might not pick up a signal. If he landed somewhere, like in a valley, the same would also be true. Look, Jack's a personal friend, and if anyone can get that plane down safely, I assure you he can."

"So you think the pilot might have put the plane down somewhere to wait out the storm?"

"That's what we're all hoping."

"I assume you dispatched search planes." Matt had already been missing for more than twelve hours.

"Normally we would have, Senator. But I'm afraid that in this case the weather made that out of the question."

"So someone's flying up there looking for my son's plane now?" He clamped down on his cigar and leaned forward, waiting for the deputy's answer.

"I'm sorry. The storm's still too bad. It would be suicide to fly in a storm like this. The only thing that makes any sense is to wait until the storm passes."

Hilton was silent for several seconds. He wasn't interested in the welfare of the other pilots, only his son. His tone became edgy. "But delaying the search could mean death for my son! Surely you can find a pilot willing to start the search? If it's a matter of money, I'll be glad to—"

"It's not that, Senator. In fact I have several pilots with me right now who are anxious to look for Jack. He is well liked by us all. But even if someone took to the air in the next five minutes, it would be like trying to find a needle in the snow, impossible. At this juncture I'm afraid sending out a search plane would be a foolhardy mission. Another downed plane won't do your son any good. With the temperature and wind like they are and the snow coming down so heavily, too many things can go wrong."

Hilton strove to keep frustration out of his voice. Normally when he told someone to jump they asked how high, but this Deputy Sheriff Douglas couldn't be moved. "What about sending out a sled? I've heard people still use dogs pulling sleds to get around in weather like you're having."

"True enough, but between here and Circle City is hundreds of miles, much of it mountainous. We couldn't begin to know where to search. I'm afraid sending out a sled would be nearly as futile as sending out a plane. No, we just have to wait."

Hilton felt like screaming. Instead he snarled, "So when exactly do you expect the search to begin?"

"Can't say. Sometimes these storms pass over quickly, sometimes not. I can only assure you that we'll set out looking as soon as it's feasible. Hopefully everything will turn out okay."

Hilton didn't feel optimistic. "Hopefully. The planes do carry survival gear with them, don't they?"

The deputy sheriff hesitated. "Yes, normally, enough for the pilot, but weight's a consideration. I understand some of the survival gear was left behind so the woman could ride. Someone told me she was his ex-wife."

"Maggie?" Hilton cut in, disgusted. "They've been divorced for years. What the hell was she doing on the plane?"

"I can't answer that one for you, sir. Perhaps she just wanted to get a view of Alaska's vastness. It truly is a wonderful sight. Remember the weather was clear when they took off. Anyway, if they did have to land, Jack will see that they all stay with the plane. If you're out in the open in a storm like this one, you're gone. You're dead. But Jack knows this."

Hilton winced and clamped his jaw. In his head he kept hearing the deputy sheriff's unvoiced thoughts—everything depended on whether the pilot had been able to set the plane down safely. "I assume the plane was carrying one of those black boxes."

There was a hesitation on the other end of the line and a shuffling of papers. "Yes, sir, apparently an Emergency Locator Transmitter was aboard, and that could be our salvation. But you do understand that the ELT has its limitations, too."

"I thought it located downed planes by satellite."

"Yes, basically that's what it's supposed to do. The ELT depends on other aircraft or a satellite picking up its signal and relaying the information to a command center so a search and rescue team can be dispatched to the site. But no planes are flying today, and I would be remiss if I didn't tell you that the

ELT is often damaged if the plane crashes. In short, they have proven not to be very effective, particularly in remote areas like Alaska."

Disheartened and angry, Hilton said, "I understand. Keep me posted." He gave the deputy his private cell phone number before hanging up.

Closing his eyes, he rocked his chair back and stayed that way for a few moments. Then he rocked forward with a bellow, "Damnit!" Both fists came down on his desk so hard that a wooden paperweight with a brass replica of the Senate Seal and his penholder bounced to the Persian carpet.

He pressed the intercom button on his telephone. "Jane! I need you to book me transport to Alaska immediately. Then get my wife on the phone."

* * * *

Will bit into the shirt he'd taken from one dead body and ripped off another length, his gaze fastened on the woman who had literally dropped out of the sky and into his life. For a while he'd thought he was going to lose her, yet here she was, lying a foot from him and looking at him like a frightened doe in headlights. Her eyes were wonderfully large and understandably troubled, her nose finely chiseled, her cheekbones angular. Without question a beautiful woman, but he wanted nothing to do with her.

Will looked to where he'd dumped Matt's body in the snow, and felt a nasty churning in his gut. The shock of seeing Matt Raine here, in the one place where he thought he was safe, still roiled inside of him even as he tried to concentrate on the matters at hand.

That Maggie had given him a false name told him immediately she had something to hide. While she'd slept, he'd searched her purse and found a police ID and a Glock. Detective Margaret Kilpatrick Raine verified his guess about her having once been married to Matt. Despite that he'd read they'd divorced, for all he knew she could have married him again, or maybe not. Not that he cared one way or the other. He'd removed the bullets from her gun before returning both items to her purse.

There was plenty of time for him to make his run. No one, not even the powerful Hilton Raine, could get anyone to fly out in a storm like this. And if the authorities opted to pursue him on sleds, they were days away, probably closer to a week, even if they pushed. By then he'd be long gone.

What was he going to do with the woman? Obviously she was an utter greenhorn in the wilds. Look at the ridiculously unsuitable clothing she'd worn. Didn't she have an inkling what the winter temperatures were like in Alaska or how many planes went down, particularly in wintertime? She must've wanted to arrest him badly, to take such a risk.

He'd done what he could for her for now, warmed her up some. But if he left her, she'd be dead within forty-eight hours. And that bothered him.

He unscrewed the top of his water skin and took a deep drink, annoyed with himself for noticing her looks and not being able to control his body's response to her. Rubbing her legs and feet had been a big mistake. But what the hell was he supposed to do? She was close to hypothermia so he had to do something to warm her. He wanted to hate her. He wanted to spit her out of his life. How was he going to do that? Oh, yes, Matt's ex-wife was a beautiful woman, but more importantly she was a very dangerous woman.

He wiped his mouth with the back of his hand. Her gaze flicked to the goatskin, unconsciously drawing the tip of her tongue over her bottom lip. He compressed his jaw and handed it over to her, holding her up so she could drink.

As she drank, he watched her speculatively, like he didn't believe what she'd told him, and her apprehension grew. He placed both hands on her injured ankle and gently probed it with his fingertips. She tried not to shake too much. He took a long time, and after a few moments she couldn't control her curiosity.

"What's wrong with it?" she asked through chattering teeth.

He shined his flashlight on her ankle for her to see. "Despite the cold, the swelling has gone clear to your knee. The inflammation would probably mask any simple fracture to the naked eye, but my guess is the injury is confined to the ankle. See how it's turning blue here and here." His flashlight beam spotted on the outside of her lower ankle as he touched them.

"When you were tossed about in the crash, you probably rolled the foot and landed your weight on it. The ankle or shin still could be broken as well, but I don't think so. This is only a guess, but you probably have some torn ligaments. Just the opinion of this layman. I could be wrong—it could merely be a bad sprain or a broken bone or all of the above. But I must warn you that a torn ligament is not necessarily good news. It's every bit as difficult to deal with as a break."

He's more than a simple layman. A man alone in this wilderness had probably versed himself in rudimentary healing from necessity. Eyeing the grotesque swelling, she thought his diagnosis correct. She shivered uncontrollably and had a hard time holding back her tears. A torn ligament took months to heal. If someone didn't come to rescue her, how was she going to find her way back to civilization?

"This probably wouldn't have happened if you'd worn your seatbelt."

The censure was mild, but there, as if to say that any fool knew better than to fly without wearing seat restraints.

"I t-took the restraint off to get a bottle of water, and I guess I didn't get a good connection when I p-put it back on. Is there anything you can do about my ankle?"

"Oh, I don't know." His eyes were suddenly bright with amusement. "It's pretty useless the way it is. Maybe I should cut it off and feed it to the wolves."

"That's n-not funny." She swung her head up to glare at him and paid for it with another sharp pain in her head. Despite the fact she wanted to hate him, the smile he shot her intrigued her. Somewhere buried behind the dark man he'd become Jamie Donovan had retained a sense of humor. But he was a man on the run, a dangerous man who had murdered his girlfriend, and she reminded herself that she'd do well never to forget that.

As if reading her thoughts, his grin slipped away, and his brow furrowed.

"If those are all the injuries you got, you're one lucky lady. Now I need to wrap that ankle."

Without waiting for permission, he uncovered the leg and began to wrap first with the flannel, then with the stiffer jean strips he'd been tearing. The bandage had been exposed to the frigid air, and the moment it touched her skin she shivered again uncontrollably.

"You may be in shock."

It was what she'd been thinking, but she was surprised at his knowledge of such things.

Finished, he sat back on his heels. "There, that's better. If you're up to it, I can add a splint, and we'll head for my place. The walking will warm you up some."

"Is your cabin c-close?" As much as she tried, she couldn't make her teeth stop chattering.

He stared at her. "Fairly close—twelve, maybe ten miles."

Twelve miles. She wanted to be brave; she hoped to be strong, but her mouth wobbled despite her best efforts. If it hadn't been so serious, she'd have laughed at his idea of close. Twelve miles.

This couldn't be happening to her. It was too surreal, a bad dream. Her foggy brain couldn't assimilate it—the plane going down, Matt and the pilot dead, this murderer her only hope for survival.

Maggie didn't want to be in this desolate wilderness. She didn't want to be so frightened. She didn't want to deal with an injury, especially in such primitive conditions. She didn't want to deal with this frightening man who looked as grim as the animal on his head. But she *did* want to live.

On hands and knees he reached across her to rummage through the duffle bags of mail, mail boxes, and debris until he came up with an old Army duffle which looked like all the other mail sacks to her. But he reached inside and fished out some batteries, a blanket, another flashlight, and a few assorted canned goods—the pilot's emergency supplies, she supposed.

"This'll help." He laid the blanket over her and tucked the thick wool around her legs and feet, then handed her a flashlight. He leaned back against the fuselage and studied her with a steely look she couldn't read, but it made a different kind of shiver churn up her insides. She pulled the blanket up to her eyes and watched him crawl backward toward the door of the plane again, carrying her bloody clothing, the ski sweater, and turtleneck.

Outside the door she could make out one of the bodies bent over like a jackknife in the snow—she thought it was Matt. She closed her eyes. Matt hadn't been a good husband, but the day they'd bought the matching ski sweaters, they'd laughed together and been happy. Once they'd loved each other, but he'd been a restless man, driven to gain his father's favor in every way possible, particularly to find the man who had murdered Ellen.

With his movie star looks and outgoing personality, women were drawn to Matt, same as they were to his famous father. Like his father, Matt couldn't turn them down. His infidelities began shortly after their marriage and multiplied, until the love she'd once harbored for him soured. Ten months after their wedding she moved out of his house and filed for divorce, vowing she'd never fall in love again. That was two and a half years ago.

Chapter Five

Jamie fiddled with some of the instruments in the front of the plane.

"What are you doing?"

"Trying to see if I can breathe a little life into the radio while you warm up." He put the earphones on and moved the dials around.

The article that landed on her desk said the men in the photo were pilots, and Will Connor's moves demonstrated he knew his way around the plane. She let out a deep sigh, not really caring that the sound was filled with self-pity and fear.

"You a pilot?" she blurted out.

He grew still and his eyes hardened. "Yes. Why do you ask?"

"You seem to know a lot about planes."

"Out here it's the best way to get around. I've flown this plane before." He propped his arm against the instrument panel and sagged back against his heels, his gaze locked with hers. "I'm afraid the radio is history. If I had some good light and a day to fiddle with it, I might be able to bring it back to life, but it's pretty badly smashed. Not likely anyone could pick up our signal here anyway."

Overwhelmed, her mouth tightened, and she looked away. It would be a miracle if she made it out of here alive. If by the grace of God she did, it would be because of his help. But never far from her conscious thought was the truth that soon as she could stand on her own two feet it would be her sworn duty to point her gun at Will Connor's heart and place him under arrest. But that was for another day. Her eyelids fluttered.

"Maggie!"

She opened her eyes only to clash head on with his icy blue ones glaring at her from beneath his frown. She thought he was going to say something more, but he didn't. Instead, he rummaged around the toolbox, drawing out a screwdriver.

With it he lifted chunks of frozen water from the belly of the plane and pitched them out the door.

When the ice chunks were mostly gone, he dumped two sacks of mail on the plane's floor, pushed it around like he was making a nest, and covered the mail with the sacks. Before he lifted her with strong arms under her back and knees he hesitated, like he expected her to resist. When she didn't, he picked her up and propped her against the wall of the plane while he moved the cushions to the nest. Then he sat her on top of the bed he'd made, pulled the hood of Matt's parka up over her head, and tied a scarf around her neck, as though he understood that right now she needed him to do such menial tasks for her.

Once Will moved Maggie to the makeshift bed, he returned his attention to Jack's radio and rumbled through the debris in the cone. He hoped to find the spare radio parts Jack usually carried, some of which might be handy to repair his own busted radio at his cabin. He fiddled with it again without much hope, his mind more on the girl than on repairing a radio that could conceivably bring the authorities down on him.

She still looked lost and scared as a rabbit about to be attacked by a wolf. His mouth compressed into a grim smile. If she knew her ex's business as he suspected, she had every reason to be afraid. If she were able, he was certain she'd have bolted long ago, though on second thought, he didn't think she was that stupid.

She had a gun, but so far she'd wisely left it in her purse. Right now his concern wasn't that she might try and take him down at any time, but rather he was afraid if she slept, she might not wake up.

With his back to her, he silently cursed her for coming into his life and himself for caring what happened to her. He didn't need the trouble, and he sure didn't want to be touched by her.

"Jack try to radio for help?" he asked without turning, mostly just to keep her awake. He figured Jack would have radioed, but radios weren't much good unless you were right over the landing field or an area where they'd put up towers. His cabin radio wouldn't work if he hadn't run the aerial up a tree at the top of the mountain. But Jack could have realized he was in trouble and reached someone *before* he got into the mountains.

"You knew the pilot—Jack?"

He nodded without elaborating. If that's the way she wanted to play it, he could carry on this charade as well as she. "You a friend of the other guy?"

"Yes." He heard her grief in the rising tenor of her voice. He was sorry he'd brought up her dead ex-husband.

She cleared her throat, and he could still hear her teeth chattering. "Jack did try the radio several times. He gave out our coordinates over and over. But I don't think he got any reception."

She could be lying, yet that had been his experience out here, too. He turned and saw she was shivering again. Forgetting about the radio, which was probably hopeless anyway, he left the plane to cover the fractured windshield with hemlock boughs and prop the metal seat frames up under the tail to minimize rocking.

Late afternoon hours slipped into night, and the wind blew hard, a cold blast from beyond the Arctic. It rattled the shattered windshield and rocked the plane. His efforts hadn't helped the plane from swaying all that much or the wind and snow from coming inside.

Will carried Maggie outside the plane so she could relieve herself, and she was so tired and weak she failed to protest. In his pack he found some ibuprofen, but concern that she might have internal injuries kept him from giving them to her. She would just have to cope with the pain as best she could. To her credit, she hadn't complained much, just that she was cold.

He handed her a piece of beef jerky and a package of peanut butter crackers. They ate in silence. Beyond the thin walls of the plane, the wind howled through the treetops with a sorrowful cry, a reminder that a terrible storm raged.

There would be no chance of returning to his cabin tonight.

As the batteries of his flashlight grew weaker, an early night, filled with dark shadows and hidden secrets, grew stronger until it devoured the last traces of light. Minutes passed slowly, measured in gusts of wind. In the belly of the plane a storm of another kind came, one storm filled with the cold winds of fear and mistrust.

A Cry From the Cold

* * * *

Gene Pryor credited that he'd been able to negotiate the mile and a half to Jack Rick's home to drop Brier and the kids there and then back again to his house without landing in a ditch to his four-wheel drive. The unplowed roads made for more of an adventure than he wanted. Once he'd returned the Toyota Four Runner to the garage, he resolved he wouldn't put it to the test again until the roads were cleared. If he had to go out, he'd go on foot.

Once safely inside, Gene and his dog, the sire of Will's husky, retired to his study on the second floor and attempted to rouse Will on the radio. After a frustrating hour of repeated attempts, he was forced to conclude that either his friend wasn't there or the storm prevented the transmission from reaching him.

He heated up some leftover beef stew, carried it in the pot to the living room, and clicked on the TV. Cable was out. He sagged onto the sofa and propped his feet on the coffee table, watching the snow on the TV and the snow outside his window with equal irritation. The stew tasted good, and he ate every lick, mulling over and over the possible scenarios of what might have happened to Jack.

The minute the weather turned sour Jack should have turned around and headed back. But, God help him, he knew how Jack's mind worked—situations like that faced pilots flying in Alaska every day. Like the moths that flew into flames, their decisions weren't always the correct ones. Jack was probably near Circle City and pressured by his clients to go on. Then suddenly the weather closed in and it was too late. He prayed Jack had found a place to put the plane down safely and wait out the storm.

Gene glanced at the clock over the mantle, not quite 10:00 p.m. He picked up a book and tried to read, but his mind wouldn't settle on the words. He marked his spot, got up, and put the empty pot in the sink to soak, then trotted upstairs to see if he'd have any better luck rousing Will. God knew if anyone could find a downed plane in that area, it was Will Connor, and he'd do it, too, no matter the weather. Will still didn't answer his radio.

He glanced at his watch. Where could the man go in the mountain wilderness at this time of night *and* in the middle of a raging blizzard? Not like he could be down the street having a beer. He rolled back his chair and shot to his feet with a growl of profanity and thudded to the window, propping a hand on the window-frame. Snow plastered against the pane, but a part still remained clear. For a long time Gene stared at the flakes whipping wildly past his security light, fighting his frustration, then he paced, before giving up. He couldn't stand doing nothing. He figured someone had to be manning the office/airport of Alaska Bush Air Transport—ABAT—and it might as well be him.

Halfway down the steps the lights went out. He groped his way to the kitchen, picked up the phone, relieved to hear a dial tone, and punched in his office number. After a short conversation with his partner Jim Foley, he retrieved a utility lantern and packed a couple of bologna sandwiches, piling on the mustard, then grabbed an apple and three cream cheese brownies. He put it all in his pack.

Then he dialed his wife.

Jack's wife answered. "Sorry, Nancy. Didn't mean to get your hopes up."

"That's all right; everyone's been calling."

"I haven't heard anything new. I guess you haven't either."

"No." He hated the disappointment in her voice.

"The lights just went out here. Is everything all right over by you?"

"Lights are out here, too. We got the generator going."

Then Brier came on the line.

"You guys all right over there?" He imagined their vigil was anything but "all right." "You have plenty of food and fuel for the generator?"

"We do. Kids are asleep. We're all set. We got a fire going, too."

"Good. I talked to Jim a few minutes ago. He's at the office, but he could use some help, so I'm heading there. I don't want to take the car out again, so I'm going to hoof it. I'll call you when I get there."

"Do that and be careful, honey. Keep us posted."

"I will, and you guys stay put."

The blast of arctic wind that hit him in his face when he opened the back door sent him back into the house for his ski goggles. Before he stepped outside again, he zipped his down jacket up over his chin and tightened the tie of the hood over his nose and mouth. In the few hours since he'd dropped Brier and the children at Jack's house, the wind had increased in intensity. In places, snow had swept into drifts as high as his boot tops.

Even with the aid of his high-beam flashlight, visibility was limited to a foot in front of his nose. He hugged the curb of the road, navigating by a few tire tracks and years of taking the same route. Several times he had to stop and shake the snow from a road sign.

No doubt about it; the weather was getting worse.

Chapter Six

Will was glad he'd saved his sleeping bag, so it was clean and dry. He knew what he must do if the two of them were to survive the night. But he didn't mention it to her just yet.

"I'll help you get inside my sleeping bag." He spread out the thick down and unzipped it. "You should rest. We have to travel come morning."

She nodded, and her trembling mouth parted into a brave smile that somehow caught in his throat. "Where will you sleep?"

Not that he'd sleep, but he needed to rest if he was to carry her to his cabin. "I'm going to bring my dogs in. They'll help keep us warm. Then I'm going to climb in the sleeping bag with you. It's the only way we'll survive the cold."

She didn't argue.

"First, I want to make another check and see if the plane is still secure. I'll add a few more Hemlock branches over the windshield to cut down on the wind."

She reached for his hand and held it, but there wasn't much strength in her grip. He looked down at their joined hands, and was surprised at the intensity of the fear that he might lose her that settled in his gut.

"You won't leave me?" Her voice was even weaker than her grip.

"I won't leave you, Maggie." *No, I won't leave you to die even though you came to arrest me and condemn me to death.* He squeezed her hand and held it and waited, waited with the sounds of her shallow breathing beating inside of him until her eyes closed and her hand fell slack. She was asleep. He backed from the plane.

The snow was three feet thick outside the plane's door. Drifts much deeper. Matt and Jack's bodies were well buried under the foot that had fallen since he got here. It was only a matter of time before the wolves got the scent of them. He hoped it wouldn't be tonight.

She was still shaking when he returned to the plane. Even in sleep she shook. Will motioned his dogs inside, then pulled off his boots and unzipped the bag. It was the mummy style and a close fit. He blew out a long sigh as he wrapped himself around Maggie's slender form, bringing her head close to his heart. Though he barely knew her, he was getting in too deep. If he wanted to remain free, it was best for him to back away.

He dragged in another deep breath and let it out slowly through his nose. His eyelids grew heavy and fell shut. Almost immediately they popped open again. What was that?

A wolf. The pack had begun its nightly hunt, and they would be here much sooner than he hoped. They would find the bodies tonight.

* * * *

Frost painted the roof of the antebellum house a gauzy white. Behind the enclosing ten-foot brick wall, naked tree branches, their red and yellow brilliance of fall having turned to brown weeks ago, had dropped to the ground. Incoming winds from Lake Michigan blew the brittle leaves that had escaped the gardener's rake through the open wrought iron gates and down the short circular drive. A few danced frantically up the front stairs to the porch. Others dropped softly past the windows of the guesthouse apartment where Libby Raine lived.

Libby was the DNA-proven consequence of one of the Senator's illicit affairs. At the age of twenty-eight, after her second ill-advised marriage ended in divorce, Libby resumed using her maiden name and moved home. In an effort to find the peace and comfort she sought, she turned to God. Every week she spent long hours volunteering at Chicago centers for children's services and found she had no trouble putting the two failed marriages firmly behind her. Furthermore, she came to the conclusion that the best way for her to make up for her errors in judgment was to have a good time without the constraints of marriage.

Upon her return, Hilton had completely renovated the guesthouse for her. Libby moved in and found the little apartment with its two-car garage and its private entry provided her the privacy and freedom she'd always craved. For the first few days in her new home, she slept soundly to the soporific drone of the little French fountain in the lily pond outside her bedroom window and to her favorite "country and western" ballads on the radio.

All too soon the nightmares that had haunted her since her sister's brutal murder came back.

Three-quarters asleep, it took several rings before Libby's mind registered that it was the phone. She groaned and glanced at the clock with one eye. Surprised that the hour was nearly noon, she pushed herself to her elbows and lifted the receiver.

"Hello."

"Hello, Libby?"

"Daddy, is that you?" She sat up and pulled the phone onto her lap. "I can't hear you very well. Are you at the house?" She pulled the sheets up over her naked breasts and held her breath.

"No, I'm using my cell phone. I think we have a bad connection. Actually I'm calling from Salt Lake City. I'm in the airport. Hold on a second, and I'll move closer to a window. There, that better?"

"Yes. Did you say Salt Lake?"

"That's right. I'm flying to Anchorage, Alaska, then to Fairbanks. Right now Salt Lake's in the middle of a sleet storm and the runways are iced. We'll take off soon as they can deice the plane and a runway—no telling how long that's going to take."

She breathed again. Phone calls from her father, rare as they were, always gave her mixed feelings of concern and pleasure. "Why are you flying to Fairbanks?"

"Actually that's why I phoned. Matt may have located Jamie Donovan there. Did he mention that to you before he left?"

Libby's face paled. "No." Yesterday afternoon Ruby, who had replaced Thea as the housekeeper at Rutland Manor right after Ellen's murder, had told her something about Matt going off for a few days, and that was fine with her.

"Maggie and a newspaper reporter are traveling with him. If he does catch Donovan, I'm sure it'll make the national newspapers, certainly Chicago's anyway. I didn't want you to hear about it from anyone else."

She fell silent, thinking back. The police, the reporters, the endless questions, the terrible feelings of loss. The long hours she spent in her room, the headaches, the anger, the tears, her unraveling. Uncomfortable, she reached for the black slip that was balled between the sheets and began to toy with the delicate ribbon straps.

"Libby, you still there?"

"Yes, Daddy, I'm here. Why was Maggie with him?"

"To get credit for the arrest, I suppose. Now I don't want any of this to upset you. If Matt brings him in alive, we'll see that he goes to jail for the rest of his life. But there's the possibility Donovan will make a run for it. If he does, I have to believe Matt will take that as license to shoot him. Either way, once Donovan is captured, you can sleep better at night. We all can put the whole unfortunate incident behind us. That's a *good* thing, sweetie. You're not to worry, you understand?"

"Yes, Daddy, but I can't help remembering how terrible that night was. Donovan scares me."

"I know, sweetheart. You just let me handle everything. Ruby taking care of you all right?"

"Yes, Daddy. She cooks and cleans and sees that the main house is kept up just like you asked her to. If I'm out, she leaves me dinner in the fridge. All I have to do is heat it up. I take it upstairs and sit at the little table overlooking the gardens. It's really nice. I like having the apartment to myself."

"Good. I thought you might. Libby, there's one other thing you should probably know. The weather's pretty terrible up here, like I said lots of snow and ice, strong winds. It's pretty much that way all over the northwest, worse in Alaska. I'm afraid Matt's plane got caught up in it. But the pilot is well thought of and has probably put the plane down somewhere, so not to worry. I just thought you should know. What time is it there, anyway? Eleven-forty? Have you gotten out of bed yet, honey? I don't want you spending all your days in bed, Libby. You know the doctor says you should get out some. You understand?"

"Yes, sir. I have been getting out, and I was just getting up. I played some golf at the club yesterday, and went out last night with some friends. I got to bed late." She glanced over at the naked man lying beside her on her pink satin sheets. He was at least fifteen years older than her, had a thick mustache and streaked gray hair tied at the back of his head. A drummer, she thought, meeting his curious gaze with a shrug of her shoulders, at the bar last night. She tried to remember the man's name, but couldn't.

* * * *

At first, Will didn't sleep. His mind churned with the journey ahead of him and of other things while he struggled not to move and disturb the woman with whom he was sharing his warmth. Increasingly, he became aware of the long, shapely legs between his, and the backside pressed into his groin that despite the thick layers of clothing was so womanly and distracting.

He fought against his body's unwelcome reaction by keeping his thoughts busy, wondering if Jack had been able to radio his location before the plane went down or if the ELT had been able to signal before it was smashed in the crash, wondering if anyone was fool enough to mount a search in this storm, fearful they might already have set out with a sled and dogs. He'd come from Fairbanks by sled many times, but only when flying wasn't an option and on the last trip before he wintered in his cabin, and he wanted his sled dogs. He'd carried in his stove by sled and a few other supplies too bulky for his plane, but he'd never traveled in weather like this. Even so, the trip had been arduous.

He decided that those familiar enough with the terrain would also be respectful of Alaska's rough weather and not easily persuaded by the powerful Senator to set out under such conditions. He hoped he was right and thought that as difficult as the storm was for him to deal with, he was grateful for the protection it provided.

Maggie stirred, shivered, and his arm tightened around her. His hand spread wide, he slowly rubbed warmth into her, carefully restricting himself to the allowable parts. But he couldn't keep from bumping her breasts now and then, and when he did, his arm burned, and his heart raced.

In her sleep she groaned and snuggled closer. He went still, holding his breath, listening intently to the deep breathing of her sleep. He remembered all the blood she'd lost from the head wound and chastised himself for not bringing his sled, even though it meant taking the long way around. Would she have the strength to endure the walk to his cabin? Or would she die as his Ellen had?

A bellowing gust of wind rocked the plane. A branch landed on the roof with a loud thud. Against his back, he felt one of his dogs lift her head. He tensed. Looking around the plane, he saw nothing. The sound of the wind filled his senses. Despite all his efforts, it blew bits of debris and snow against the plane and through the shattered windshield.

Something frozen hit his face. He wiped it away with his fingers. After a moment Hilde nuzzled her cold nose against his cheek and licked him.

"Good dog." The air he drew into his lungs was painfully glacial.

Thinking of frostbite, he checked to see that the hood and sleeping bag were tightly secured around Maggie's head. He adjusted his scarf over his own mouth and nose. After a while he drifted into an uneasy sleep.

The feeling that something was wrong hit him suddenly.

Instantly he was wide awake. He couldn't put his finger on what was wrong, but something had changed while he'd slept. He glanced toward the door where low and ominous growls rumbled from his dogs. It was black as tar inside the plane, but he pictured them standing at attention, their hackles raised. He lowered his scarf from around his nose, lifted his cap from his ear, and listened for what had gotten their attention. The wind still howled, spitting snow against the plane same as before. He heard no other worrisome sound hiding within the wind's cry.

Then abruptly, terrifyingly, he heard it. He knew what his dogs sensed, and his fingers closed around the butt of his gun. Some creature, man or animal, was moving around outside. Hardly able to draw a breath, he rose on his elbows and levered himself from the sleeping bag to his hands and knees. He thought of the frozen bodies under the new snow: one of a friend, the other an enemy. He picked up the flashlight without turning it on. That was a mistake many made. To turn on a light prematurely or stare into a fire destroyed one's night vision.

He cracked the door. Immediately, he turned on the beam and four pairs of glowing, yellow eyes stared back at him. Wolves. Probably more than four. For a moment the wolves froze, then as if someone had given them a signal they merged back in with the trees and snow like ghosts. Then they were gone—but they'd be back.

After that Will had little trouble staying awake.

* * * *

When day finally came, a feeble wash of gray spilling over the treetops, it brought no warmth or end to the snowfall. The wind whined across the mountain. Will shivered and flexed his stiff joints inside the sleeping bag, stretching, working his cramped muscles to get the blood moving. He peered over Maggie's shoulder at the frost-coated plane, relieved the long night had finally ended, but dreading the ordeal still to follow.

When Maggie didn't show signs of waking, he touched her face with his gloved hand. "We have to leave. Daylight won't hold long."

Maggie's head twisted around, her lids flew open, and he looked into disquieting eyes.

"Who—" she began, then stopped abruptly. Her gaze darted from him and swept around the plane in an effort to orient herself. "Oh . . . I remember." Her brow knit. "I must have fallen asleep."

"You did, the whole night through." She turned within the circle of his arms, and somehow they drew so close their lips almost touched. He pulled back, his heart pounding in his ears. "How are you feeling this morning?"

He pulled his gaze away and unzipped the bag. Watching her was doing something to his insides. He slipped out, crawled to his pack, rummaged through it until he found a couple of packages and a tin pot that looked like a miniature pail then headed out into the storm.

"Where're you going?" She rose on her elbows.

"I've got some sterno and these mixes, so I thought I'd scoop up snow and make some warm soup. I can still smell the hint of gas in here so I don't want to chance lighting it inside. Chicken noodle all right with you?"

He glanced back at her and saw a genuine smile and that her eyes were green.

"Chicken soup sounds wonderful."

He turned away, tamping down the unwanted tingle surging through him and kicked his boot against the frozen door.

When he returned, Maggie sat with the sleeping bag wrapped around her, cocoon style, looking vulnerable and exhausted, but far better than last night. He thought about a travois to carry her, then decided against it. Constructing a travois would take time, more time than they had, considering the rate at which the snow was mounting, the shortness of daylight hours, and that his food supply was almost gone. Besides, it would be difficult if not impossible for one man to drag a travois down the steep mountainside to the riverbed below, then pull it along the treacherous river valley with its hidden rocks and fallen tree limbs concealed beneath the snow, and up the other side where in places the climb was hand-over-hand.

Desperately Will Connor wanted to remain a free man, but Maggie's former husband was dead, and she was alone. He'd have to do whatever it took to keep her safe. Then he would run. Tomorrow or the next day, when the planes once again were overhead, he would run.

Chapter Seven

A bloody arm stuck out of a drift of snow. Maggie crawled behind Will to exit the plane, and when he stepped down into the snow, the arm couldn't be missed. Unprepared for the sight, she reeled back, though she'd seen far worse.

Suddenly she knew. The growling she'd heard during the night she'd mistakenly attributed to his dogs. While Will trudged through the snow to the little stove he'd set up on a log, she held onto the side of the plane and closed her eyes.

"I thought I heard your dogs growling last night."

Will glanced at her, his black brows drawn together in a frown. He retraced his steps back to where she'd sagged on the floor of the plane and handed her a tin of soup, a spoon, and some crackers. "Careful, it's hot."

Maggie thanked him and looked into blue eyes fringed with lashes long enough to catch snowflakes. There was something compelling about his eyes, about him. It pulled her, and she turned away.

"Wolves," he said as though it were of no importance, then returned to where the flame from his sterno stove was melting down a tiny cook pot of snow. "They didn't do much damage. I'll put the bodies in the plane before we leave."

Maggie cupped her hands around the tin of soup, relishing the warmth. Was he lying about how much damage the wolves had done? Did she really want to know? With her back to the unnerving sight, she finished every last noodle of her soup then ate the frozen crackers.

A few feet away, Will dismantled the cooking gear and loaded it into his pack. She studied him anew. Taller than she first thought, he was a rough-looking man, rugged, with a dark growth of beard over his cheeks and chin that gave him every bit the appearance of the criminal she thought him. He was a hard man. Life on the run had made him strong and self-reliant.

He caught her staring, and his mouth twitched with a hint of a smile. A faint blush warmed her cheeks before she twisted away.

"I was hoping the snow would stop and the wind would die down," he said, walking up to her. She'd hoped the same thing and prayed that come tomorrow she'd be greeted with the sounds of aircraft flying overhead.

"I'm afraid neither happened. Unless I miss my guess, today's going to be every bit as bitterly cold as yesterday. For the first three-fourths mile or so the hike is steeply downhill. I know you're feeling better, but how's that ankle of yours?"

"Better, too." She didn't miss the worry in his eyes, the same worry she felt in the pit of her stomach. "Not throbbing as much."

"Good." He held out his arms. "All right then, slide out of the plane, and we'll test it out."

He had replaced her boots with the pilot's. The boots came up to her calf, and he'd laced them tightly over three pairs of socks, insisting they'd give additional support to her ankle than the heeled ones she'd been wearing. She looked at the boots, at the deep bank of snow, and his open hands, and hesitated. Out of the blue, a photo of Jamie Donovan and Ellen snapped into her mind. The picture, taken on a weekend ski trip to Ontonagon, Michigan, was filed away with dozens of others in one of the cold case evidence boxes. She particularly remembered the photo because Jamie and Ellen had appeared so happy. The photo was taken three months before Jamie Donovan knifed Ellen Raine to death.

On an exhale of breath, she pushed back the image, but couldn't rid herself of the ever-present sense of concern. That she was all alone in the wilderness with a man wanted for murder. She would do well not to be drawn to trust him.

"Come on, sweetheart." The hint of a smile returned and dimpled his cheeks in a way that made her forget to be afraid of him. "You slept in my arms last night. If I were going to kill you, I would have already done it and eaten the second package of soup myself."

She smiled and let him hand her to the ground. Despite all she'd learned from Hilton and Matt about him to the contrary, he was damn appealing. No wonder testimony after testimony from the girls at Montgomery Academy indicated half of them had crushes on him.

Not letting go of her hand, he grabbed a stick resting against the fuselage and handed it to her. "Hold on to my arm and to this crutch and take a step."

The forked stick he'd cut fit neatly under her arm. At about hip level a five inch stub, trimmed of its bark, stuck out for her hand. She took one tentative step with her crutch and when her knee didn't buckle, she took another and another and found the snow more of a hindrance than the pain in her ankle. "I'm good to go."

"Are you quite certain? I can carry you."

Keenly aware that a misstep or fall could cause more severe damage to her ankle, she considered taking up his offer. But it simply was too much to ask of him to carry her.

She clenched her jaw with determination. "I can walk." She took a few more steps to prove it. "You've got enough to carry with that pack."

"I can leave the pack in the plane and transfer a few essentials into my pockets. But if you're okay with walking, try not to put weight on your injured ankle. I could be wrong and it could be broken. If it is and you land on it hard, you could compound the break. That splint I made is only of the most rudimentary sort."

"I understand. Lead the way."

"All right, give me a couple of minutes to put the bodies in the plane, and we'll start."

In no time he was back at her side and not even breathing heavy. "We'll take it real slow. When we get to the bottom of this hill, we follow along the relatively flat lands by the river, and it'll be easier." Without another word he hefted his pack, whistled to his dogs, and started walking downhill.

In her overlarge boots Maggie followed awkwardly. Almost immediately she slipped and fell, and caught her forearm on a broken branch sticking straight up from the ground. It began to throb. She pulled her sleeve back down over it and kept her mouth shut about the stab of pain. In seconds he climbed back to her and lifted her to her feet. After that he pointed out branches of small shrubs and trees for her to hold onto, and she mostly managed to keep on her good foot and the crutch.

He moved down the mountainside like his dogs, sure-footed, like he'd been born to hiking like this. And it occurred to her that in some ways, he was probably enjoying it.

She wasn't. She spent all her days at a desk, and her legs were screaming with each step. In no time the boost of energy she'd gotten from the soup and crackers fled. An overwhelming feeling of exhaustion set in. Her lungs labored to fill with the thin air. Even with the frigid temperature, very soon she was sweating. Tiny droplets formed between her breasts and at her hairline. How was it possible to sweat when it was so terribly cold?

The snow was over two feet deep. In places where it had been swept by the wind, it came up to her waist. Moving through it was like trying to walk through water. In no time her legs grew weak, then numb. Her borrowed boots were several sizes too big and in spite of the extra socks didn't tie close enough around her slim ankles to keep the snow out. Very quickly her socks and feet were wet with chunks of ice and aching with the cold. She began to shiver again. And they weren't even to the bottom of the mountain.

She stopped to rub her thighs and calves. "How many miles do you think we've gone?" She panted to catch her breath.

"Can't say exactly—maybe half a mile, more or less."

And his place was twelve miles away? She groaned and forgot to hold on to the spruce branch he'd shown her. Her feet slipped out from under her, and she didn't stop sliding until she hit the back of his legs. Immediately her head began to pound, but somehow her ankle was okay. "I'm so sorry."

He smiled and lifted her. "That's one way to come downhill. We're nearly at the bottom now. I see my snowshoes over there."

Only the tips of his snowshoes were visible. If he hadn't pointed them out to her, she'd have thought them just more sticks.

"Your ankle all right?"

She nodded.

"You still sure you want to walk?"

"Yes," she lied. Darned if she'd let him know how weak she really was. If he could walk carrying a huge pack, then she ought to be able to make her way on her own one and a half feet. But she felt so extraordinarily weak.

He handed her a skin flask from inside his parka. "Here, drink some water."

She took it with clumsy fingers and drank, spilling some down her front. When she'd finished, he took several swallows himself. "Well, if you're certain you're able, we better get going. We can't afford to stop for more than a few minutes at a time if we're to reach the cabin before dark."

He adjusted her scarf. "Keep that up over your nose. Frostbite is a very real possibility in this kind of cold."

She thought of her aching feet, but kept her mouth shut.

At the base of the mountain they stopped again while he tied the snowshoes onto her boots. "Have you ever used snowshoes?"

She shook her head.

"They should make it a lot easier for you to walk. You won't have to try and move all that snow with each step, but can walk on top of it instead. Just don't come down with your foot toe first or you'll topple over."

The cumbersome looking contraptions were little more than strings of some sort woven between two bowed sticks. Having something so large attached to her feet felt awkward. She fell again almost immediately.

He helped her up and dusted her off. "It'll take a few minutes to get used to them. You're doing fine."

Once more she tried and managed a few steps before one snowshoe came down on top of the other, and she toppled face-first into the snow. "I'm hopeless." She giggled, surprised that she could.

He bent over and gave her his hand. There was strength in his hand, and kindness. The kindness unnerved her, and to her dismay sudden tears rolled down her cheeks, warm rivers against her frozen face. What was the matter with her? She was a police woman. She'd been trained to handle crises; she'd been through crises before and not dissolved into tears like this. Annoyed with herself, she swiped the back of her hand over her cheeks and set her jaw with determination. "I'll do it right this time."

A bit more practice and she managed to stay upright with the aid of her crutch. He led the way beside the frozen river, walking through snow that in places was thigh-high with apparent ease. From time to time he paused to look at her and let her catch up. Those times he brought out his water bladder and they drank. Then he'd tediously refill it with snow and put it under his parka to melt against his body.

She on the other hand, despite sweating from the exertion, was also shivering from the cold. Deep down in the marrow of her bones she shivered. All too soon the placing of one foot in front of the other became a monumental effort. Breathing the thin air made her lungs hurt. She needed rest desperately, preferably in a place where there wasn't any snow, a place out of the cutting wind. If only she could get warm. It seemed a long, long time since she'd been warm.

He glanced back at her. "You all right?"

She was numb from the cold. Her feet were numb. Her brain was numb.

"Yes . . ." It seemed too much effort to say more. Lost in her thoughts, she failed to concentrate on lifting her feet and stumbled like a hobbled bull into the deep snow.

Once more he lifted her to her feet. His hands lingered on her arms, then his grip suddenly tensed. His eyes narrowed with something, maybe fear, and he stilled, staring at the trail they'd trampled in the snow behind them.

Maggie's breath leapt from her mouth, then jerked to a stop against the lump of fear lodged in her throat. "What? What's wrong?"

* * * *

Hilton was furious. After delay after delay he'd managed to make it all the way to Anchorage only to be told that because of the weather no planes were flying in or out of Fairbanks. Even the train had been shut down due to the snow and fallen trees on the tracks. He stood in the loading zone outside the airport where the maze of construction cones and detours made it impossible to find a cab, and cursed the falling snow. His options boiled down to waiting in the airport until a flight materialized or booking a hotel.

Ignoring the customers waiting in line in front of him, Hilton bullied his way past them, slapped a fifty dollar bill on the counter, and prevailed upon the harried information agent to use his computer and search out places where he could stay the night.

"I'm sorry, sir," the agent said fifteen minutes later. "There just doesn't seem to be a single room available in the city tonight."

"You tried all the B&Bs?" He'd stoop to that degree of inconvenience if it kept him from sitting endless hours in the airport.

"Yes, sir, as many as are listed in the computer. There may be others, but it would take hours to search them out, and others are waiting."

Hilton was forced to face the real possibility of spending the night in a hard plastic chair at the airport. Many of the car rental counters and food vendors were already closed. The bar was closed. The airport was shutting down. About the time the gray-haired, stoop-shouldered man at a magazine kiosk called him over, Hilton was desperate.

The man didn't crack a smile when he suggested that if Hilton couldn't wait, he could hire someone to take him to Fairbanks by dog sled.

"Of course," the man amended with a chuckle, "by the time your sled gets to Fairbanks, you'll be half frozen, and the storm will be long over. Me, I'd wait out the storm and fly in soon as the planes can take off. I couldn't help hearing Barry tell you the hotels are full. That's to be expected with the bad weather n' all and it being off-season and many already closed, but I can probably book you a room at a place my cousin runs up the road apiece. Usually it's pretty dead up there this time of year. It's up to you."

The "hotel" took over an hour for the cabby, another of the man's relatives, to drive. The blue two-story clapboard construction was cattycorner to the only other building within sight—a gas station. There wasn't a tree or a shrub within twenty yards.

The view outside Hilton's window was of a dump. A dump! He cringed. Without the pristine covering of snow, the place would look even worse. The room was marginally acceptable: clean sheets, bare bones furnishings, unadorned walls.

But miracle of miracles, the hotel had a bar, and soon as he dropped his carry-on on the bed, he retraced his steps down the wooden stairs to the dimly-lit, smoke-filled room.

The only occupant and source of the smoke sat on a rickety stool at a bar painted the same sky blue as the building. An old fellow with long, crinkly white hair and beard puffed and lit one cigarette from the other like he had a death wish. He was reading a motorcycle magazine. Hilton lit up a Cuban and sat at the other end of the bar. He saw no bartender.

Badly in need of a drink, he went to the front desk and spoke with the same Aleut woman missing her two front teeth who had smiled a greeting to him at the front door. She was sitting on a chair with her feet propped up on a stool, also smoking cigarettes. After some discussion, Hilton got his drink, a Johnny Walker neat, and was directed to the dining room for supper.

The room was large and as blue and barren of decoration as the rest of the establishment. Only two of the vinyl-topped tables were occupied. After ten minutes, a rail thin middle-aged woman brought Hilton a menu with two pages of selections.

"Because of the storm there are a few things that aren't available tonight." The list she rattled off was so long Hilton lost track.

"Well then, do please tell me what *is* available."

"The fried chicken and the meatloaf."

"Fine. I'll take the meatloaf and another Johnny Walker. Make it a double."

Even with his expectations at rock-bottom levels, he was surprised meatloaf could taste so much like sawdust. He drowned it in ketchup, ate quickly, and retired to his room with another double scotch and some magazines he found in the lobby.

On the bedside table a single lamp gave off an orange glow that didn't reach the corners of the room, far too dim to read by. He flicked on the TV, tuned to some news, and sat back on the bed to see what was happening in the real world.

Moments after he'd hung up his suit, the light and TV went off. Hilton hissed a string of oaths. The chair in the airport was beginning to look good. He groped for a phone to call room service, couldn't locate one, so put his pants back on and trekked down the uncarpeted steps to the lobby where an elderly woman with blue-gray hair now manned the desk by candlelight. The vendor's cousin he presumed.

"Surprised the lights didn't go out sooner," she greeted cheerfully, testing his temper right away. "Haven't seen this much snow in years." After a monologue on how hard the foul weather was for business, she gave him a candle and promised to have her nephew deliver more to his room right away.

"Be careful with those candles. Don't want to burn the place down," she said.

That was precisely what Hilton had on his mind when he returned to his room. Fortunately for the other guests, he wasn't quite drunk enough.

* * * *

"Damn it, Maggie, you're bleeding." Will's gaze bored into her. "You've left a trail of blood. Why didn't you tell me?"

"I didn't know. I smacked my arm on that first fall, but it didn't seem like much, just a scrape. I didn't realize I'd actually cut it. The blood doesn't show up on this dark parka—I thought the sting was from the snow, so I didn't think about it." For the first time Maggie noticed the blood dripping from her sleeve. The cut must have been pretty deep, because where she'd fallen just now, the snow was pink.

"I've been worried about my feet. I think they may be frozen," she blurted, then immediately her face heated from embarrassment. "I'm sorry. I don't want to be any more trouble than I already am. I thought I could do it, walk . . . such a simple thing . . ." Her voice cracked. She tried to smile, but the look on his face told her she'd made a poor job of it.

He touched two fingers to her chin. "You're doing fine."

He squinted toward the sky, into the heavily falling snow, then without a word lifted her from her feet and sat her on a fallen tree. Slipping the pack from his shoulders, he took hold of her hand and examined it. "It doesn't look too serious."

"I'm grateful you're such a good Boy Scout."

He barked a laugh and shook his head. "No one ever accused me of being a Boy Scout before," he said, bringing a smile to her face. Then the laughter left him. He rummaged through his pack and spoke without looking at her. "I'm afraid everything I know I learned the hard way. I learned to carry bandages and disinfectant when I tried to free an eagle caught in a hunter's snare, and he bit me. I learned to carry spare clothing after I fell through thin ice when I was out hunting and nearly froze to death. Here's what I need."

He pulled a roll of gauze from his pack and took her wrist in his hand. "I just need to cover it with a bandage to keep it from bleeding."

He never moved anywhere without his rifle, but it was the lethal-looking eight-inch blade he pulled from a sheath at his waist that riveted every ounce of her attention. The knife was precisely the kind that had killed Ellen and had his fingerprints all over it. Maggie froze, unable to breathe. If she ran, there was no way she could out-distance him. She slipped her hand into her pocket where she'd moved her gun and hesitated with her gloved forefinger over the trigger. She was a good shot—hours and hours of practice at a shooting range had given her confidence she could hit what she aimed at, but if she shot him, her chances of survival were slight to none. She had no idea where his cabin was and no skills to survive in such a harsh environment.

He must have sensed her unease, for he looked up suddenly and met her eyes. Then his head dipped, and he looked at the knife in his hand and stilled. She thought he might be seeing ghosts of that night so long ago when he had just such a knife in his hand and killed his sweetheart before he'd run from Chicago. For a long time he didn't move. Around them the wind howled, and the leaves rattled and chunks of ice dropped from the trees like broken tears.

At last he straightened, pulling a large piece of jerky from his pack. Sucking in a deep breath, he cut off a couple of chunks, handed one to her and put the other in his mouth then sheathed the knife. She let go of the gun and breathed.

The jerky finished, he told her to sit on the fallen tree, and he gave each foot a good rub to get the circulation going before putting dry wool socks on her feet. Edgy, she watched his every move as he watched hers. After a while she began to think something must have caught his eye, for he repeatedly bent back his head, kneading the muscles at the base of his neck, and stared back at the mountainside where the plane had gone down.

What was making him frown? She looked where he did and all of a sudden it dawned on her what he was seeing—nothing. The plane was no longer visible. Snow had covered it. The thought depressed her, and her mind returned to the crash and to Matt, lying dead in the tomb of the plane where Will assured her he'd be safe from predators until a rescue could be mounted.

As he ripped open the Velcro straps that held the sleeping bag onto his pack, she keep staring back the way they'd come.

"Something in particular bothering you?" he asked.

She bit her lip to keep it from trembling. "I can't see the plane."

While he unzipped the sleeping bag, he glanced back at the mountainside. "Not surprising. About eighteen inches of snow fell on it since it went down."

"But how will the search plane find me?"

He tossed the bag onto her lap. "Don't know. But for certain, they're not likely to spot the plane from the sky until spring. Now go on and wrap that bag over your shoulders. You're shaking so much right now, you're making me cold."

She almost smiled. He was teasing her. Here they were in the middle of nowhere with him looking like the abominable snowman and just about as frightening, with snow hammering them and miles still to walk, and he was trying to cheer her up. She was still afraid of him, but not as much as before.

"Don't worry." His tone softened along with his eyes. "Someone'll come looking for you. The pilot—I knew him. He was a good man and a good pilot. Some of his friends will come searching for him soon as the weather clears enough for them to fly. You can count on that."

He adjusted the sleeping bag over her head and shoulders. "I've got a few more peanut butter crackers you can munch as you gather your strength."

They sat side-by-side on a downed tree beneath a wind-cracked pine, its thick evergreen branches providing a little shelter from the snow and wind, and ate without talking. Around them the bitterly cold wind came down the river valley, howling like a steam engine.

Finished eating, Will loaded his pockets with what food he could stuff into them. Then he carried his pack to a nearby spruce where he concealed it between branches and came to stand in front of her. Even after eating she felt weak, woozy, but she filled her lungs and resolved she'd walk the rest of the way without complaint.

He went down onto one knee and began to take the snowshoes from her boots.

"Why are you doing that? I'm beginning to get the hang of them."

Will gave her a hard look. "I know you are, but for the last couple of miles you've been staggering. I'm going to wear the snowshoes and carry you."

She dropped her gaze to the blood colored snow and knew he was right.

He took the sleeping bag from her shoulders and held it open. "Now sit back down, and I'm going to slip you into this. When you're not moving on your own, the air feels a lot colder."

It was galling to have to be carried, especially by this man, but she knew how done-in she was. Her protest was weak. "No, I can't ask . . ."

"You're not asking. I'm telling. Now get into the bag." His tone brooked no argument.

Reluctantly, Maggie complied and tried not to wince when he hoisted her across his shoulders, fireman style.

"I'm afraid this won't be very comfortable for you." Lifting his rifle, he set out with a steady gate.

She squeezed her eyes shut, embarrassed that she who took such pride in being so self-reliant could now seem to do nothing without the help of this man. Only because of him was she alive.

She bounced against his back, watching his footprints in the snow, and dreamed for a moment . . .

"You all right back there?" The sound of his voice shook Maggie out of her reverie. "We'll take another short rest."

"Yes," she said softly, unable to summon the strength to say more. She closed her eyes. Her ears rang; blood pounded in her head almost as bad as it had last night.

He set her on her feet and held her upright with an arm behind her back while he took the sleeping bag from around her. She was glad for his support, unsure if she had the power to remain standing without it. He lifted her into his arms and deposited her on a stump. Then he glanced at the sky as if gauging the amount of remaining light, and she thought the sky looked darker than before, bleaker. Was it her imagination?

"How long since our last stop?"

"Roughly three hours."

Three hours riding and bouncing on his back . . . she didn't remember any of it. How could she not remember it?

While she rested, he stood looking up at the mountain ridge they'd been walking along. The storm hadn't abated, if anything the snow seemed to be coming down harder than before. His dogs were close at hand, rummaging through the snow on the frozen river. The mountains facing them were a little higher than where the plane had gone down. But she couldn't see what had caught his eye. She followed the direction of his gaze to an overhanging edge that curled above a steep slope. Beneath it was a litter of fallen trees and rock that might have broken from the ledge.

She looked to the mountaintop where his attention was snared. In the wind and falling snow everything was movement, a kaleidoscope of black and white and gray. Then she saw it, a definite shape moving deliberately along the ridge, against the wind, and her breath caught.

"What is it?"

"Wolves." He came with his gun in his hand to sit close beside her. "They've been following us for some time now. They smell your blood."

Chapter Eight

Hilton awoke to a frigid room, socked in skies, and far from rested. He waited ten minutes for the water to turn hot; decided it wasn't going to and forwent taking a shower, redressing in yesterday's suit. His watch read noon, but he wouldn't have guessed it from looking outside. Power had been restored, but he couldn't get the TV to work. His cell phone battery was dead. The charger was in his bag that hadn't made it to Alaska yet, or at least not to him. That, he mused, rendered his cell phone a worthless piece of hi-tech junk.

Thinking, outside Anchorage, the region had failed to move into the Twentieth Century, Hilton picked up his wallet and headed downstairs to find a pay phone. There were several. He picked up one, then another. All dead.

"Lines are all down on account of the storm," the railway agent's cousin cheerfully informed him.

"Well, does someone have a cell phone I might borrow? I have an important call to make."

"Sure, I have a cell phone, but we're pretty much out of range. No towers nearby. Don't forget you're in Alaska."

Not likely, he thought bitterly.

"Sorry about the TV not working. Cable doesn't come out this far, and the antenna's blown over in the wind. Nothing but snow on your TV screen." She laughed at her silly joke. When he maintained his stony silence, she cleared her throat.

"Any word on the airport, whether planes are flying in and out?"

"Radio says all flights are canceled until at least 5:00 p.m., maybe longer if the wind doesn't slow."

He walked away, cursing under his breath. An hour later he tried the phones again, and an hour after that, until finally at four that afternoon he got a working line. Three rings later a male voice answered the other end of the line.

Ann Merritt

* * * *

By the time Will left the riverbed and began the trudge up the steep mountainside toward his cabin, he no longer worried about the wolves—his dogs were keeping them at bay. He was worried whether he had enough in him to make the last climb. Exhausted and spent, he sucked air and drained off the last vestiges of his strength, his movements rote, mechanical.

Dotted with trees, large outcrops of rock, and hidden holes, the climb to his cabin from the eastern side was difficult even on a summer day, impossible for a sled and dogs. He'd chosen the spot specifically for those reasons. Tonight the climb was treacherous, the approach dark as a cave.

His thighs and calves burned. The shoulder Maggie lay across throbbed unmercifully. His feet were numb with the cold. He fumbled along, picking his way over the pitfalls.

At first he worried about the footprints he was leaving in the snow and swept the path behind him with a spruce branch. His energy sapped, he threw the branch away, praying that with the swirling winds and heavily falling snow, the footprints would be gone come daylight. What he needed, what his woeful little party desperately needed, was food and warmth. Would he ever be warm again?

To his own ears, his breathing sounded loud, labored. His lungs burned.

Maggie's sudden moan startled him. His snowshoe slipped across an ice-crusted rock. For a perilous moment he teetered, but quickly his hand found a branch, and he regained his balance. At least she was alive. Since she hadn't responded to him over the past hour, he hadn't been sure.

The soft whimpering worried him so he stopped, propped his weary shoulder against the trunk of a tree, and let her slide to the ground.

He touched her cheek. "Hang in there, sweetheart. We're almost home." She didn't respond. Nothing he could do now, so he hefted her back up to his shoulder and set out again.

His mind was numb with fatigue. At a time when he must be extra careful, he couldn't think clearly, and that scared him. If the authorities were waiting, a sound from Maggie could alert them to his coming. But could they have gotten here in such a blizzard as this? And would they stoop so low as to shoot him with Maggie on his back? How would they know who he was carrying? Maybe it was a good thing she was making sounds in her semi-conscious state. God, he was so tired his thoughts no longer made sense.

Nose lifted, he sniffed the air for the scent of smoke. Would the authorities be smart enough not to light a fire? He figured they would.

Stark still, he listened to the night sounds for a careless whisper and studied the way ahead in an effort to detect movement inconsistent with the storm. Daylight long gone, the night was so pitch black it was hard to tell if the movement he sensed was from the wind or man. But his dogs seemed relaxed, anxious to be home, and hungry. He would take his cue from his dogs. Even so, he moved ahead slowly, from fatigue as much as caution, searching for fresh tracks without any hope of seeing them even as he walked over them.

He was still a good three hundred yards from his cabin, when he heard the first rumble from his sled dogs. He lifted his head sharply and stopped, his mouth dry from exertion and worry. He stood for a moment, listening to the crescendo rise. It was normal for his dogs to bark a warning. He started again, staggering the first few steps.

As he approached the cabin, a heavy and unexpected sadness entered his heart. Every tree felled, every nail hammered, every stone carried, chiseled, or blasted for the fireplace had been done by his two hands. With the exception of the stove and the glass for the windows he'd brought in by sled two years ago, he'd made every piece of furniture from trees he'd dragged sometimes for miles so as not to disturb the natural setting around his cabin. And now he would have to leave it all behind.

For the most part, the years spent in his cabin had been if not exactly happy ones, certainly chore-filled and peaceful, and accompanied by a growing feeling that in the wilderness of Alaska he had at last found a place where he was safe.

But the statute of limitations for murder never expired.

No light showed from the cabin windows; no scent of a wood fire came from the chimney. All good signs. He was certain no one was there to take him into custody tonight. Not this time. Not yet. Still, when he stepped inside the dark cabin, he tensed, his finger on the Winchester's trigger. Nothing. No movement. Nudging the door closed with his elbow, he stood in the dark, breathing heavily, listening for any unfamiliar movement. When there was none, he let the tension slowly leave his body. He'd made it.

He let Matt's wife slide across his shoulder, bracing her against a chair to keep her from falling. She crumpled to the chair and slid to the floor at his feet without any sign of life. He groped for the lantern on the table just inside the door, fired it, and turned up the wick. Everything appeared to be just as he'd left it.

He felt for a pulse, found one, and softly shook her. "Maggie, wake up. We're at the cabin. Soon you'll be warm and able to rest."

She was silent, her head sagging to her chest, her face drawn and pale. He pulled her gently across the floor nearer to the hearth, looked around for a place to make her comfortable but ended up leaving her there, leaning against his chair. Getting warmth into the freezing cabin was a priority, and he went to work building a fire.

The jugs of water he kept on hand were frozen solid. He set them on the hearth to melt, went outside, packed a cooking pot with snow, returned and hung it on a hook over the fire. That done, he turned his attention to Maggie. Alarmed at the pallor of her skin and that she seemed comatose, he pulled the quilt from his bed and covered her in the sleeping bag.

He steeled himself against the pull her presence was having on him. When he thought of her courage and guts, he felt a small jolt of pride. He felt responsible for her, and he cursed himself for the feeling. What he should be thinking of was packing and making a run for it. He didn't want to be touched by a woman ever again. Couldn't afford to be, not if he wanted to live. The capacity for caring should have been torn out of him. But it was still there, so he had to find a way to deal with it. God help him.

How had Hilton Raine's son found him way out here? Did Maggie realize he was the man her husband was searching for? More than likely she did.

He sat beside Maggie and pulled her close, sharing the quilt with her. Bracing a pillow under his arm, he fought the overwhelming fatigue that pulled him toward sleep. Think, think out a plan for the morning because come first light he must leave. His eyelids grew heavy. He rubbed his fingers over them, stretched his arms up in an effort to stay awake. A battle he couldn't win—his eyelids drifted closed, and he didn't have the energy to move them.

* * * *

"Dad, that you?" Paul Raine dropped the heavy law book onto his desk and breathed an audible sigh. "Where are you? I've been worried sick. I've been sitting by the phone for two days waiting to hear back from you and listening to the TV newscasters go on and on about the terrible storm hitting Alaska. Have you found him? Is Matt okay?"

"Wish I knew. Last contact I had with the Fairbanks police was right after I called you. They didn't have any new information so I didn't bother to call you back. I'm in Anchorage, trying to find a way to get to Fairbanks. The bad weather has shut down everything. Phones just got restored a few minutes ago, and my bag with my cell charger was located at the airport at about the same time. Someone's on his way here with it right now—so things are looking up. But it's touch and go whether cells will work up here—not enough towers except in the heart of the cities."

Paul stared out the window of the swank stucco office building of Wilson, Casey and Raine at the vast, noisy metropolis of Los Angeles. "So I suppose you don't know any more about Jamie either?" Since his father's first call, Paul had been thinking a lot about Jamie, remembering things about him, like how much he liked him and how they'd won the state football championship together, and inconsequential things like how in his four years of playing football at Northwestern University Paul had never found another who could match Jamie's sure hands or his uncanny ability to be at the right place at the right time. He'd been thinking more about Jamie than he'd been thinking about Matt.

"According to the deputy sheriff in Fairbanks, they only know him as Will Connor."

"But you're pretty sure the guy is Jamie?"

"I don't know if the guy is Jamie or not, Paul. I haven't seen the photo the Chicago police say they have, but Matt sure as hell thought he was or he wouldn't have set out after him like he did. I hope he is. And I hope we nail him and put him away for good."

Paul took a swallow of his coffee, swiping a hand over the ring it left on one of the stacks of papers on his littered desk. "If a court of law finds him guilty, yes, I agree. I just hope Matt doesn't get trigger happy to please you. I hope he brings Jamie back alive. I'd like the chance to talk with him face to face. There are lots of questions I'd like to ask him, things I'd like to get straight. I know you never approved of him, Dad, but I always liked and trusted him. You know that. And to be honest, I've always thought Jamie was innocent just like I've always thought that the MVP trophy awarded me at the high school state football championship should have gone to him."

"That's foolish. You deserved the trophy."

"Well, I have it, so I guess the point is moot." Paul looked over at the place where the impressive trophy once was displayed. Some years ago he'd taken it home and put it in a box. "You know Mother used to have Jamie to dinner on many of the nights when you were out of town?"

"I found that out when the police were interrogating her after the murder. It was the first I knew of it, and I can assure you we had words about it afterward. Look where all that charity for that young man landed her."

"It wasn't charitable feelings that drove Mother. From the first day I brought Jamie home after football practice, she took to him. Half the girls at school were after him. Libby baked him a birth—"

"Damn it, Paul, right now I don't give a damn what you or your mother thought of Jamie or who the hell had a crush on him or baked for him. Right now I'm not even thinking about the man. I'm worried about Matt. And just you remember when your thoughts turn soft on your high school buddy, your sister was murdered by him, brutally—don't you ever forget that! I was there, by God. I saw the results of Donovan's knife. His prints were everywhere, and he tried to murder me, too, before he ran. I hope they put him away where he'll rot for the rest of his days."

A Cry From the Cold

"All right, Dad." Paul exhaled. "You win." He changed the subject to safer ground. "The newspapers are calling the blizzard you're experiencing the worst in a century."

"Damn inconvenient is what it is."

"Speaking of newspapers reminds me. Remember the state congressman's daughter who went missing a couple of months ago?"

"Lester Stern's daughter, hell yes—how could I forget when the newspapers haven't stopped going on about her since she failed to show up at her house after the party that night? Have they found her?"

"Unfortunately, yes. I thought you might have missed seeing it. It was in the Chicago papers this morning. Her body washed up on Lake Michigan's shore, not far from our house. Captain Oswald called me from Chicago a couple of hours ago."

"You talked to the police?"

"I guess they're questioning everyone who attended that party which was the last place she was seen alive, so that included me. You, Libby, and Celia can look forward to hearing from him, too. Seems her death doesn't look like an accident, but Captain Oswald was tight-lipped about details. After he brushed me off, he asked if we'd heard from Matt. I guess he read in the papers his plane was missing."

"I called him shortly after my first conversation with Fairbanks. I hoped he could expedite the search for Matt's plane."

"Maybe Oswald didn't have any better luck with the Fairbanks department than you did. The weather's the culprit," Paul went on. "I guess there wasn't much else he could do, but he said to tell you he hoped Matt and Maggie were all right. Then he asked me a few questions about the evening when Stern's daughter disappeared. Not much I could tell him. I didn't even remember what the girl looked like until I saw her picture in the paper. I think he hoped to ask Matt a few questions, too. According to those in attendance, Matt spent quite a bit of time talking with her that night. Oswald was hoping Matt might have an idea if she were meeting someone and if so, who."

"Hell, people are always getting murdered in Chicago. That's nothing new. She probably had a fight with her boyfriend. I hope Oswald's not inferring that Matt went off with her that night?"

"I don't think so. Anyway I got to worrying about Libby there in the house all alone, especially with that creep murderer still out there preying on classy women. You know the one the newspapers are calling the Lakeshore Murderer? Anyway, I hope Libby's all right."

His dad was quiet for a second. "Ruby's there with her. She comes in every day. She'll keep an eye on her. Libby'll be fine. I talked with her right after I talked with you, and she seemed fine. Anyway, I can't get any definite picture of when the weather's going to clear enough for the planes to start flying so I'm thinking I'll get a cab to the train depot soon as my suitcase arrives. They tell me the train to Fairbanks should be running late this afternoon. Any chance you can find your way up here and meet me in Fairbanks? If Matt hasn't been able to capture Donovan, I've decided that I'm going after the bastard myself."

For a few seconds the line went silent except for the crackle. Paul cradled his head in his hand, massaging his forehead.

"You still there, son?"

"I'm here, but I don't know about coming . . . I'm pretty busy . . . I have a big case. You remember me mentioning the rising starlet, Marilyn Rose. I'm representing her in a big case against MGM."

"I know her, sure. Spent an evening with her as a matter of fact. A beautiful woman. I'm the one who sent her your way. Did she tell you that?"

"No, she didn't mention it—I thought it was my intelligence and good reputation that attracted her." He laughed. His father chuckled on the other end of the line, and Paul's own smile widened. He knew his father well, was aware of his appetite for young women with beautiful bodies. Paul hadn't followed in his father's footsteps. Though the opportunities for affairs with famous Hollywood starlets that were the downfall of many, were numerous, it wasn't a roving eye that had broken up his own marriage. He rubbed his thumb over the place where his wedding band once resided. It had been his compulsion for long hours of overwork that sent his wife into the arms of someone else.

Paul glanced at a photo of his six-year-old daughter and raked a hand over his mouth and chin. He'd worked hard and sacrificed a great deal to make partner. He'd also lost a lot. Had it been worth it? He cleared his throat.

"Dad, I've been thinking a lot about bringing Jamie Donovan back to Chicago. I don't think it's a good idea. You should forget about him and just bring Matt back home. Jamie has stayed clear of us and made another life for himself. Why bring all that scandal back into the open? It's not going to do any of our careers any good. Don't you think after all this time Jamie's paid his dues?"

"As far as I'm concerned, he'll not have paid enough until he's dead. My sweet Ellen is dead on account of him, and he should get no less."

"But, Dad . . ." He drew in a deep breath and spoke in a rush. "Okay, I'll see what I can do about coming. Give me some numbers where I can reach you."

There was nothing to be nervous about, Paul told himself as he hung up the phone. Surely Matt would be found somewhere safe and warm, weathering out the storm. Matt always landed on his feet. Frowning, he took a swallow of the coffee his secretary had brought in earlier, found it cold and replaced it on the desk with a thump. Perhaps the guy Matt thought was Jamie might not be him at all.

He carried his musings and worries to the private washroom adjacent to his office, washed his hands and splashed water on his face. That fatal night, Paul had been in the little garden behind the house making out with his date. He and his girlfriend had heard the gunshot and ran around the house in time to see Jamie run down the front walkway. He hadn't seen what happened inside the house. Since then he'd heard about it nearly every day of his life, but he hadn't *seen* anything except Jamie running and the bruises on his father's body that he attributed to Jamie. Paul blotted the water from his face with a monogrammed towel and dreaded having to testify in court against his friend.

Back in his office, he pressed the intercom on his desk. "Julie, please book me on the next flight to Anchorage, then on to Fairbanks."

83

"Yes, sir. Will you be back in time for your appointment in court day after tomorrow? You also have a couple appearances to make on Friday."

"No. See if you can get Ron Sanders to take those. Although I hope to return within the week, leave the return flight open."

"Ms. Rose just walked in, sir—she's conferring with the receptionist. Will you see her? And what about the date with Harry Wilson and his wife tonight? He told me he's bringing a date for you."

Paul laughed. "Harry's always fixing me up with a hot date. The last one wanted me to introduce her to Matt Damon."

"So I gather you don't mind postponing the date?"

"Cancel it. And Mrs. Atwater, don't think I don't know you've been putting him up to setting up these dates."

This time she laughed. "Well, how else are you going to meet a wife?"

"Thank you for your confidence in me, *Mother,*" he joked. "I already know the 'you need a good wife' and the 'your daughter needs a mother' lectures by heart. Just get me to Alaska. If there's no connecting flight to Fairbanks, get me on a train. Rearrange the appointments as you see fit. Now, please send Ms. Rose in, and then see if Ron has a few minutes so I can go over these cases with him."

"Yes, sir, I'll take care of everything right away, and shall I send for some lunch? You haven't eaten anything today."

Paul chuckled. "Make it a Philly cheese and beef and a large unsweetened tea."

"And I didn't have anything to do with that date who thought you were a friend of Matt Damon's."

"Likely story."

* * * *

Dog-tired and red from the cold, Gene Pryor entered the ABAT Service building behind the Fairbanks airport terminal, stamping snow from his feet. A couple inches short of six feet, wiry build, Gene's face was hallow-cheeked and weathered, and his normally friendly expression was grim.

A single bulb shining from the overhead fixture in the small waiting room fused with the twilight from outside, lighting he equated with the sterile look of a police station or a military barracks. Except for the low moan of the wind, the room was so quiet it seemed eerie. He looked around to see if anyone had come in since he'd gone home earlier in the day for a few hours sleep and some chow.

Off in a corner beside the window, Jack Ricks' wife Nancy sat on a wooden chair, looking very pregnant and very tired, her eyes puffy and red. Her temple rested against the windowpane, a bag of necessities camped at her feet.

Jack had been missing for more than thirty-six hours.

Gene shook his head and crossed the room, taking her hands in his. "Brier told me you were coming. I'm so very sorry, Nancy. I wish to God I could tell you I've heard from Jack. Don't give up on him. You know he always carried emergency food and blankets. Hopefully, he's holed up somewhere."

Nancy's mouth quivered. "I'm praying for that . . ." A fresh wave of tears washed from her eyes. "What's the latest on the weather forecast?"

Gene swallowed and knelt to bring her into his arms. He held her, then rocked back on his heels. "Unfortunately, calling for continued snow and more winds. The front stalled over half of Alaska, but if Jack got his plane down when the weather came in, he'll be fine for days. Soon as we can get into the air we'll go looking."

"I know . . . how's Jenny?"

"You're not to worry about your daughter. She's doing just fine at the house."

"Thank you so much for keeping her. I don't know what I'd do without you and Brier. I don't want Jenny seeing me like this. I just can't seem to stop crying. Oh, God, I hope he's safe."

"We're all praying for him. But night's coming in, and we're not going to be able to take to the air for a while. You should let me take you to the house for some rest. You're all done in, and we don't want to have to deliver that baby of yours until after Jack returns." He offered her a smile, but it was weak. "We'll keep you informed, I promise. Plow's just been through so the roads are mostly passable for now. Why don't you get your things together, and I'll drive you to our house?"

"Thank you, maybe that's a good idea. I *am* all done in—I couldn't sleep at all last night."

* * * *

Paul Raine drove to the airport, the possibility of coming face to face with Jamie after all these years still on his mind. There was so much baggage between them.

Ironically, Jamie had attended the prestigious Montgomery Academy on a scholarship that in a tight election year Paul's father had sponsored. But his father had never expected his own children to cavort with Donovan's sort off the football field. In the privileged society of the Raines, his father had made it abundantly clear "Jamie Donovan had nothing to offer but trouble." Paul sighed heavily. How accurate his father's prediction had been.

He rubbed four fingers over his brow, remembering the first day he'd laid eyes on Jamie Donovan. Introduced at an assembly as the recipient of the Raine-Proctor Scholarship, Jamie, unsmiling and forbidding, already close to six feet tall, stood in obviously hand-me-down clothes like a presence awaiting expected doom, his broad shoulders hunched forward. Aware of Jamie's noticeable social shortcomings and his father's dire warnings, Paul had felt uneasy.

It was on the football field that Paul recognized the toughness inside of Jamie. And he admired that. Their friendship came later and grew strong over the four years Jamie attended Montgomery Academy.

Shortly after Ellen's murder, a newspaper article revealed Jamie had a record with the police prior to his acceptance at Montgomery Academy. Apparently he'd climbed out of St. Mary's through an upstairs dormitory window in the middle of the night, made his way to downtown Chicago on foot, and picked a fight in a back alley with some gang members.

According to the story, several individuals were beaten badly in the incident, Jamie included. Aside from his lacerations and bruises, he had suffered a life-threatening knife wound in his gut. Two of the combatants he'd fought had also been hospitalized, one with a severe concussion, the other less seriously injured. The article gave no motivation for Jamie's precipitous action. Jamie hadn't denied the fight. Consequently, he'd taken the rap.

Only fifteen at the time, with no prior convictions, the judge had let Jamie off with probation and community service. Reading the story in the newspaper a few days after Ellen's murder had shocked Paul, forcing him to realize he hadn't really known his friend as well as he thought.

Not surprising that Jamie had been able to hide from the law all these years. Paul often wondered how the running had changed him, what kind of life he'd made for himself. A bush pilot, his father told him. Paul figured he'd be a damn good one, facing up to the dangers of Alaska like he faced the big bruisers on and off the football field.

At the busy airport Paul left his car for valet parking, and easily went through security with his Gold Medallion pass. He sank into the comfortable seat of business class and watched Los Angeles grow small as the plane took off and gained altitude.

By now Ellen's murder was classified a cold case. If Matt hadn't been so obsessed with finding Jamie, the whole unfortunate tragedy would have ultimately withered and died. Not that it sat well with Paul that his sister's murderer was still at large, but his brother's preoccupation with the case had always disturbed him. He prayed Matt's efforts to shine in his father's eyes wouldn't come at the cost of either man's life.

When Paul looked out the window at the vast empty sky, the uneasiness he'd felt the first day he laid eyes on Jamie settled on him once again.

Chapter Nine

Maggie awakened to the golden light of the ebbing fire in a dark room. Lying on a fur in front of the fireplace, she had no recollection of how she'd gotten there. A brown animal pelt was tucked under her head. The sleeping bag they'd spent the night in was still around her. On the floor a foot away, Will lay on his side, his back resting against a low table, his cheek fallen to his shoulder, his breathing a soft whisper.

One of his dogs, the one called Hilde, was between them, tucked up close to Will's hip. The husky licked her arm. Maggie smiled and reached over to give the dog a few pats. From her position at Will's feet, the dog Lucy that looked pure wolf raised her head and stared at Maggie speculatively.

The light from the fire was soft, the heat warm and comforting on her skin. The air was rich with the scent of burning logs and pine from the stout log walls. She closed her eyes, then opened them again and found herself studying this strange world where cold clung to the air and little had been purchased at a store. She'd have been infinitely more comfortable in her crowded Chicago office with its rattle of conversations, telephones ringing, keyboards clacking, filled with the smell of coffee and overworked people.

The break in Ellen Raine's murder case came a week ago, when a clipping cut from the *San Francisco Chronicle's* Sunday edition lay on Maggie's desk. Someone had printed her name on a post-it and paper-clipped it to the envelope containing an article about bush pilots. Upon further inspection, the envelope was addressed not to her, but to Matt. Postmarked Chicago, there was no return address, no indication of who'd sent the clipping or why. After rereading the article and using a magnifying glass to examine the photo of four pilots standing in front of a plane, in particular the one circled, Maggie had pondered the names listed for the best part of an afternoon without coming any closer to solving why the article had landed on her desk.

When queried, no one in the office could solve the mystery. After Matt returned to the office and she'd shown him the clipping, waiting at his side while he examined the article and photo, his reaction had taken her off guard. He'd hugged and kissed her like she'd handed him the moon, like he still cared.

"Can't you see? It's Jamie Donovan." He propelled her to the bulletin board where Jamie's wanted poster was displayed, and held up the clipping of the pilots. "Look. He's the tallest one of the two standing in the middle. Add some years. I'm sure it's Jamie, and so was whoever sent the clipping."

In a flurry of excitement Matt had dropped all the other cases he'd been working on to act on the tip. Though to Matt the arrest was personal, a task laid out by his father when the scandal had first sullied the Senator's name, some of his excitement had rubbed off on her.

Part of her job was an observer of people, an evaluator, and she was good at it. It hadn't taken her long to realize this man who called himself Will Connor was at ease in the hostile Alaska wilderness. Self-assured and capable in many ways, he was also guarded and prepared. Now as she lay beside him she couldn't quite make herself believe he was a murderer. But she was pretty sure he was hiding something.

The wind outside the cabin howled and sent a puff of smoke back down the chimney and a chill through her. She shivered and fanned the smoke away, arching her head back until it touched the rough-hewn legs of the sofa behind her. The sofa was like no other she'd ever seen. Obviously hand made, its hide-covered cushions were filled with spruce or some sort of fresh-smelling pine. She breathed deeply of the scent, deciding she liked it.

Whoever this Will Connor was, in order for her to get out of this mess and back to the lower forty-eight, she had to formulate an escape plan. But with her head still pounding, her mind was too fatigued to think coherently, let alone plan a viable escape. For now, she prayed the storm would pass quickly and one of the planes Hilton had undoubtedly dispatched to find his son would soon find her.

She offered her face to the warmth of the glowing embers in the hearth, and her attention was drawn to the huge stone fireplace. Stones meticulously stacked without any evidence of mortar rose up through the roof. She imagined that Will Connor had built the fireplace and marveled that his hands had broken all those stones and chiseled them to fit so precisely. Was it possible those same hands belonged to a man who'd brutally stabbed his pregnant girlfriend?

Above a rough-hewn timber mantle, a rather large painting of a lone polar bear crossing the Alaskan tundra caught her attention. The artist had transformed a desolate scene with its dark and cloudy sky and barren reaches of snow-covered ground into one of breathtaking magnificence. As she continued to survey the log walls of the cabin she noticed more paintings, many without glass or frames, most of them of the wilderness and its wildlife. Surprised that this rugged bear of a man possessed such a compelling collection of art, she could hardly wait to get a closer look. The warmth and spectacular beauty of the paintings was in direct contrast to the disorderly mess and blatant masculinity of the rest of the place and brought a smile to Maggie's face.

Without warning, her mind darted to her ex-husband, the man she'd left behind in the plane—a corpse, literally frozen stiff and stripped even of the dignity of wearing clothes—and her smile fled. How had it all come to this? She reran the last week in her mind, imagined the many different decisions she could have made to prevent this disaster from happening. For one, she should have insisted Matt postpone the trip until spring, when conditions were better. Would he have listened to her? Matt had one priority—finding the man who'd murdered his sister.

Years ago, before she faced up to Matt, she'd suspected he was sleeping with the pretty rookie cop who'd been helping him search for his sister's killer. Stubborn and spoiled to the end, he'd denied it, but she'd done her homework and confronted him with the evidence.

The same night she moved out of Rutland Manor. Other than her clothes, few things in the exquisite suite of rooms she shared with Matt belonged to her. Only one thing in that house would she miss—Celia.

Hilton's wife had chosen to stay with her philandering husband, but she'd supported Maggie's decision to leave, maybe because she valued her friendship, or because she didn't have the strength to leave herself. Maybe simply because she knew Matt, better even than Maggie did.

As divorces went, the meetings between her and Matt and their respective lawyers were amicable—after all, they had to work together. Even though well rid of him, tensions ran high, and although their ranks of detective were the same, to keep the peace she often found herself acquiescing to his demands.

The morning before they boarded the plane for Seattle was a prime example. They'd argued about the reporter. He'd been adamant Vera accompany them, insisting he wanted her to cover the capture for the newspapers and for a book he intended to write with pictures and documentation. Maggie had argued against it, saying a reporter could be found in Fairbanks. In the end Matt had his way—Vera came and shared a room with Matt.

The trip from Chicago had been tedious. They had flown to San Francisco where they'd hoped to meet with the author of the article that accompanied the photograph of the three pilots to get more information. Upon arrival at the journalist's office, however, they were told Mr. Ralph Wayne was on assignment and not expected to return for a week or more. The editor, a portly man with a rosy nose and a wealth of white whiskers that reminded Maggie of Santa Claus, told them Wayne had conducted the interview in Fairbanks.

Matt decided they wouldn't wait for Wayne's return, but head directly to Fairbanks. They flew into Anchorage without incident, but had to wait eighteen hours to catch a heavily-booked commuter plane to their destination.

The next few days in Fairbanks were spent canvassing the town together, tracking down the three men standing beside Will in the photo, particularly looking for the one who might or might not be Jamie Donovan but called himself Will Connor. As it turned out, two of the pilots hadn't been difficult to locate.

In separate interviews, Jack Ricks and Gene Pryor remembered the incident and the reporter who'd written the story on the bush pilots that formed ABAT some years before. In fact, a large reproduction of the photo that appeared in the article was mounted over the desk in the office they shared. Both pilots spoke highly of Will Connor's skills as a pilot, recalling his reluctance to be included in the article, but neither admitted to knowing precisely where in the White Mountains Will Connor retired during the winter months.

The last pilot was Jim Foley. But before Maggie and Matt could locate Foley, they were directed to Evegeny Zemkov who'd been flying with ABAT for a number of years and was a good friend of Will Connor. With Vera and her camera along, they found Evegeny in front of his house in Fairbanks. He'd just returned from a week in Anchorage. Nearly six feet tall and barrel-chested, Evegeny had a face full of salt n' pepper whiskers that needed a trim. At their approach, he brushed a hand over his forehead as if to drive away an annoying fly.

"I heard about you three," he said. "You've been asking questions all over the office about Will. Well, let me save you some trouble. I don't know where he is."

"Is there anything you can tell us about him?" Matt queried as Vera snapped the man's photo without asking.

He glared at her for a second. "I don't know a thing about Will Connor's personal life. He's a damn good pilot, I work for him, and that's all I need to know. But I'll tell you something you might not know. The photograph printed in the newspaper isn't the photo Ralph Wayne took that day."

Hand on her hood to keep the wind from blowing it off, Maggie said, "You're right. We didn't know that."

"The one Mr. Wayne took didn't include Will at all, at Will's insistence," Evegeny admitted. "Will pretty much keeps to himself, doesn't like publicity of any sort. He's a loner, always giving credit to others, and taking none for himself. I thought Will was just being reserved, not wanting to be included in the article. He deserved credit for making the same mail runs as the others. His plane had gone down a time or two, too. When a couple weeks later I came upon a photo of the four of them I'd taken the year before, I sent the photo to Wayne. I guess I shouldn't have done that. Why are you looking for Will anyway? Is he in some sort of trouble?"

"We don't know, Mr. Zemkov, we're just trying to find him."

Finally, they located Jim Foley, laid up in the hospital, recovering from pneumonia and taking a lot of medication. The visit with him revealed no new information.

Everyone who knew Will—and most everyone did—said he wintered in the mountains somewhere. But everyone was either unable or unwilling to reveal precisely where. Several hazarded a guess. "Thought I heard once he built somewheres in the mountains along the Yukon. He's gotta have built where he could set his plane down, so it's likely you'll find his cabin on a river or some lake. But I can't say I know a body that's been to Will's cabin. I sure haven't."

Somewhere in the mountains along the Yukon covered a lot of territory. With the Yukon River almost two thousand miles long, and more than three million lakes in Alaska, the information was next to useless. Maggie learned a plane could land on the frozen tundra. Will Connor could be anywhere.

No one expected to see Will Connor in Fairbanks again until March or April. Matt came close to scrapping the investigation until spring, but she agreed with him—odds were strong that before they could return, someone would alert the man that the authorities were asking questions about him. Once again he would slip away.

Since they were still in Fairbanks, they decided to widen their search. Questioning the office workers provided no new information.

Then they got lucky.

While interviewing a pilot who occasionally flew for ABAT, a female clerk at the store where the pilot was currently employed approached them. She'd overheard their questions and the inference that an inheritance was due Will and offered that last winter her cousin had seen Connor in Circle City. Perhaps they'd find him there.

Granted, not much to go on. They hired Jack Ricks to take them to Circle City. Because of the unusually large weight of mail for delivery that day, Jack limited his passengers to two. Matt had wanted Vera along to take photographs. Maggie insisted she had more priority.

Now she found herself stranded in a one-room cabin with the murderer she'd come to arrest. To her further chagrin, Vera was very much alive and presumably comfortable in Fairbanks.

Maggie breathed deeply. What was done was done. She must take each problem one at a time. So far Will Connor had extended her nothing but kindness and more. She was alive because of him, and that was enough. For now.

Will's rhythmic breathing changed. He awoke with a start, jerking his chin from his shoulder. "*Damn*, I fell asleep," he said, half under his breath. He rubbed the sleep from his eyes then propped himself on his elbow to scratch Hilde, who rolled onto her back and whined happily.

In the firelight the dark beard on his chin and cheeks had taken on an orange hue; a swath of blood was smeared under one eye. Maggie thought he looked half asleep, disheveled, completely masculine, disturbing, and not at all the sort who could commit murder.

He gave her a quick glance. "You awake?"

"Uh huh . . ."

"Doing all right? How's the ankle?" He sat up.

"Sore, but not bad, considering. Actually, I'm feeling pretty good, much better than before, but I haven't tried to walk yet." She looked up into his face.

For the length of a breath, he smiled at her. His smile washed over her, releasing a tiny shiver through her. She swallowed and her gaze skittered away from him to the dog he petted. "I owe you thanks."

He pushed to his feet and turned to the fire, stirred up the coals, added some kindling and a log, then stood back to watch the wood ignite. "Anyone would have done the same."

He was dead wrong about that. In her line of work, she came across many men, fellow cops who thought themselves pretty tough, more criminals who made their livings by frightening others into submission. She couldn't imagine any of them would have shown such courage or stamina as Will Connor.

"What time do you think it is?" she asked.

After placing another couple of logs onto the flames, he walked over to his desk and rummaged through a stack of papers until he found his watch. "I can tell you exactly. It's a little after three." He tossed the watch back. "By my reckoning, there's a good six hours left of night."

He walked back to the fireplace and sat on the floor across from her with his back against a chair, his long legs stretched out in front of him. His dogs came up beside him and lay with their heads on his thighs, one on each side like they were accustomed to doing so, and he began to scratch them. Across from him she sensed the love he had for his dogs, the strong bond between them.

"Go to sleep. No one will be flying while it's dark."

Already she felt herself drifting back to sleep. Her voice, when it came, was hardly above a whisper. "When do you think they'll come for me?"

He let the question die. "Go to sleep."

Chapter Ten

Throughout the night the blizzard raged. At one point Maggie awoke to the wind wailing outside the walls. She burrowed deeper into her cocoon of fur and drifted back to sleep.

Later, the tantalizing aroma of something cooking brought her fully awake. She rose to her elbows, and for a moment she studied the broad shoulders of the man bent over a large pot set on a cast-iron range that was surely an antique fifty years ago. He was clean, his hair still wet, and wearing jeans, brown boots, and a red plaid shirt that stuck out from under a worn, brown leather pilot's jacket.

She'd never witnessed a man at home in a kitchen. Though the little space where Will cut up potatoes could hardly be described as a kitchen, she enjoyed seeing him there. Growing up, her mother had done all the cooking. After college she'd been intent on moving up the ladder in law enforcement. That required long hours on the job and never left time to learn to cook more than the simplest of things.

"Good afternoon," he said without turning. "Hungry?"

The smell of whatever was in that big cast iron pot made her mouth water. "Famished."

"Just a few more minutes, and it'll be ready."

"How long have I slept?"

"The night and half the day. This'll be late lunch or early supper. You needed it—the sleep."

She had expected to be uncomfortable in this place in the desolate wilds of Alaska, the place that belonged to a man who'd committed murder. Instead she found herself drawn into his cozy, strange world, where daylight glowed faintly outside his single window, and where the paintings and sketches and Eskimo artifacts were quiet and friendly, as was the man who'd put them there. The complete opposite of what she'd expected to find in him.

"I like your paintings," she said, primarily to start up a conversation and keep her mind off her problems for a while. "Were they all painted by Alaskans?"

He stirred the pot and turned, a guarded look in his eyes. "I suppose you could say that. I suppose I've been here long enough to be considered an Alaskan."

She rose and hobbled to the fireplace. "You painted them? All of them? But the name on the painting over the mantle is Wilding." She looked back at him.

He shrugged dismissively. "A pen name. Painting's a hobby of mine."

Did others know of his talent? That he used another name to sign his works indicated not. "Do you market any of your works?"

"A friend of mine has sold several from her restaurant."

A woman. More than a casual acquaintance she suspected, for she doubted he'd open up to just anyone with his private paintings. Drawn to a painting of a wolf standing at the edge of a river, she crossed the room.

"That ankle of yours must be feeling better this morning."

"Yes. I don't think it's broken."

He nodded. She braced her hands on a table littered with paints and brushes and sketches done in pencil and in ink and studied the lovely little watercolor of a wolf hanging over the desk. Light and airy, it was painted with a caring hand and with an understanding and appreciation of the power and intelligence of the solitary wolf. She sensed an underlying loneliness there, too.

When she looked back, she caught him watching her. His eyes, a rich blue that stole little glints of gold from the flames, held hers. His dark, bold good looks marred slightly by a scar that ran from his hairline through his eyebrow, barely missing his eye. She dragged her attention from him to his painting, quickly assuring herself that the fluttering in her stomach was nothing more than hunger. Heavens! The blow to her head must have knocked her good sense clear out of her.

"I particularly like this." She pointed out the unframed watercolor.

"You saw him yesterday—the wolf—when we were walking along the river. Do you remember? You were pretty out of it by then."

She remembered, but she hadn't seen the beauty in the beast as he did, only the threat. It surprised her that he had seen it and expressed it so eloquently.

"He and I have become friends of a sort. I think he has his eye on my Lucy." He tucked his chin and reaching down to pet his dog, chuckled to himself like he was used to doing it that way. "Come spring I'm expecting a visit from him."

He crossed to the far side of the room and opened a jar, pouring a bit of a crushed herb into the palm of his hand. He brought it to his nose and smelled. "Oregano. My friend who runs the restaurant insisted I take several jars of herbs she put up last summer. I didn't have the courage to tell her I haven't a clue how to use them. But this smells good." He tipped his hand over the pot and stirred.

A full five minutes passed before he spoke again. "When you leave here, you can take the picture of the wolf with you if you like, a souvenir of Alaska. For now, you should sit down while this cooks and rest that ankle."

He carried a wood-framed dinette chair, one of the few items that didn't look handmade, and placed it close to the fire.

She recalled how confident Matt had been that they could arrest Jamie Donovan and bring him back to Chicago. "The bastard will be caught off guard," Matt had said, "and we'll bring him in without much fuss." But then she hadn't met Jamie Donovan, hadn't known the man he'd become, if indeed, this was Jamie Donovan. Even if Jack Ricks had landed their plane without mishap, she very much doubted they'd have taken this man back without a fight. What's more, she wasn't at all certain it was a fight they'd have won.

He took a walking stick from against the hearth and twisted it through his fingers. For several moments he contemplated it, and then, as though he felt her tension, he glanced at her with a slightly amused look. He crossed the room and handed the stick to her.

"This might help you get around."

A snake was carved around the shaft of the stick, the natural bend at the top its head. The crown of the shaft came up to the top of her head, too tall to be comfortable for her but a perfect fit for him. She ran her fingers over the perfectly carved scales of the snake. Had a friend made it for him? She wondered at the story behind it.

"Up here things are pretty crude. No bathroom like you're used to. When you need it, there's a pot in my bedroom. I rigged up a blanket to give you a little privacy. Sorry I can't do better for you." His slow grin renewed the tension in her stomach.

Glancing over in the direction he nodded, she smiled. The bedroom that he'd generously turned over to her was beside the fireplace. It consisted of a wooden shelf supported by four legs between the stone chimney and wall and served as his bed. A faded green blanket was pinned to a clothesline with clothespins and bunched up to one side.

Darn, but her head throbbed. She leaned heavily on the stick and held back a grimace of pain as she awkwardly made her way to the chair he'd placed by the fire. Hilde came up beside her and nudged her thigh. She ran her fingers through the dog's thick fur while she watched the dog's master, looking totally masculine and at ease in his makeshift kitchen, wiping out two bowls with a cloth.

Out of the blue she remembered her gun. When he wasn't looking, she slid her hand over the pockets of the parka and frowned. Before she exited the plane the gun was in one of the pockets, but it wasn't there now. Where was it? A shiver of apprehension skittered down her spine. Yesterday, the arrest warrant for Jamie Donovan had been in the inside pocket of Matt's parka. The inside pocket was empty; all the pockets were empty. If he ever left the cabin, she'd try to locate her gun and the warrant.

Will poured two bowls of stew and handed her one. Then he stoked the fire, took his bowl, and sat on a stool across the room from her.

"The oregano okay?"

"Tastes good to me, but I'm not much of a cook, therefore not much of a judge."

"I thought all women could cook. Thought it was bred into them, some kind of cooking gene they inherited or something." His mouth twitched and almost smiled.

Maggie flashed a quick smile before she could stop herself. "Actually, I like to cook, but it seems like stuff goes wrong when I do—like I get sidetracked or too busy or the telephone rings, and I forget to turn on the oven or to add the sugar. Truth is, my mother was an excellent cook, but rarely used a cookbook. When she passed on, her recipes were lost."

He made no comment, just went on eating.

She wasn't used to silence, but he certainly didn't have much to say. No idle conversation, no interrogation, not even a query about the gun he must've found on Matt or her own gun that was no longer where she'd put it.

Which was for the best, she reminded herself. If she didn't have to, she didn't want to try to foist off a story about the gun, and she didn't want to know any more about him than necessary. She'd just have to make the best of a bad situation, keep her wits about her, bide her time until she figured out a way to get free. She was a cop with a strong sense of right and wrong. There were rules and laws, and consequences for when they were broken. He was wanted for murder and when the opportunity presented itself, it was her sworn duty to arrest him, but she realized with a nudge of surprise she was no longer looking forward to the job.

She'd never killed anyone, never even drawn her gun on anybody. She worked in the office, canvassed crime scenes, poured through forensic evidence, sorted through police reports, files—old and new. When necessary, she followed the clues to the streets, anything to find the right puzzle pieces. Before she was promoted to detective she'd been in acute danger a few times, but she'd always had backup.

She breathed a little harder. Will Connor wouldn't be taken in without a fight. She reached down for the glass of water at her feet, drank half, then wiped her mouth with a fingertip.

Will was a big man, a tough man of the mountains. Whether she had her gun or not, if he wanted, he could keep her here. Make her his hostage and have his way with her, if his mind was set on that. She needed help. But until help came, she was on her own.

"Do you think they've sent someone to look for the plane yet?"

He rose and looked at her for several seconds as if measuring her concerns before he stepped to the kitchen corner and served himself a second helping. "Not a chance, not until the storm quits. In a wind like this a plane would be more likely to be blown off the runway than to get off the ground. If by some miracle a plane did manage to take off, in this snow, the pilot would be flying blind. Would you like more stew?"

She shook her head. "No thanks."

Tears threatened—from frustration, from physical weakness, from knowing she was no match for this man. But tears wouldn't bring strength or someone to rescue her, or heal her aches and pains. She sniffed them back, annoyed by the weak moment.

"How long do these storms usually last?"

He turned and smiled, the amusement making his eyes friendly. "There's nothing usual about *this* storm. It could be over in a few hours or last for a week."

So, she might be stuck here for some time. She wanted desperately to go home to the little house on Chestnut Street where she'd grown up and had lived since her parents' deaths.

Will was cooking something else on his little potbellied stove. Her gaze went past him to the window. It was snowing harder than ever, or else it had blown clear up over the window. The wind still blew with a mournful sound that tapped a desire inside of her, something she rarely dwelt on. Will Connor lived alone, but for her, even married to Matt, she had essentially been alone.

Unless she misjudged him, he was content with his way of life, the strength and character within him enough to get along without others. But sadly, she wasn't.

Willing her self-absorbed thoughts away, she sat quietly. That's when she heard them, the sounds he lived with: the cheerful crackle of the fire, the soughs of Hilde and Lucy sleeping close to the hearth, the occasional creak of the log walls as they shifted ever so slightly in the wind, and the intermittent bark of other dogs he kept outside to pull the sled he mentioned. Comforting sounds. In springtime he probably opened the door and window. Birds would be singing, the creek where he fetched his water babbling, the wind not a sorrowful cry from the cold, but a gentle whisper.

Suddenly she understood how he had made this place his home and found peace.

* * * *

A blasting of snow obliterated the sign outside the wooden building, but the path trampled to the front door told Hilton he'd found the right place. Paul opened the door for him, and the two men were greeted by the welcome scent of fresh coffee and frying sausage. After the first night's debacle in Alaska, Hilton secured a decent hotel, but not transportation to Fairbanks. His third day in Anchorage, he met Paul at the airport. The following afternoon, the rails opened briefly, and they caught a train to Fairbanks before another wave of bad weather hit.

Hilton followed his son into the warm restaurant and closed the door behind him, glad to be out of the frigid cold and wind. The room wasn't large, but eight or nine wooden tables were crammed inside, all filled. Three men stood just inside the door, waiting for a seat.

A stout woman holding a tray was engaged in conversation with three men sitting at a table as she collected their empty dishes. A younger woman served up plates of eggs and sausage from a large fry pan. Only one other woman was in the restaurant, and she was having breakfast with a man and two small children.

After Hilton and Paul's arrival in Fairbanks the previous night, Hilton's first stop had been the sheriff's office. Since Jack Ricks was a friend, Deputy Sheriff Brad Douglas appeared as anxious for the search for the downed plane to begin as Hilton. Deputy Douglas contacted the airport and confirmed that search planes and pilots were on standby to take to the air as soon as the storm permitted.

Hilton showed Deputy Douglas a copy of Jamie Donovan's wanted poster. To his disappointment, the man saw no likeness to Will Connor and insisted the man had never been in trouble in all the eight years he'd known him. According to the deputy, Will had made several daring rescues in his plane, *Everhawk*, and was highly thought of by one and all.

Clearly, the deputy wasn't interested in a man who'd been accused of a crime thirteen years ago. Hilton concluded that if he was going to find Jamie Donovan he'd have to prod the investigation along himself.

This morning, as he shaved, Hilton recalled Paul's recent remarks that Jamie Donovan had always had a way with women. His own daughters and his wife had been charmed by him. He reasoned that a man like Donovan would have found himself a woman. A few subtle questions to the proprietor of the Fairbanks Lodge, where he was staying, he discovered that Connor did indeed have a girlfriend. One Tracy Kora, owner and operator of a popular local restaurant.

Leaving Paul to hang up their coats, Hilton headed for the woman who was filling the plates. A man stood behind her washing dishes. Another used a wooden spoon to beat batter in an earthen bowl. Hilton didn't want his conversation overheard, but he would be careful with this initial contact.

The woman had ash-blonde hair pulled neatly back from her face. Beneath a no-frills apron, she wore a simple and crisp white blouse with a chocolate brown skirt. She hadn't bothered with lipstick or mascara. Her mouth was wide and smiling at him cautiously like she maybe knew who he was.

"Hello," she said while she continued to fill the plates. "I don't believe we've met. I'm Tracy Kora. Is there something I can do for you?"

"Senator Hilton Raine." He held out his hand, watching her face closely for a reaction to his name. He was disappointed to see a flicker of recognition. If Donovan had mentioned his name it could work to his disadvantage. "My son and I just got in last night, and your restaurant was recommended to us as the best place for breakfast."

"Pleased to meet you, Senator. It was on the news last night that you were in our city for a few days. We don't get many visitors in Fairbanks during the winter. Welcome. Karla will find you and your son a seat in just a few minutes. Meanwhile, if you don't mind waiting by the door with the others, it'll make it just that much easier for Karla and me to get the customers in and out."

As Tracy Kora promised, the restaurant thinned out within fifteen minutes; only a couple of elderly men lingered over coffee and sweet rolls. With a clean mug and a coffeepot in one hand, Tracy walked over to where Paul and Hilton were finishing the last of their breakfast.

After refilling their mugs with steaming coffee, she set the coffeepot on the table and sat in the chair across from them.

"Thank you, Ms. Kora. We appreciate you giving us your time," Paul said.

"Please, it's Tracy. Ms. Kora is way too formal around here."

"My son was a passenger on that plane that Jack Ricks was flying," Hilton said without preamble.

"We're all praying they'll be found alive." She took a swallow of her coffee, and the tone of her voice flattened. "You've got to understand, Senator, this is a small town, particularly in the wintertime, and people asking questions about a person around town don't go unnoticed. I recognized you the moment you came in. In case I hadn't, several of my customers have brought you to my attention. I'm sincerely sorry your son was on the plane that's missing. A friend of mine was the pilot of that plane, so we're all very concerned, but it doesn't explain why your son has been asking about Will Connor all over town. What really brought you gentlemen to Alaska in the middle of the worst storm in years?"

"First and foremost we came in hopes of finding my son alive. But we're also looking for Will Connor. We were told he's your boyfriend, so we thought you might be able to help us locate him."

She let his assertion pass without comment. "We have a small TV in the kitchen, Senator, and just now Fox news was interviewing someone from the Chicago Police Department. I heard your name mentioned, but not much of the story. I wondered if it had anything to do with Will Connor and your son. Perhaps you can clear it up for me."

"Will Connor is suspected of using a false name and coming to Alaska to hide from the authorities. We think his real name is Jamie Donovan. If so, he murdered my daughter thirteen years ago. And we intend that he pay for his crimes."

Paul heard the rising anger in his father's voice and placed a hand on his arm. "Please, Dad, let me—"

"So are you going to tell us where the hell your boyfriend is hiding?" Hilton demanded, shaking off Paul's hand.

"Enough!" Paul turned and looked into the worried eyes of this attractive, industrious woman. "Tracy, my father is understandably upset by my sister's murder, but I'm sure he meant to say that if Will Connor is really Jamie Donovan, then he is a suspect in her unsolved murder. None of us witnessed the crime. Whether he's guilty or not would be determined in a court of law."

"I can't believe that of him," Tracy said. "Will wouldn't knowingly hurt anyone!"

"If it's any consolation, I don't believe he killed my sister either, but all the evidence points his way." Surprised by his own admission, he glanced at his father. "He needs to come back to Chicago and help the authorities clear the matter up."

"Just tell us where the hell he's hiding," Hilton repeated. "I'll see your name is kept out of it."

"I told you earlier. I don't know where he is." Tracy pushed her chair back and began to gather the mugs. "That still stands. And quite frankly, if I did know, I wouldn't tell you. I'll be honest with you. Will isn't my boyfriend. He's just my friend. But if Will had wanted me, I would've married him years ago. Men like Will don't come along but once in a lifetime. I sincerely hope you don't find him."

Tucked in the back seat of the lodge's limo, an ancient Jeep Cherokee, Paul and his father left for the airport. The sky was dark gray and thick with fog; the road clogged with snow and barely passable.

Hilton turned toward his son and smiled. "I'm excited. I have a strong feeling we're getting close to finding Donovan."

* * * *

Maggie sat with her feet propped on the hearth, trying to ease her tension, to think, but even after three days of recuperation her head still ached uncomfortably, a constant reminder that the ordeal she'd been through had taken everything out of her. And now worry kept her off balance. Opportunity to search for the arrest warrant or for her gun hadn't presented itself. With each passing hour she became more certain Will must have found them and knew exactly who she was. So why didn't he pack up and leave?

An open book in her hands, she tried to ignore him working at his potbellied stove. She didn't want to notice the little things about him: eyes that twinkled when he allowed himself to smile, or his hands, large and capable, when they cut up potatoes, when they tended the fire, when they checked her ankle each day and rewrapped it. It took Herculean effort to remember those same hands had stabbed a pretty young girl to death.

Maggie leaned against the back of the chair with a sigh, uncomfortably aware of the strange sense of uneasiness growing between them. There was something damnably compelling about him, and she couldn't ignore it.

She swallowed and tried again to read, but it was no use. "What are you cooking over there? It looks like enough to feed an army."

He turned, and his eyes flashed with tension as though aware she'd been watching him. His expression softened. "I've got six hungry dogs outside. Sled dogs expend a lot of energy, so they need a lot of food. I try to get a week's worth of cooking done all at once."

"Why don't you just feed them some Alpo or Purina kibble? Wouldn't that be a whole lot easier?"

"Yes, but a whole lot less nutritious."

"Oh." She rested back against the pillows on the chair, and he turned back to his cooking. After a while the images around her began to blur, and her eyelids grew heavy. If she closed her eyes and emptied her mind for a minute or two, she'd better be able to deal with him, with her plight. Her eyes blinked, once, twice, and then they stayed closed.

Vaguely she remembered him lifting her. On the edge of sleep she breathed in his scent—the wood smoke, the meat he was cooking—as he carried her to his bed. She forgot all about searching his cabin for her gun and the warrant. He laid a blanket over her, and she thought she mumbled, "Thanks," but wasn't sure.

She never heard him leave, never registered the high-pitched barking of his dogs as he ran them and fed them. Only when he returned to the cabin after sunset did she awaken. She eased up on her elbow to look at him standing just inside the cabin door, his parka white with fresh snow.

He hung his jacket on a peg behind the door, then came over to her. For a long time he just stared at her, then with his fingertips he brushed a few stray hairs from her brow. Inside her something shivered and cracked.

"You hungry? There's more stew."

She nodded. "Yes." But her opportunity to check for the gun and the warrant had passed, and she was angry at herself that she'd been so weak.

Chapter Eleven

Gene Pryor decided the senator looked like hell. He'd aged twenty years in the eight since he'd last seen him. Though the mane of white hair was the same, even groomed to perfection, the dark bags under the man's eyes showed his worry and lack of sleep. The web of tiny blood vessels on his nose and cheeks revealed excesses. Not even the year-round tan he sported improved his appearance. In the winter light the tan looked sallow.

From a few feet behind the ABAT counter, Gene stood as the senator's entourage stared at him as though he should have something more for them, some shred of hope. He wished to God he did; that he could believe his good friend and business partner was still alive.

He came out from behind the desk and held out his hand. "Senator, I don't know if you recall, but we met once before at a military awards ceremony at the White House about eight years ago." Gene remembered that Will was supposed to receive an award at that ceremony, too, but no amount of urging could convince him to attend.

"I remember." The senator shook Gene's hand. "Libby spoke of you in glowing terms for days afterward. She was disappointed you never called her again."

"I lived in California at the time." The senator was still the same pompous SOB Gene remembered. But right now his company was in the SOB's employ and being paid well for service. Working the counter at Bank's Hardware for extra cash during the winter months was a lot less enjoyable than flying a search and rescue. He smiled. "How's Libby doing these days? She ever get married?"

"Twice. Didn't work out either time. But she's doing well, thank you."

Gene nodded. "Tell her I asked after her, and that I'm married and have two kids."

"I'll do that. Have you met my son, Paul? And this is Vera Phillips from the *Sun Times*."

Gene shook hands with each. Vera reminded him of the senator's daughter—dark hair, sexy figure, sensual mouth.

The men outside the terminal with fancy video cameras were reporters, too. Gene wondered if the senator had called them in or if the reporter had. The senator's missing son was headline news. Suddenly Gene pictured the two cops sitting in the back room—they weren't from around here, he was damn sure of that. He snickered under his breath. Not like planes didn't go down all the time in the Alaska wilds. If those crashes were reported in the lower forty-eight at all, it was a tiny story buried on a back page. But let a plane go down carrying a senator's son, and suddenly it's a regular three-ringed circus.

* * * *

Will wore faded jeans and the top of his long johns, unbuttoned at the neck, sleeves pushed up. His wool plaid shirt was tossed carelessly beside a jacket over the end of the table where he worked, his hair tied back at the nape of his neck, a few strands wandering across his face; a peanut butter and jelly sandwich and an apple forgotten at his elbow. He sat working from some photographs he'd lined up in front of him.

From across the room Maggie sensed his concentration, his isolation, an intense stream of it flowing from him. She limped up behind to look over his shoulder. "Mind if I watch?"

Will's hand stilled as if waking from a daze. "I'm not sure. No one's ever watched me paint before."

"Am I your first visitor?"

For a second or two he just stared at her, then she almost saw the protective shutter close as his gaze turned flat and unreadable. He never spoke of himself, held back everything.

"You're not the first visitor."

She thought he'd offer no more, but when he turned back to his drawing he continued. "A friend of mine has come a few times. Once in a while a hunter friend stops by when he's looking for a meal or a little conversation. He hunts and traps along the Yukon and through these mountains. Several years ago when he was down on his luck, he came across my cabin by accident. We've been friends ever since. But he's the only one besides my other friend and now you."

The thought of such isolation saddened her. Annoyed with herself, she bent over the table to study the animal photographs—birds, wolves, a few bears. Another pile was of Native Alaskans. All of them, including the animals, had an attitude and a story. "These are excellent photos."

"Mostly I take them in the summer when I fly into small villages in the remote areas with hunters or mail or whoever wants to hire a plane."

"I don't see any pictures of the villages themselves. Why is that?"

Preoccupied, he opened a tube of brown and squeezed a dollop onto his pallet. "I take them, but I like the animal and native ones best."

"Then during winter you come here and paint from your photographs?"

"That's about it." He glanced at her then went back to work.

She pulled up a chair and sat silently behind him. Before her eyes his visions took shape and color on the paper. After a few minutes, she realized he wasn't in the cabin with her. He was in the painting. To watch him paint was like having a glimpse into his soul. She found the experience intense, heady, and strangely sexual.

For this painting he used watercolors, but also on his worktable were tubes of acrylic, oils, a box of colored pencils, a penholder, dozens of penpoints, and a bottle of India ink. The photo of a black bear had been taken on a sunny day on wide open tundra. In his painting the bear, emerging from a cave, looked thin from months of hibernation. Above the bear the sky no longer appeared sunny, but dark with storm clouds. She could almost hear the thunder rumbling in the distance, feel the stiff wind blustering through the barren trees. But there at the base of the cave against the stone, peeking through the winter-browned grass, he painted the fresh green blades and the delicate violet-colored bloom of a wild iris, conveying the promise that spring was close.

The painting was moving, captivating, the message powerful. She told herself to move away from him, to give him space, to sit on the bed he'd given up for her with the book she'd borrowed from him. She was an intruder, trespassing on the personal relationship between him and his painting. Watching him, she was being drawn too close. But she couldn't pull herself away. She kept watching as he dipped his brushes into his paints, building the storm in the sky with bold, daring strokes, then using delicate ones to bring out the minute detail, every little hair on the bear's back, his hungry eyes, the barren trees.

After a while a pile of sketches and paintings he'd left under the table drew her from the chair, and she sat cross-legged on the floor beside them. This was the fourth day she'd spent with him, and still the storm raged outside without showing any signs of weakening. They'd talked of inconsequential things. She'd failed to find the right opportunity to search for her missing items. Possibly her gun fell from her pocket during one of her frequent falls and now lay rusting in some snowbank. The corner of her mouth tightened in a wry smile. Not likely.

In tucking a stray strand of hair behind her ear, she touched the small bandage over the gash in her forehead. The wound was healing, the headache nearly gone, and her ankle, too, felt better, the swelling down, the wrap he replaced each day keeping it stable and relatively comfortable.

She shuffled through the watercolors and pen and ink drawings; the head of a woman staring out a window at the sea drew her. He'd painted the woman's face with the strong features of an Aleut Indian, her long black hair hanging over one shoulder. Around her neck a collar of beads and tiny fish bones were drawn in meticulous detail.

Some paintings were only half finished, but each seemed to speak of isolation. Studying them, she learned more about him than he ever revealed in their conversations. Thirteen years on the run would do that to a man, make him wary, keep him from talking about himself, particularly to a woman who had literally dropped out of the sky and into his remote mountain hideaway. But then who could really know a man capable of seeing such beauty within such desolation, who had the talent to convey those feelings onto paper, a man who kept so much stored inside?

She ached for the man he'd become, the pilot who defied death because he didn't care about his life, the artist who spoke of his loneliness through his paintings, the hunted man. Whatever life he'd built up had been destroyed by hunters as soon as they got a whiff of his trail.

Now, she seriously doubted he'd committed the brutal murder. Couldn't imagine him losing control like that, but then years on the run must have taught him many things. Maybe concealing a fiery temper was one of the things he'd learned.

Matt had colored her opinion of Jamie Donovan. Yet Maggie found herself rationalizing the facts that had been presented to her by her former husband and Hilton Raine, and in the endless police reports. Annoyed with herself, she rose to fill her mug with coffee. She pictured the crime scene photos. They'd been hard to look at. At Matt's insistence, she'd studied them, not really to solve the case, because as far as her department was concerned, the case was solved. All that remained was to apprehend the guilty party—Jamie Donovan.

Photograph after photograph showed Ellen's face, her upper body and arms clearly swollen and discolored from someone's fists and/or from some instrument. Several items found at the scene—a baseball bat that belonged to Paul, a Tiffany lamp—were possible weapons, though neither of those items bore traces of Ellen's blood. Jamie Donovan's blood was on the lamp along with Hilton's and several other family members' prints, proving only that they had turned on the lamp. The lack of destruction to the room indicated minimal struggle. Did it also suggest the murder had been committed in sudden anger and without premeditation? Surely Ellen must have called out when first struck. Or had she known the killer so well she didn't see the danger until it was too late? Something more than met the eye happened that deadly night at Rutland Manor.

Will moved, catching her attention. He swished a brush through the water to clean it, then took up another.

Mug in hand she settled onto the floor to continue her perusal of his drawings, her thoughts full of him. His rescue of her was beyond courageous. No doubt the existence he had carved out for himself in Alaska provided a measure of contentment, but living in hiding carried a heavy price. Clearly, he'd concealed his past from those who called him friend in Fairbanks.

She wanted to know more about him. If he were innocent as she suspected, why hadn't he ever gone back to clear his name?

With a stack of drawings in her hand she pushed to her feet and pulled up her chair, sagging into it, and watched him work on, while the fire died and his sandwich grew stale, until the details of his painting grew finite and exquisite, until her head grew light from feeling the emotions in him and the contradictory ones in her. A drawing slipped from her lap. When she leaned over to retrieve it, she noticed under the table a radio against the wall, mostly-covered by an artist's portfolio.

"Is that a two-way radio I see hidden under the table?" Anxiety made her voice sharper than she intended.

He lifted his head to look back at her, like a man awakening. He rubbed the muscles at the base of his neck, then flexed his fingers. "It's not hidden—if I'd wanted to hide it, there are plenty of places I could have. But yes, it's a radio."

"Why didn't you tell me you had a radio? Why haven't you radioed Fairbanks and let them know where I am?" She was worn out, testy, and her confusing feelings about him weren't making it any easier for her to sort out exactly what was going on here.

Unperturbed, he pushed strands of hair from his face. "The radio's busted."

Her frown flashed, and her jaw set in an uncompromising way before she lowered her gaze back to the radio. "You sure it's broken?"

He didn't answer, but leaned closer to his painting, touched up a spot on the bear with his finger.

"So you're not sure it's broken?" she snapped.

"Of course I'm sure it's broken. But even if I had been able to get through on the radio, no sane person is flying in these conditions. Feel free to see if you can make it work."

"What other sort of equipment you got hidden around here? A computer?"

For a few seconds he just sat there, staring at her, something tough in his eyes, and something sad, too. He sat for a long time, then he put his brush down and leaned back in his chair.

"I have a laptop, yes. It's in the drawer under my bed with a stack of batteries, but if you're looking for internet service, it's not possible here. I also happen to have a printer, the newest HP desk jet—it runs on batteries, too. I would have a battery-powered TV, but there's no reception. I also have a cell phone, but it's only good in Fairbanks. So, I'm not exactly living in the dark ages, just without electricity and a radio tower or satellite dish. But that's not what's on your mind, is it, sweetheart? That's not what's making you ask all these questions and frown at me like you're deciding between busting the radio over my head or trying it out yourself?"

His tone and expression would have intimidated most anyone, but her emotions about him were already a mayhem of conflicts. The air between them charged with more than the unmentioned radio.

He swore and pushed away from the table like a wolf had just snapped at his shins. Two steps away he turned and came back. Without a further word he grabbed her arm and jerked her to her feet and against his chest. Then he cupped his hands to the sides of her head and pulled her closer and kissed her, hard, but briefly, shoving her back to her chair just when the warmth of him made her legs weak.

Before she could shake the dizzying effect of his kiss, he reached into the pocket of the jacket he'd earlier put onto the end of his worktable and pulled out her Glock.

She couldn't move, couldn't draw a breath. He handed her the gun. In her hands it felt heavy and cold. She stared at it, resisting the urge to see if it was loaded, fighting to regain her equilibrium.

"As far as I'm concerned, you can take this little peashooter and point it at my heart anytime you want. I'll even give you some bullets which I took the liberty of removing some days ago. Oh, you're surprised I know about the gun, are you?"

"Yes, I suppose." She breathed. "I guess I thought you would have mentioned it if you knew I had a gun."

"Hell, the damn thing was banging against my back when I carried you here. Of course I know about the gun, and the guns your ex-husband was carrying, too."

He knew who she was. Of course he did. He'd probably seen her ID, too. He was no fool. She had been the fool to delude herself into thinking maybe he didn't know, that maybe he hadn't recognized Matt.

He turned his back on her and grabbed a log from the pile beside the hearth, carefully adding it to the fire. "As far as I'm concerned you can leave anytime you want." He looked at her, his face lost in shadows, but she could feel his gaze locked on her, and her heartbeat skidded.

She needed to dislike him, to arrest him, but what she felt was far from dislike. How had it come to this, this attraction to him, in so short a time?

"I gave you credit for having more sense than to try and make the trip on your own. You don't need a gun to get past me, sweetheart. Just go. Take everything you can carry—food, blankets, the sled and dogs, everything, and go. You have no idea where you are, and it's a hell of a long way from here to Fairbanks. You'll be dead in forty-eight hours. If you leave me alive, I'll follow you and bring back my dogs."

Not knowing exactly how to respond, Maggie nodded. Never mind that she was a police detective, he was in control here. Since the plane went down she'd been powerless, and she suspected he would hate it if the situation were reversed. In fact, he had gone to great lengths to see he wasn't caught unprepared.

He returned to the table, and bit off a quarter of his sandwich and chewed. She rose, her mouth tight, and started to walk away.

He pulled her around by the shoulders to face him, then pushed her into the chair and glared at her until he'd swallowed. "No you don't. Stay right where you are. I'm damn sick of playing this cat and mouse game with you. It's time to get a few things clarified." He arranged the other chair directly across from her and sat so close to her their knees touched. "For instance, I'd like to know when exactly you planned to tell me your name is Maggie Raine and that you and Matt came up here to make an arrest? When you tried to cuff me?"

Her eyes grew wide. "How long have you known?"

"Hell, you were carrying your Chicago Police Department ID and a gun in your purse. It's the first thing I checked. And even if I hadn't recognized Matt, which I did, he was carrying his ID, too. As a cop you should have figured I would check the wallets first."

She sank back against the seat. "I wasn't thinking straight."

He leaned forward. "But you're thinking straight now, and since you started thinking, it's eating at you because you want to know if I'm the man you and Matt came to arrest. Well, I'll save you any more anxiety. Yes, I am. The name on the note in my blanket when I was found on the steps of St. Mary's is James William Donovan—Jamie Donovan. I'm wanted for murder. Feel better?"

Her chin dropped. "I think I knew you were Jamie after I got a good look at your face. At least now there's no question." That was true enough, and it left no room for doubt about what she had to do. His admission made her sick inside.

She was pretty naïve. She rubbed her hand over her eyes unable to ignore the hollowness inside her, the fear that had nothing to do with the murder and missing diamonds, but everything to do with the man sitting across from her. What had she been thinking? The truth—she didn't want to believe him a murderer. Sure, he'd been nothing but kind to her, but she of all people knew that an intelligent criminal, even a murderer, could present himself well. If Will had committed the crime, some part of her didn't really want to know.

She drew up her chin, and it wobbled a little. "I was afraid if you knew Matt and I had come to arrest you that you'd go off and leave me to die."

He didn't affirm or deny her accusation, and right now he looked perfectly capable of murder.

She wrapped her arms under her breasts and rocked forward then stilled and lifted her gaze to meet his. "When you never said anything, never confronted me about the false name, I began to hope I was wrong about you, that maybe you were simply a man of the mountains, and who I was didn't matter to you. I deluded myself into believing you hadn't searched my purse. I remembered putting the gun in my pocket before we left the plane, but when I couldn't find it, I thought maybe it'd fallen out when I fell in the snow. After that it seemed easier, safer, to keep up with the pretense until rescuers found me."

"Now you're wondering what you're going to do about me and what's to become of you. Is that right, Maggie?"

She said nothing, wishing she was safe and far away from this cabin and this man who so disturbed her, far away from the fear that hadn't left her since the plane first showed signs of having engine trouble. Of course, the thought had crossed her mind to run many times, but he was right. She'd never survive in this cold even if she knew how to manage his sled or where she was going. Unfortunately, she needed Will Connor.

She swallowed and looked into the flames then at him. "I've heard the stories of all the others who were there that night in Chicago when Ellen was murdered. I'd like to hear yours."

Chapter Twelve

Will froze. His life was built on secrets. For thirteen years he'd been living a lie. But since Maggie came into his life, every feeling he'd thought dead had resurrected. He disliked that, and when he looked at her it was no longer with anger or fear. It was frustration that the case had never been solved, and disappointment that, after so many years of avoiding detection, he'd been found. But it was more than that—there was relief. And a feeling of warmth and caring that had no place being in a hunted man.

Despite the danger she represented to him, he realized he trusted her. He wanted no secrets between them.

He rocked forward until his elbows touched his knees, his hands clasped between them. For several long moments he stayed that way, his insides knotted, his breaths coming in and out of him in little quivering steps. He who prided himself with the ability to face danger head-on was afraid of this, of giving up his secret.

"I've never talked to a soul about it, Maggie. I don't even know if I can."

"But you remember it?"

"That night? Of course I do, like it was yesterday. I'll tell you the story, but I'm not certain it will shed any new light on the case. First I want you to know that although I've been tried and convicted in the press and by Hilton Raine and Matt, too, I didn't murder Ellen."

She reached out and took his hand. Surprised, he looked at their joined hands, then away, but he kept hold of her hand.

"Nevertheless, she's still dead," he said.

"If you didn't kill her, you're not responsible for her death."

"I impregnated her, and I came to the party. I knew Hilton would be angry, but I allowed my desire to see Ellen convince me her invitation and Paul's were enough. No, in many ways I'm responsible."

"You're hard on yourself, Will."

"I'm just trying to be honest with you."

"I believe you. I understand that circumstances have forced you to live a life of lies. Even though I was afraid of you when you showed up at the crash site, I felt your courage, your integrity. When you knew I was a cop, you could have easily left me to die, and no one would have known, except you . . ." She looked at their joined hands then back at him. "But you risked your life to stay. That required a great deal of integrity and compassion. Despite the hand life dealt you, I think those things mean more to you than anything else. I admire that in you."

He rubbed his fingertips over their joined hands, pleased she cared enough to say that because right now what he felt for her was more than he'd ever dreamed of feeling again.

For a long time he held her hand, saying nothing, his thoughts running wild.

Suddenly he tossed his head back and barked a laugh. He drew in a deep breath. "It happened so quickly, so unexpectedly. One moment I was whistling down the walkway of Ellen's house. The next moment I was in the middle of hell, struggling to save my life."

In slow motion the nightmare of that night reran through his mind. He took back his hand and tucked both hands up under his armpits, rocking back and forth "When I walked into that front foyer, Ellen's father stepped out of the shadows, ambush like. I was struck by the hatred in his eyes. I've never seen the kind of malevolence I saw in the congressman's eyes that night, and I hope never again to see it. He went right after me, shoved me into a table and I landed on the floor. I was itching to give him as good or better than I got, but I had to admit he had reason to be angry. To his way of thinking I was in his house at a party I hadn't been invited to and looking for a daughter who had been forbidden to see me, so I restrained myself.

"I asked Hilton why he'd shoved me. He declined to answer. When I asked where Ellen was, that's when he let me know in so many words that 'Ellen was dead and I damn well knew it.'"

Will closed his eyes and arched his head back. While his silence stretched out, she maintained her own, and he thought she knew he needed this time to compose himself. His dogs sensed his need, too, and moved in beside him. Absently, he reached down and ran his fingers through their fur.

He kept his description of Ellen's dead body to a minimum, but when he mentioned that the corsage of baby roses he'd sent her was still pinned to her pink gown, his voice broke. He rose and stood before the fire, staring into the flames for several moments before he resumed his story. He paced the length of the cabin as he talked.

He kept his story short and as impersonal as he could, glossing over the details of his blows with Hilton and Hilton's shot that had missed his head by mere inches. "Well, that's about it. After that I ran, and that's a whole other story." He swung around to look at her. "The papers said I murdered Ellen because she refused to marry me after I knocked her up—those are the paper's words, not mine. I didn't even know she was pregnant . . ." He broke off, shutting his eyes. "The papers went into great detail about how after the Raines' welcomed me into their home on numerous occasions, I'd turned on them."

She came to stand directly in front of him and wrapped her arms tightly around him and held on. He breathed in her scent and ached inside.

"I don't believe you murdered Ellen."

He held her back from him and looked into her eyes. "Because of what I just told you? I could have made it all up to get your sympathy."

"Based on the incompetence I've displayed these past few days, you must think me an utter fool of a detective, but let me assure you my intuition is good. And after that first few hours spent with you, I began to doubt you were the killer. Do you know who *did* kill Ellen?"

Emotionally drained, he shook his head, sighed deeply, and sat on the hearth, clasping his head between both hands. "If only I did. At first, even though Hilton wasted no time in accusing me of killing her, I thought it was all some kind of bad joke. I didn't think it possible she was *really* dead. Hilton's accusation went right over my head—and for him to think I'd killed her was preposterous. Even when I lifted her lifeless hand, I didn't believe she was dead. The whole scenario was too unreal, too macabre, like I was dreaming about some TV crime drama, only I was in it. When I looked under the blanket laid over her, and saw she'd been cut up in a terrible way, then I knew it was true."

"Why do you think Hilton thought you killed her even though you came in after the fact?"

He looked up at her. "I've given that a lot of thought. I don't have a good answer for you, unless he killed her himself and was looking for a scapegoat, which, incidentally is the most plausible scenario I can come up with. Sure as hell, Hilton didn't think I was good enough to associate with his Ellen. And sure as hell knowing I had impregnated her would have put him into a rage. When he met up with me in the foyer he would have been experiencing all those emotions a father would feel after finding his daughter's dead body—shock, grief, anger. If he didn't kill Ellen, considering his low opinion of me, he probably thought I had killed her and that I was trying to flee or had come back for my knife. Whatever he thought, I know he knew Ellen was dead."

"Oh, hell," He templed his fingertips under his chin, propping up his head, and closed his eyes. "I've been over this scenario so many times I sometimes think I'm reading things into things that aren't there. But there's another thing about my encounter with Hilton that night that's always bothered me. Before I arrived someone had already covered Ellen with a blanket. I assumed that someone was Hilton. But if he had time to cover Ellen with a blanket, why hadn't he called in his wife to be at her daughter's side, and why hadn't the ambulance and police already been summoned? He called the police while I was there."

She sat on the wooden arm of the sofa. "You're quite certain about that?"

"Hell, yes. He had a gun pointed at my face, and he dialed with his left hand. It's not something I'd likely forget. It *is* possible, of course, that the ambulance had been called and just hadn't arrived. You would know about that better than I. I sure as hell didn't stick around to find out, and I do know Mary wasn't there, and that always struck me as odd because I knew

Mary well enough to know that if her daughter was hurt, she wouldn't have left her side until forced to."

"Off the top of my head, several other possibilities come to mind as to why Hilton could have been in the front foyer," she said. "He could have been on his way to find Mary, or he may have decided to bar his wife and children from viewing the sight you describe as being horrific. Also, he may have thought someone might have been hiding there and been anxious to identify that person."

He gave her a small grin. "You're beginning to sound like a cop. Why'd you become a cop anyway?"

Her green eyes gleamed a smile. "My father was a cop. My brother's Military Police with the Navy. I guess it runs in the family."

He looked at her—smart, beautiful, and a cop. He had just bared his soul to her, and in the worst way he wanted to kiss her again. But that first kiss had been ill advised. Another kiss would be disastrous, and he didn't need the trouble.

"If I'm to help clear your name," she said, "I'll need every detail you can remember. Sometimes the smallest fact can lead to a solution. Your class graduated that afternoon, but you missed it. Why was that?"

He lifted his shoulders. "Nothing sinister. I just didn't care if I went to the ceremony or not. I didn't expect anyone to be there on my behalf because I didn't send out any of the printed graduation invitations I'd ordered, so I picked up an extra shift at a local auto repair shop for a friend of mine."

"It might surprise you to know that you had several friends from St. Mary's who went to your graduation. When the murder was reported in the newspaper, all of them came forward to testify on your behalf, even though their testimony wasn't solicited."

"I didn't know that. Anyway, I needed the money. That's mainly why I picked up the extra shift, and that afternoon, just as I was closing the shop, a woman brought her car in with a busted carburetor. She was desperate for her car, so I stayed late, and she gave me a forty dollar tip for fixing it—a fortune for me. I've always been grateful. Without her tip I don't know if I'd have had enough money to survive that first week. Point is, I arrived at the party about an hour after it started, but Ellen wasn't waiting for me on the front porch where I expected her."

"Tell me about Ellen's siblings—do you recall where they were that night?"

"Can't help you there. I don't know where any of the others were." He crossed the room to the stove and filled a cup with coffee. "Care for some?"

She shook her head.

"Any other questions?" Rather than returning to the hearth, he sat at his worktable.

"I will have, but first let me jot down everything you told me and mull it over. From what I recall from the files, your account differs at several points from what others have told the police. But it's a classic 'he said' versus 'she said.' Clearly, it'll take more than your word to convince a jury of your innocence, especially as it'll be going against Hilton's word. With luck and hard work maybe I can unearth the real killer. Right now all the evidence points to you. All I can tell you is that I'll try." She shifted her gaze from the notes she'd been writing on a blank piece of his drawing paper to him. "So where do we go from here?"

He smiled wryly. "Well, I'm not planning on killing you, but I'm not going to try and get you back to Fairbanks, at least not yet. I haven't exactly decided what to do with you. I figure my friend and partner who knows where this place is, will be faced with jail-time for aiding and abetting if he doesn't cooperate, so sooner or later he'll have to, but only under duress. He'll put them off for as long as he can, hoping I'll get the hell out of here, and I plan to do just that. More than likely he's tried to reach me on that radio you don't believe is busted."

She had the good grace to look abashed.

"Sounds have a funny way of carrying around here, so we should hear the posse before it reaches the cabin. About that time, or before, I plan on hightailing it out of here." He bit into his apple and changed the subject. "Now that you've apparently decided to accept my hospitality a little longer without shooting me, and in case I have to leave you unannounced before they arrive, you might like to know that I keep the meat outside and some frozen veggies in a locked box about a hundred yards from the cabin."

"You don't have to feel responsible for me."

"The hell I don't. If you want to use some of the meat to try your hand at cooking, you'll find the key hanging on a nail beside the box. I leave it there so if anyone's in need and I'm not around, he can borrow some."

For a few minutes neither spoke. She rose and busied herself stacking the paintings she'd looked at earlier, like she was thinking on all the things he'd told her and feeling a little uneasy with him. But he must have been wrong about what she was thinking because when he returned to the table after pitching the core of his apple into the fire, she reached out and stopped him.

"If I hand over my gun,"—she turned the Glock over in her hand, a little smile on her lips—"do you think I might use that tub you have hanging out there to take a proper bath tomorrow?"

The tub was an antique affair with decorations stamped into the brass around the edges. He'd paid $2.00 for it at a garage sale. Left standing against a shed for a number of years, it had needed a lot of work. He'd refinished and hauled it here.

"That's what it's for. Much as I'd like to stay and watch, I'll give you privacy. I've been meaning to go back and retrieve my pack. I'll do it while you're bathing."

* * * *

In the thin daylight the following morning, Will cracked the ice in the outside tub. He hefted the tub to his shoulder and lugged it inside to the hearth, and he thought of Maggie's perfectly shaped breasts and long athletic legs and not that she was a cop and not that she had come to arrest him.

This was the fifth day she'd been living with him. With her ankle tightly wrapped, she was getting around pretty well. He stoked the fire, added chunks of ice to a cast iron pot that swung on a long arm over the flames. Maggie was on his bed and had failed to close the curtain he'd hung for her. The gas lamp hanging over the bed was lit, and by the bowed angle of her head, he suspected she was reading. He wondered which of the many titles on the shelves had caught her fancy this time. Books, lamp fuel, his airplane, and the pot-bellied stove, were the few luxuries he'd allowed himself.

Over the years he'd saved most of what he earned and had it stashed in an Anchorage bank under another name, though what use it would be to him when he made his run into the vast Alaska tundra, he couldn't imagine. Endurance was what he would need, and he'd need that in abundance.

Five years ago, Will spotted this tract of land in the White Mountains from the air, decided it suited his purpose, and began to build. It took two years to complete. For the past three years he'd spent his winters here. He'd lived a pretty comfortable life, he thought, glancing around his place appreciatively, but what he had were only things, personal possessions that weighed a man down. His gaze came to rest again on Maggie. He thought of the kind of life denied him where a man and a woman lived together, cared for each other, and raised their children. Everything inside of him ached.

Maggie complicated things.

Stretched out in a pair of his old jeans under a lap blanket, he remembered the feel of her legs, long and shapely, as he lay close beside her in his sleeping bag. Her hair, red, slightly curly, and disheveled, fell across her face in disarray. Her oval-shaped eyes were large and bright with intelligence and warmth she couldn't hide; her mouth was wide and generous.

"You have a cribbage board hanging on your wall." She glanced up at him. "It looks handmade—another of your accomplishments?"

"An Aleut friend gave it to me. He made it from a walrus tusk."

"I've never seen one quite like it—it's marvelous. You must be a good friend for him to part with it."

He wandered to his dresser to hunt a pair of socks without looking at her, but suddenly he pictured the empty kayak and his friend's leg trapped in his fishing net, dragging him down into the frigid Arctic waters. "I did him a favor once."

"How did this Aleut friend come to know how to play cribbage?"

"When he was a boy, a missionary taught him. He built the board, then after the missionaries left, his cards got ruined, and he forgot how to play."

"Where'd he live that he couldn't get new playing cards?" Her green eyes sparkled.

"You ask a lot of questions."

As he pulled off a boot and added the second pair of socks, he studied her. He delighted in her adjustment to his Spartan living accommodations. Would she take to living in this wilderness? Who was he kidding? Despite that he'd come to care for her, she was a cop. If he were here when the posse arrived, it was her duty to arrest him. He would run and find another place to hide. She would return to the city. And that would be that.

Had he waited too long to make his escape?

"So, do you get the chance to play cribbage?"

"I'm ashamed to admit I've never used the board. I don't really recall the rules either." He shrugged. "Besides, it takes two to play."

"Do you have cards? If you like, I'll teach you to play when you get back."

"You've got yourself a date. I should have a deck somewhere. I play a mean game of solitaire."

"You cheat?"

He smiled, couldn't help himself. "At solitaire? Sometimes. Do you?"

She lifted her eyebrows. "I never cheat,"—she grinned sheepishly—"well, hardly ever, I did cheat a little when I was a kid, but there's not much reward if you don't win on your own."

Leaning back, he clasped his hands behind his neck, stretched, then pushed himself to his feet. He'd already wasted too much time. He needed to leave.

He filled his canteen with water and his pockets with emergency food. "Well, I'm on my way. Water should be heated for your bath soon, soap's right beside the tub—you'll like the soap, some sweet-smelling stuff a friend gave me. Don't forget to bolt the door from the inside soon as I'm gone. And don't let anyone in unless you know him."

"Yes, sir." She gave him a jaunty salute as she swung her legs off the bed. "I'll be fine and clean when you get back. You be careful."

"I always am. I'm taking Hilde and Lucy with me, but the sled dogs will let you know if trouble's outside. I've fed them already so you won't need to do that."

"You're not taking the sled?"

"No, the sled's no good on that side of the mountain—too steep and too rough. I'll try and be back by dinnertime."

He hefted his rifle and put more cartridges inside his pockets. Outside, he stood under the eaves to strap on his snowshoes, then whistled to his dogs and pulled his scarf tighter around his neck. Will frowned, no longer certain exactly what he dreaded most—having the authorities arrive to cuff him and cart him off to jail or running out the door and out of Maggie's life forever.

The sky shimmered with cold, gray half-light. Hunched over, he headed into the frigid wind and snow without looking back. Alaska winters were ruthless, and this one was just beginning. Living outside in the raw elements of an Alaska winter would be a challenge, but he was no stranger to harsh conditions. He'd survived them before. He would again, if necessary. But by staying with her so long he had cast the die, tempted fate, and the odds weren't in his favor. Planes would be airborne soon, perhaps today. Still, he was reluctant to leave before he was certain she would be found. Once he left it would take him days to reach a place where he could phone her whereabouts to the authorities. Anything could happen in that time. In truth, she was quite capable of taking care of herself. He simply did not want to leave her.

He trudged over the drifts swept up against his cabin and headed downhill. Below, the gorge was a river of snow, rimmed with jagged rocks worn down by centuries of the river's flow. Even without a pack, trekking down the steep slope was difficult. But he knew the land, knew the rocks underneath, where the sheets of it were and the likely patches of ice, and he let the wild, wind-torn trees that leaned in the prevailing winds guide him through his unmarked trail.

Near the bottom, he saw the riverbed more clearly; the wind had swooped down the river between the mountainsides, sweeping the river, creating man-sized drifts of snow against the banks providing a definite corridor. If at a later date he decided to return to his cabin, clearing a landing strip might not be as much of a problem as he'd originally thought. But of course once he was on the run, returning to his cabin would be a huge risk. Even if the authorities didn't have the manpower or the resources to see that someone was left behind to ambush him, Hilton would find a way to ensure that avenue was closed. But Will knew how to wait. He knew how to make the most of opportunities that came along.

At the base of the mountain, he looked back at the way he had just covered then forward the way he was about to negotiate, studying the terrain for anything that appeared out of the ordinary. If the search for Jack's plane were up to him, he'd have dispatched dog sleds already. Were they even now combing the flatlands?

For days the front had been stalled over the mountains, but it was weakening, and soon it would pass. His time was short.

Seeing that the riverbed could accommodate his plane was a double-edged sword. If it were good enough for him, it would be good enough for them. A trained pilot would spot a landing place in a minute. For Jim Foley or Gene Pryor, it would be a piece of cake. He had to be careful how he sabotaged it.

He rolled a couple logs into well-placed positions across the runway. It wouldn't stop them, but it would make landing more difficult. Before continuing on, he glanced back at where he normally parked his plane during the summer, assuring himself that his tanks of spare gas were well camouflaged beneath the Hemlock branches and snow.

For the next few miles he followed the riverbed. He saw no signs of a search. Still, he wondered if a sled were around the next bend or the corner after that. Every once in a while he cocked his head to listen for dogs or a man's voice. Nothing but the wind.

Maggie said she and Matt informed Jack of their plans mere minutes before takeoff. When Jack balked, they'd showed him the arrest warrant, and in the end Jack cooperated. Though only Gene Pryor had been to his cabin, both Jack and Jim Foley had a general idea of its location. That Jack had found it with only a few passes destroyed any illusions Will harbored that Jim would need much time to locate the cabin once he took to the air. Will picked up his pace. Ghostlike, he slipped through the snow, nearly invisible in his off-white parka.

Chapter Thirteen

Maggie stepped into the tub with a sigh. She washed her hair and soaked until the water grew cold before reluctantly toweling off. After dressing, she swept through the house, snatching up Will's socks, his long johns, and t-shirts, and threw them all in the washtub to soak along with her panties, bra, and blouse. She found some rope hanging by the door, made a clothesline, and strung it from the rafters in front of the fireplace. After she'd washed out the dirty clothes and hung them over the line to dry, she braved the cold to reach his outdoor freezer and garnered some meat for supper, pulled out a bag of green peas from a crate, and was careful to relock the freezer and the cabin door.

She wasn't exactly sure what the meat was because none of the paper-wrapped pieces were labeled. So like a man. Hoping it was beef, she put it in a pot with water and some onions she found on a shelf, and set it on the stove which he'd fired up before he left.

Several times as the thin light of day faded into darkness, she rubbed her shirtsleeve over the frosted window pane to look out. Snow-covered trees waved at her. When dinnertime came and went, she began to worry. By 9:00 p.m. she was agitated, and anger set in. By eleven, she figured he wasn't coming back. In truth, she couldn't blame him.

With a sigh, she served herself a bowl of stew and sagged into his one comfortable chair to eat. She expected to be afraid, to be furious, but neither emotion was true. No longer did she want Will caught. Realization set in. She was in love with Will Connor and wanted him to escape so she could prove his innocence.

The sled dogs barking jolted Maggie awake. Pounding on the door shot her to her feet. Fear slammed against her chest.

She grabbed the Glock and stumbled across the room. At the door she paused. "Who's there?"

A man's voice was carried away by the wind. Surely it was Will. Who else could it be?

"Will?" she shouted. "That you?"

Again the wind carried away the single-word reply. She lowered the gun and threw the bolt, jerking the door open. A cold blast of wind-driven snow slammed into her face, momentarily blinding her.

A snow-whitened man stood inches in front of her, a big man, the hood he wore revealing only a black void. He put his foot in the doorway. She held her ground and raised her gun, her mind racing with several scenarios, none good.

Red spots were splattered over the man's jacket, contrasting ominously with the white of the snow. Blood. She smelled it. The dogs continued barking. Dread took her breath away.

"It's me," Will said at the same moment she released the safety on her gun. "Now get back inside before you freeze to death."

"Oh, Will, you're splattered in—"

"Blood. Yes, I know."

"Are you all right?"

When he spoke, his voice sounded tired. "Yes. Lucy killed a hare and brought it to me, looking for praise, no doubt. Before she dropped it at my feet, she shook it and splattered the blood all over me. I tried to wipe it away with snow. I'm afraid I only made matters worse."

Not a stranger, but Will back safe and sound. The surge of relief was so great she sagged, suddenly boneless. His strong hands on her arms prevented her from falling. She looked up into the face that had become so important to her in so short a time.

"I'm so relieved you're okay. I admit that at first when I saw you standing outside the door, I worried it was someone else. I thought I'd made a mistake. I couldn't see your face. And the dogs didn't quit barking."

"What were you thinking opening the door unless you were damn sure who it was? With the light liming you, you made a perfect target standing in the doorway. Someone wanting to do you harm could have hidden in the trees and shot you stone dead. You're not in Chicago, Maggie. The dogs weren't barking at the postman. For all that, a bear could have been waiting outside the door. Many things could have caused the dogs to bark, very few of them boding anything good. Don't ever take a chance like that again."

He took his hands from her and one by one pitched the gloves to the floor by the door, then pushed back his hood.

Her head fell forward, her cheek resting on his ice laden jacket, and beneath that the soft texture and underlying steadying strength of his arm. Relief poured through her that he was back safely. "I'm sorry. I knew better." She grinned up at him sheepishly. "You said there were two reasons you're so late. What's the other? You forgot about our date and stopped at the local pub to have a few beers with your buds, did you?"

He laughed out loud, then grew still, looking into her eyes. "I hid my pack a little too well." He pushed a length of hair back from her face. "I had the devil of a time finding it."

She waited for him to kiss her, but he turned away and walked the rest of the way into the cabin.

Over her head Will saw she'd tidied up his worktable and set out two places for dinner. The candle she'd lit was burned to a nub, but the sprigs of Holly she'd put in a glass gave the table a homey touch that made his heartbeat falter. He honed in on the scent of beef. She'd cooked for them.

Then he suddenly spotted the clothes, his and hers, hanging from a rope strung from the rafters. He inhaled through his nose and laughed. "Good God, woman, this place smells like a boudoir. What have you done?"

She started to walk away, but he took her face in both his hands and stopped her.

"It was your fault." Her lopsided grin made his heart turn over. "You gave me that soap. After my bath I merely used it to clean up a few other things. It was all I could find. I hoped you wouldn't notice the scent."

His chest tightened with the bittersweet ache it had every time he looked at her. For a moment they stared at each other, their smiles fading. Need welled up in him with so much urgency it took his breath away.

He wound his fingers around a soft red curl and pulled her close. She lifted her face to him, and he saw the luminous glow in her eyes.

"Oh, hell," he breathed and gave up trying to keep his distance. He kissed her on the lips, kissed her hard and long. When he released her, she staggered a bit. It pleased him that the kiss had affected her in the same way it did him.

But it was unlikely they would ever talk about the feelings going on between them, nevertheless act on them. He couldn't escape the spider web of his past. But she had broken through his defenses, and he knew he'd already stayed with her too long.

"I'm going to get more firewood." He walked toward the door, stopping halfway to turn and look at her. Her back was to him as she struggled to put a fresh candle in the piece of twisted branch he'd cut and bored with holes. In one of his old flannel shirts and worn pants she'd tied with a rope around her waist, she looked as hand-hewn as the rest of the things in his cabin.

His mind filled with the possibilities of her staying with him, but the storm was weakening. Unless he missed his guess, at daylight planes would be in the air. They were coming for him. And despite her assertion that she didn't believe he'd committed murder, she was a cop.

"While I was gone, I did a lot of thinking. I want you to know I never had any beef with Matt. He was about thirteen when I left Chicago, almost four years younger than me. So far as I knew him, he was a nice kid."

"He could be awfully charming when he wanted to be, but his father always had a hold over him. I often wondered if he were afraid of Hilton. It would have been better for our marriage if we'd moved out of Hilton's realm."

"Hilton kept them all in check. But when he was out of town, Mary relaxed the rules and often invited me to dinner. We'd sit around the kitchen table, and Mary made me feel a part of the family. I'd known them for a couple of years before Ellen told me her sister Libby was a stray. Hilton sired Libby while Mary was pregnant with Matt."

She nodded. "I didn't know that until after Matt and I were married. I knew Libby and Matt were less than a year apart, but not that Hilton had gotten another woman pregnant. The family's very protective of Libby, and she appears to feel the same way about them, most particularly about her father."

"Somehow Mary found out about Hilton's affair, and when Libby's mother died shortly after having Libby, Mary refused to allow the baby to go to an orphanage. She took her in and treated her as one of her own. That's what Ellen told me. She had a kind heart, Mary did. She was the closest thing I ever had to a mother. I loved her, but I never got to tell her." The last words caught in his throat.

"I never got the chance to meet Mary, so I never interviewed her. I guess you know she died within the year after the murder. From all I've heard about her, she was a gracious and lovely lady."

He zipped his jacket. "She was, and kindhearted. I feared Hilton would learn Mary had taken me under her wing, and put a stop to it. My background didn't measure up. No one spilled the beans about how she had cared for me until after Ellen's murder." He slipped on his gloves and nodded at the pot on the stove. "Save some of that dinner for me. I could eat a horse."

"For all I know, horse may be what I cooked."

Grinning, his gaze dropped to his bloody gloves. "If I bring in more ice, would you mind heating water for a bath before we eat?"

"I thought you mountain men bathed in ice water."

He chuckled. "When there's nothing else." He stared at her, smoldering inside. "After I clean up, I'd like to continue where we left off . . . you know where you were kissing me."

He closed the door on her laughter, the sound of it carrying on the wind. God, he was going to miss that.

* * * *

Gene Pryor stood in the opening of his office door and looked out into the fog. He could barely make out the red windsock not 100 yards away and couldn't see the cars parked across the street. For a long time he stared into the dreary sky, wishing he'd see Jack's Cessna part the clouds. He fought his ongoing battle against the insidious feelings of false invincibility that he could beat the odds and fly out to search for his friend.

A stiff gust of wind lifted his baseball cap off his head and hurled it halfway across the parking lot. He chased it down.

Until that moment, he'd actually been considering making a reconnaissance flight. Bad thinking.

Even on days with calm winds and good visibility, winter flights were dangerous. Gene knew the risks. So did the other men who flew in Alaska. Many of them, himself included, thought they could overcome the danger.

Facing facts, he assumed Jack's plane was down. Bottom line—he was tired of waiting, but taking to the air in this weather was a mistake and he damn well knew it. A deadly mistake. He, Jim Foley, Jack Ricks, and Will—all of them had been forced down at one time or another. They were lucky. They lived to talk about it.

But Gene seethed about something else. A few minutes ago Tracy Kora phoned from the diner with disturbing news about Will Connor. She informed him in angry, tearful words that the senator and his son were looking for Will to arrest him on charges of murder. Will wanted for murder? The notion was laughable, only he didn't feel like laughing. He shook his head.

Inside, he closed the door and walked down the hall to the small sitting room. Gloomy, he needed a stiff drink. As he looked at the sorry little group sitting against the wall, his mouth tightened. He rubbed his chin and shifted his weight to one foot.

"I'm sorry," he announced. "It's not the news you've been waiting for, but Deputy Douglas informed me a dog sled and crew left Circle City around 11:00 this morning. They're combing the area along the Yukon, where we think Jack's plane might have gone down. The snow has nearly stopped. Weather forecasters predict the winds will die down during the night. If that's the case, Jim Foley and I will fly out toward Circle City at first light."

A door behind Gene opened, and he turned to see Deputy Sheriff Brad Douglas come out of the small office carrying a coffeepot full of water. The deputy's brows lifted in question. Gene shook his head. "Not in this wind. Besides, not enough daylight left."

The deputy nodded. "Wise decision. Stupid to risk it. No use having another plane go down. You tell 'em about the sled on its way?"

Gene nodded. "Just did, but they might have some questions for you."

The deputy turned to the people in the sitting room. "Sorry it's so cold in here. The heater's old. Days like this it can't quite keep up. But coffee'll be ready in a few minutes."

Gene poured himself a cup before the pot stopped perking and turned back to the senator and his son, and Nancy's heartbreaking face. "Jack's plane had navigational tools, a compass and a radio, altimeter, all the usual stuff. He knew how to fly with instruments. He also was carrying the ELT—the little black box."

"The plane was equipped with the black box?" Paul rose and joined Gene at the counter.

"Yes, all of our planes at Alaska Bush are, but we haven't been able to pick up a signal from it yet."

"If you didn't pick up a signal, wouldn't that mean his plane didn't go down in that area?" Paul asked.

Gene scratched his head. "Not necessarily. In theory when a plane goes down, the ELT transmits a signal to nearby aircraft or satellite, which in turn sends the location to a command center. Problem is, much of Alaska doesn't have radar or satellite coverage."

"Then where exactly will the dog team be searching?" Paul poured himself a cup of coffee.

Gene turned to Brad. "You can answer that better than I."

"Can't say precisely, but they know the area and they know the plane was headed for Circle City. My guess is they'll go along the Yukon if the snow's not too deep for the dogs. That's what I'd do."

Gene noticed the questioning faces. "Those who aren't from around here don't know about Circle City so I'll tell you a little. It's not a city at all, but a very small village. Less than ninety permanent residents, mostly Native Alaskan Gwitch'in Indians. There *is* a road called the Steese Highway that connects Circle with Fairbanks, but after a storm like this, the road will be impassable."

"Circle City," Douglas added, "is only fifty miles from the Arctic Circle. Right now the temperature's around minus fifty degrees Fahrenheit, pretty harsh conditions for anyone trying to run a sled."

"Isn't it possible the plane was heading somewhere else before dropping off the mail?" Paul asked.

"It wasn't in Jack's flight plan." Gene sipped his coffee. "I've wondered the same thing. Why exactly did your brother and his ex-wife hire on with Jack in the first place?"

Paul and the senator began talking at once. Hilton stood slowly, held his hand up for his son to be quiet. "I can answer that." Hilton puffed on his cigar despite the *No Smoking* sign prominently displayed. "My son's a Chicago detective, and he and his ex-wife, also a cop, are looking for a man named Will Connor. The deputy here knows about it."

Gene glanced at Douglas.

The deputy nodded. "Yeah, my office called a Captain Oswald at the Chicago PD who confirmed Matthew Raine is a detective there and on assignment to locate Will. I had Oswald's office fax over Raine's creds, and they look legit." The deputy's mouth was tight, and his eyes didn't quite meet Gene's.

Gene's gut tightened. They *were* looking for Will, not to receive an inheritance due him as Matt Raine had said when he questioned everyone at the office, but something else. And it must be a damn serious offense to bring cops and reporters all the way to Alaska in the thick of winter.

"Why are they looking for Will?" He'd heard Tracy's story, but wanted them to voice it.

"I'll answer that in a minute," Hilton said before the deputy could speak. "But first let me get a little information from you. I understand Will Connor has a cabin somewhere in the mountains near Circle City where he spends the winter. And since he's your partner, I'm going to assume as a pilot you know where his place is and can help us out."

Gene let the senator's words dangle in space and sipped his coffee. If he refused to cooperate with the law, they could indict him for aiding and abetting. But he sure as hell couldn't just lead them to Will's place—he owed the man his life.

"I've been thinking that if this Jack Ricks is as good a pilot as billed," Hilton went on, seeming willing for the moment to let his assumption pass unconfirmed, "there's a chance he brought the plane down safely and guided my son and his ex-wife to Connor's place on foot."

"What makes you think Jack knew where Will is wintering?" Gene asked.

"Will has a radio," Deputy Douglas said before Hilton could answer. "I've tried to raise him to let him know Jack's plane had gone missing. I never got through, but in the mountains radios are—"

"I know . . . unreliable." Hilton sneered.

"You're learning, Senator." Douglas smirked in return "Will's a very private man and it wouldn't surprise me if he changed his call letters."

"Did it occur to you that maybe this man you all seem so eager to protect has deliberately chosen not to answer or to call for help if my son and the others made it to his cabin? Perhaps forcibly holding Matt and Maggie there?"

Gene set his cup down so hard coffee splashed over the lip. Nothing riled him more than some city fellow making allegations about his friends. Raine was beginning to rub him the wrong way.

"That's a mighty big *perhaps* you're throwing out there, Senator. What exactly are you insinuating—that Will would forcibly detain your son and the other cop at gunpoint? And confine Ricks, his partner and good friend? If that's the case, you can just go to hell."

Hilton's eyes flashed anger. "Now you listen to me, flyboy." He snatched the cigar from his mouth and stabbed it at Gene. "And listen good. Just because you screwed around with my daughter six years ago doesn't give you license to speak to me that way."

Gene struggled to control his temper. "And just because you're a senator in the lower forty-eight doesn't give you license to come up here and insinuate that a friend of mine would forcibly hold your son and some woman cop. Let me tell you something. If your son and his former wife found Will or were found by Will, they'd be damn lucky. If Ricks is dead, Will's the only one around those parts who might be able to get your son out alive."

He turned his back to the senator, but Hilton grabbed his arm and swung him around. Gene shook him off easily and shot the senator a hard stare. "You don't want to have a fight with me, Raine, so back off."

"Gentlemen! Please." Paul stepped between them. "Everyone's understandably upset, but we're on the same side."

"I'm not finished with you, Pryor." Hilton ignored his son. "A few moments ago you asked why the police were looking for this friend of yours. Well, I'm going to answer in terms even you can understand. The Chicago PD has good reason to believe this Will Connor is really James Donovan. And Donovan is wanted for murdering my oldest daughter in Chicago thirteen years ago."

It was true! Clasping both hands on the counter, Gene stared blankly at the aerial photo of Alaska's coastline framed behind the desk, mulling over the senator's shocking information. If Will had gotten himself into trouble, it had happened a long time ago. Lots of Alaska's residents were looking to put their pasts behind them. He himself had come to Alaska to get away from an abusive, alcoholic father.

Gene met Will when they trained together in the Naval Air Force. Before that Gene worked briefly in naval intelligence and law enforcement, but the wide open skies called to him, and before two years were up, he requested a transfer into the Naval Air Force. During the Gulf War, he and Will flew side-by-side in the same squadron. He figured Will's uncanny sense of danger and superior piloting skills had a lot to do with why they survived the war. Not to mention the time Will led troops to rescue him when his plane went down. After the war they resigned the Navy and came to Alaska together, flying for Alaska Airlines.

Paul broke into Gene's thoughts. "Right now, our prime concern is for my brother and Maggie and for the pilot. But, Gene, if you know where Connor's cabin is, please tell us. We need to find out if he's Jamie Donovan. We could be mistaken. It certainly wouldn't be the first time we've followed clues that led us nowhere. I knew Jamie well. If he's the right man, I'll recognize him."

Gene lifted the hot coffee and drank slowly. The senator and his son had a hidden agenda.

Hilton tapped his fingers on the counter impatiently. Gene slurped noisily, then swiped the back of his sleeve across his lips. "My wife is expecting me for dinner. Talk to you two gentlemen in the morning."

"If you know where Connor is and don't tell us, you could be aiding and abetting a criminal. You could go to jail."

"The senator's right, Gene," Deputy Douglas said. "Didn't you fly up with Will one summer to help him build the place?"

"That was a long time ago." Gene shrugged and walked out of the terminal. He pulled his hat down and his collar up, but Gene recognized the chill he felt inside for what it was—apprehension.

Late in the summer when Will first started building his cabin, he asked Gene for help to lever logs into position for the walls. Will had helped Gene build his own home. Gene accepted readily.

They finished in six days, then spent another four enjoying each other's company and the crisp, cool sunshine of Alaska's summer. Gene knew exactly where Will's cabin was located.

Chapter Fourteen

Nearly 1:00 a.m., Maggie filled the coffeepot with grounds as Will splashed in the tub in front of the fire. Heat from of his eyes burned into her back. Outside, the wind blew a constant melancholy cry.

"The weather's clearing."

Her head jerked around to stare at him. "So, when do you think the search planes will start looking?"

"Daybreak—soon as the wind dies down you can expect to hear them." He reached for his towel, then shot to his feet, sending a wave of water cascading over the sides of the tub. In his powerful nude body she saw not only his virility but the hardships he'd survived on the run. He looked unbearably masculine. With a quick intake of breath, she turned away.

She crossed to the window and rubbed a spot clear of frost. Through the clouds, moonlight gave a cold, silver-blue cast to the snow. She sighed and rested her forehead against the icy pane. Innocent or guilty, Will was a wanted man. As a police officer she had to uphold the law, whatever the cost to herself. She worried that her honor was at stake here, and the worry spread through her like the cold from the glass. She wanted to lean on this man whose broad shoulders and quiet smile called to her. She couldn't deny it. She wanted to stay with him. Love for him squeezed her heart, clouding her eyes with unshed tears. She was in love with Will Connor. But she was duty-bound to turn him over to the authorities.

Behind her she heard a rustle of movement and turned. He'd put on his jeans but not a shirt, and the few stray drops of water on his chest gleamed. His hair dripped. His smiling eyes glittered at her, glowing and hot as the coals in the fire. A melting took hold of her heart so that she could hardly think.

He hung his parka close to the fire to dry, then came back to her and dropped a hand to her arm and gave it a gentle rub.

"They won't land while it's still dark, if that's what you're worried about. We still have the rest of tonight."

"I'm scared, Will. You should be leaving . . ."

He smiled and put his fingertips over her lips, cutting off her words. The smile he gave her was wistful and sad, and full of yearning. "I should have left a long time ago, sweetheart." He kissed her hair.

She lifted her face to his, and his mouth was there, everything she wanted, everything she needed. His arms came around her, and she closed her eyes and wrapped her arms around him, pulling him against her, loving the hard muscles of him.

His lips opened as he slid his tongue between her teeth. The kiss deepened, and when it was over he pulled her shirt up over her head and loosened the string that held up her pants, coaxing the worn jeans to slip to her ankles. He lifted her into his arms and carried her to the carpet of skins in front of the fireplace.

His long legs stretched out beside hers, he propped himself on his elbows above her and stared at her with the intensity of a wild animal that knew he was about to be caged, and her breath left her chest in a low groan. This man who never showed what he was feeling was looking at her with his heart and his loneliness naked in his eyes. And between them the tension became unbearable.

She touched the corner of his mouth with a finger, and he took that finger in his hand and brought it to his mouth, kissing it. She thought he would take her now, at last, and she was eager to let him. She wanted his arms around her forever, wanted to touch every little part of him.

Just looking at him looking at her made her blood burn. She cupped his face with her hands and pulled him back to her mouth. His kiss was hungry and demanding, his hands leaving trails of fire wherever they touched. Then just when she thought she would expire from her need, he was inside her. Together they rode the hot waves of their passion, while above the snow-capped roof of the cabin that hid them the clouds blew out, and stars began to fill the night sky.

* * * *

141

At noon the following day Gene Pryor stretched his tired muscles and entered the back room at ABAT to have a look at the radar screen, wondering if Jim Foley's plane was within range yet. He fiddled with the dials until he brought up the distinctive bleep-bleep of yellow light.

Gracie Palmer, a thin, middle-aged woman with long, black hair pulled back at the nape of her neck, came up beside Gene and offered up a tray of sandwiches. Gracie had been the office manager since ABAT's inception and assumed the role of mother to all the pilots.

"It must have been a bumpy ride up there today," she said.

Gene helped himself to a sandwich. "It was. Just ask the deputy here." He slapped Brad Douglas on the back. "He almost lost it a time or two."

The deputy laughed uneasily. "I don't mind telling you that I thought *you* were going to lose it in some of those air pockets. Never could figure out what you flyboys love so damn much about being up there. Me, I prefer to keep my feet on the ground. I think I'll assign Tumlin to take this afternoon's run with you."

"Fine with me." Gene helped himself to another sandwich, and waved it at Gracie. "Thanks, you're too good to us."

"Damn right I am, and don't you forget it."

Gene headed for the waiting room. He risked breaking the law when he deliberately avoided the airspace over Will's cabin. Twice he flew close, hoping, if Will were listening, he'd know planes were near and get out. He tried to signal Will by dipping his wings and flying upside-down. Gene chuckled. His antics had scared the spit out of Deputy Douglas.

Word that Gene had helped Will build his cabin had gotten around, and soon he'd have no choice but fly to the cabin. He couldn't stall much longer. The senator would have him arrested if he continued to pussyfoot around. Aside from that, Gene wanted to find Jack, and find him alive. By all accounts Jack was probably in the vicinity of Will's cabin. This afternoon he'd take the long route to the cabin and set down.

Gene reached for the coffeemaker, but before filling his cup he paused and turned to the senator and Nancy Ricks, who were still waiting. Paul Raine had flown out with Jim Foley after Gene returned.

"I made a couple runs over the area between here and Circle City and part way down the Yukon." He grimaced, remembering how the wind had buffeted his plane. "Searched it back and forth, low as I dared. Didn't spot a thing—no sign of a signal fire, no sign of Jack's red plane. I didn't pick up a signal from the ELT either.

"Foley and your son are still out there. Maybe he's having better luck than I, but don't count on it. There's lots of land out there and that land's under several feet of snow. We get lucky and get a little thaw, maybe Jack's red plane'll show up. What I was looking for was some sort of signal fire."

"And your partner's cabin, I hope," Hilton said.

Gene took a bite from his sandwich and nodded. "Jim should be landing any minute. I'll see if he needs any help." He zipped up his jacket. He was still chilled to the bone.

The little biplane touched down then made a sideways skid for a good hundred yards before stopping in a snowbank. The landing was pretty smooth, considering. Gene let out his breath.

Jim jumped to the ground.

"Need a hand?" Gene got behind a wing to help push the plane to a place where it could be tied down.

"Wouldn't say no to it."

Gene was breathing hard in the icy cold, pushing behind the plane. His legs felt like rubber. "I must be getting old. Once upon a time, this was easy. I guess you didn't find anything then?"

"I didn't say that. No sign of Jack's plane, but I think I located Will's cabin. I left the senator's son up there—at his insistence. Landing on the riverbed was no small challenge because someone had rolled a couple of logs across it. Once we set down Deputy Sweeny and Paul helped me move them. Sweeny opted to stay with Paul."

Chapter Fifteen

Will sat on a chair beside his backpack. He looked over where Maggie lay propped up on a pillow in front of the fireplace, watching him. Her dark eyes were flecked with gold from the firelight, her lips soft from their night of lovemaking. Warmth glowed in her cheeks. All these years he'd missed having someone special with whom to talk, to share his life, and to share a home. More than anything, he wanted to join her and take her into his arms. For a moment he just sat with his head in his hand looking at her, his fingers clenching and unclenching his hair, wishing, dreaming, and listening to the fire's cozy crackle and the soft sounds of his sleeping dogs.

He let out a breath, slowly, and straightened. "You said you might have more questions. Time's running short, so go ahead and ask while I gather a few things."

She turned away to shrug into his L.L. Bean shirt. She rose and retrieved the jeans she'd worn earlier, pulled them on, then sat back down on the fur with her back against the chair, her feet tucked under her. She reached for a pad and pen on a nearby crate.

"First, I'd like to confirm that you believe Hilton to be the prime suspect." She sounded very much like a cop.

"If someone had asked me that right after the murder, I would have sworn it was Hilton."

"But now you're not so sure?" She seemed surprised.

"I've had a lot of time to think it over." He paused, worried about finding just the right words to separate his dislike of Hilton from the facts. "No doubt, Hilton is a vainglorious, ambitious SOB. Yet in his own way he was fond of Ellen. His reaction to her death is what I would expect from a father who just found his daughter murdered. If he did kill her, he did it in a fit of anger, when he learned she was pregnant and I was the father.

"Perhaps the fury he directed at me in the foyer was anger directed at himself for letting his temper get out of control, for killing the wrong person. There I was—the perfect scapegoat, a way for him to save his reputation, his career, his life. If Ellen died from a shove and hit something that broke her neck, I'd say look no further than Hilton. But to retrieve my knife from her car and kill her,"—Will shook his head—"as much I dislike the man, I can't imagine him plotting to kill his daughter— not even to frame me. Using the knife on me would have served his purposes better."

"Could he have blamed the murder on you to protect someone else?"

"Possibly. He must have found Ellen too late to save her. I arrived at the wrong place at the wrong time. Already furious at me before I arrived, seeing me could have sent him over the edge. Once he'd accused me, it was convenient not to change his story. I don't know who killed her, Maggie. I simply don't know. I wish I did.

"Of course, the obvious motive is theft. But why the knife? I can think of easier ways to kill someone."

"So can I. Theft wasn't the prime reason for the murder, but it's still a possibility." She wrote on the pad. "Forensics narrowed the murder to within an hour or two of the time you arrived, but it's not precise. According to interview transcripts, everyone associated with the household accounted for his or her whereabouts at the time Ellen was killed. They all checked out."

He shook his head. It was the same old story. Everything pointed to his guilt. "Whoever killed her would have gotten blood on his clothes."

"Hilton's clothes were the only ones with blood on them, and that could have happened when he found his daughter's body. Most of the search and analysis was concentrated in the parlor where the body was found, so blood on the rug in the laundry room wasn't discovered for several days into the investigation. It seems Mary, not wanting herself or members of her staff subjected to the chore, hired a crew to clean the front parlor. And bloody towels were rinsed in the laundry room sink before being taken away."

"Was it Ellen's blood?"

"Yes. Analysis also identified some cleaning agent, supporting the theory that the blood came from the cleaning crew."

"And the cleaning agent was one the crew used?"

Maggie shook her head. "That wasn't conclusive."

Will harrumphed. The police, supposing him the killer, hadn't looked for evidence to the contrary. He said nothing. Whatever evidence there might have been was long gone after thirteen years.

"Also, a trace of blood was in the sink of the bathroom that joined the sisters' bedrooms. Someone had attempted to clean that, too, and did a pretty thorough job. Sample analysis results were also inconclusive. Later, authorities learned Ellen had cut herself peeling an apple the day before, so that trace of blood was dismissed as inconsequential. A Band-Aid on Ellen's finger confirmed the cut. No other bloody clothes were ever found." Maggie consulted her notes. "You said Hilton had forbidden his family to associate with you. So when Hilton learned you and Ellen were seeing each other, it must have been a shock."

Will looked from her to the small pile of essentials he would be taking with him, then back at her. "He warned Ellen I was no good and she was to stay away from me."

"But she didn't. You continued to see her behind his back. When he learned Ellen was pregnant, I assume he was incensed?"

"Yeah, you could say that. Hilton expected orders to be followed. When I appeared at the door, he wanted revenge for Ellen's death. I actually think he picked the fight with me hoping I'd make a run for it and give him the excuse to kill me. If that shoe I threw had missed its mark, he would've shot me dead—I'm sure of it."

"Shot while fleeing the scene—open and shut case," she said.

"You got it. A justified and tidy end to his daughter's murder. No blame pointing at him."

"Perhaps someone else heard it and told him."

"Perhapses, could haves, might haves . . . it all boils down to the fact that I'm only speculating . . ."

"Yeah, but it's a good place to start. I know what you think Hilton's reaction was, but how do you think Mary would react to the news that Ellen was pregnant?"

"Not pleased, mostly because Ellen was so young. But I can't imagine Mary laying a hand on her daughter—stab her—not possible." He arched his neck and stared at the ceiling. "Truth is, I believe the shock and horror of Ellen's murder killed Mary. I read in the papers she had a heart attack, but I think she died of grief."

"What about Libby, Paul, and Matt? Do you think any of them would have had a violent reaction against their sister because she got pregnant?"

"Paul would have been disappointed, but he understood Ellen and I were in love. I don't honestly know what Libby would think. If one can trust locker room scuttlebutt, Libby had been laid a time or two herself. And as far as Matt is concerned, I suspect you would know that better than I would."

"I'm curious about the timeframe." Maggie jotted something down. "How long do you think Ellen had been dead before you got there? Was she still warm when you touched her? Did her arm move easily when you lifted it?"

He scrubbed a hand over his face and answered slowly. "Yeah, she was warm. From the doorway, she looked to be reclining. I thought she had a headache. She suffered from them occasionally. She hadn't been dead very long. She was still bleeding."

"Police reports put Libby upstairs in her room on the phone with classmates. There's no indication she had even come down to the party by the time her sister was killed. Would you say that was normal . . . for her to stay away from her brother's graduation party?"

"Knowing Libby, she was probably trying to decide what to wear. Mary monitored her dressing to be certain she wore something appropriate, and Libby pushed the envelope as far as she dared. I expect she would have joined the party sooner or later. Libby was quite the flirt."

"Meaning her skirts were too short or her tops too tight?"

"Exactly. Libby was only fourteen, but well endowed. She looked older. And she liked the attention the boys gave her." He pulled some packets of dehydrated food from a box and placed them into his pack.

"Did she ever flirt with you?"

He glanced across at her and couldn't help but smile. "You asking professionally?"

She grinned. "Mostly."

"Yes, she flirted with me, but there were few guys she didn't flirt with. Ellen once told me Libby had a crush on me. I never took it seriously. As far as I was concerned Libby and I were just friends."

The wind blew a gust down the chimney, sending a puff of smoke into the room. He fanned away the smoke and snatched a lap robe made of rabbit skins from the back of a chair and tossed it to her. "Better put this over you. Today, we'll have to go without a fire, and it's going to get mighty cold in here."

"Just a few more questions and I'll let you get some sleep."

Abruptly he stilled, then ran past her to the window. Cocking his head, he leaned closer, listening with his ear inches from the pane.

"What?" she said.

He shook his head. "For a second I thought I heard a plane."

She came to his side by the window and took his hand. He stared at their joined fingers and brought them to his lips, smiling to cover the urgency making his heart beat overtime.

"Night's over, Maggie. If you have more questions, you better hurry and ask, because if that was a plane, they'll be back soon."

From the scared look on her face perhaps her heart was beating fast like his was, waiting for the sound of the plane to return. But was she more afraid the searchers might not find her or that they might find him?

"I'm curious about the knife. How do you suppose Hilton came to have your knife?"

"I left it in Ellen's car. I didn't have a car of my own back then."

"Did you normally carry a knife of that size with you?"

He smiled. "I bought it when I was just a kid—it was for protection then, though it was too big to conceal well, and I never used it. About a week before the party, Ellen and I had a picnic in the park near her home. I remembered the knife and brought it along to cut up twigs for a fire."

"Was Ellen in the habit of locking her car?"

"Not when it was parked in her drive. They had a gate."

"So pretty much anyone could have found the knife that night."

He nodded.

"What about Paul? How does he fit into the picture?"

"I never saw him. I suppose he could have murdered Ellen. But I'd put my money that he and Sherry were making out just out of view of the party. You'd have to be some kind of psycho to murder your sister and start making out with your girl a few minutes after that. You know Paul. I'm sure you'll agree he's not that kind of guy. But he might know who did kill his sister."

"Yes, he might. Theoretically they could all know—everyone except Matt. That weekend he opted to stay at a friend's lake house instead of going to the party, and his friend's parents signed a statement that confirmed the boys were with them watching videos. That's about all I can think of right now. Thanks for confiding in me."

Smiling, he cupped his hands to either side of her face, his thumbs smoothing her jaw. "It felt good to get it off my chest. Thanks for trying to help."

"I just hope I can." She tore the pages of notes from the pad. She glanced at her watch. "Goodness, it's nearly noon."

They'd been up all night and then some.

He placed both hands on her waist and pulled her against him. His hands cruised down her back. His lips rubbed hers. He meant it to be affectionate, just a gentle see-you-later kiss, but the time slipping away made it far more than he planned.

The soft, throaty sounds she made raced through his veins like a raging fever. The leap from lighthearted to hot, hard urgency was so fast, he didn't have time to do anything but cling to her. He wanted to memorize the way it felt to have her in his arms. He needed to remember exactly this for the rest of his life without her.

He was so deeply immersed in the sensations she was creating in him that he nearly missed the steady drone of a plane. His heartbeat faltered. Abruptly, he broke the kiss, listening. There was no doubt. He sagged against her, letting his brow rest on hers. He'd hoped they could have another day together. It wasn't to be.

His breath tumbled out, low and anguished. "They've found us."

The odds had always been against him.

Gently he eased her from his arms and bent to reach her coat she'd left on the chair behind her. In the pocket was her gun. He lifted it and held it out to her. "I doubt they know who I am, Maggie. Right now Hilton and his cohorts are only guessing. My friends are looking for Jack Ricks, you, and Matt. But then maybe I'm wrong. Maybe Hilton's told them who I was and has enlisted the help of the Fairbanks police force. Maybe my friend Gene has been forced to lead them here. Understand that I'm not going to let them take me in for questioning. With Hilton at the reins, they're likely to shoot first and then ask questions. If you're going to place me under arrest, you better do it now. Otherwise, I'm gone."

She stared at the gun then at him. He looked into her eyes. Despair, worry, and caring fought with her sense of duty. Her eyes teared. She looked away.

"Go on. Get out of here. Take my gun. I'll tell them you held it on me."

Will smiled and pocketed the gun. He wasn't afraid to die. But he preferred to live. He wouldn't stay meekly in his cabin waiting for them. If they caught him, they would win. And he intended to win. That was how he'd always played the game. It was how he would play it now. He would escape. Or die trying.

"Good, because I wasn't going to let you take me in. I enjoy my freedom too much."

He kissed her forehead and she trembled.

"Take care. I'm going to try as hard as I can to prove your innocence."

He dressed in his outdoor gear, tied his sleeping bag to his rucksack, added a few more supplies, and shouldered the pack.

Outside he walked quickly to his dogs and harnessed them to the sled. They began to bark with anticipation. He loaded some meat from the lock box onto the sled, then the rucksack with his laptop and batteries, and then the backpack. That done, he turned back to look at her. Standing at the door watching him, tears ran down her cheeks. She took a step forward, then another, then ran awkwardly across the snow and into his arms. He moved into her like a wildcat pouncing and wrapped his arms tightly around her. He hauled her up against him and his mouth came down on hers hard. Their mouths locked together in a desperate kiss.

He groaned into her open mouth. "Oh, Maggie, don't cry." He rubbed his lips over the tears on her cheeks and rocked her gently in his arms. "We both knew it had to end this way."

"Hold me. Just hold on for one minute more," she whispered.

His gloved hands came up to frame her cheek, his thumbs stroking the line of her jaw, catching the teardrops. Their breaths intertwined then disappeared in the wind. "No more tears. I'll see you again."

"Promise me."

"I promise, God willing."

"But it's too dangerous for you to come to Chicago. We'll meet somewhere else. Tell me where."

"I'll contact you. You told me you're a crack detective. I'm trusting you to clear my name."

"Oh, Will, I'll do my best."

"That's good enough for me."

He walked her back to the cabin with his arm around her, and suddenly the pitch of his dogs' barking raised a notch, sending a jolt of urgency up his spine. Just outside the door, he paused long enough to take one last look at his cabin that had come close to being the home he longed for, the embers of the dying fire, the pictures he painted, the smell of pine from the log walls, and for less than a week the woman he would like to share it all with for the rest of his life. Homey sounds and smells he would sorely miss.

A branch cracked not far away. Men were coming up the mountainside. No time to dally. "Get back inside, Maggie. Time for me to go."

One quick kiss and Will ran. At the sled he looked back and saw her standing in the doorway, framed by the light of the fire. He lifted his hand in a last wave, when a shot rang out. His head swung around to the path alongside the cabin as a man stepped from the trees, a gun pointed directly at Will. It was too late.

Chapter Sixteen

Will froze in place. Once again he had underestimated Hilton. The man had hired pilots and pushed them to start the search before prudent. Given an equal playing field, Will could match his wits and skills against any men Hilton hired, but as always the senator saw to it that the field favored his team.

"Sorry, Will, but I got to take you in. Put the brake back on that sled and walk on over here real slow like." The deputy panted heavily, and his hands shook in an effort to catch his breath.

"Sweeny, that you?" Will straightened, his fingers closing over the gun in his pocket, and noticed a second man stood to the deputy's side.

Will walked at a normal pace toward the cabin then stopped in front of the men. Paul Raine was the last person Will imagined would be the first one up the hill, but here he was. Perhaps Paul was merely the fittest, the fastest. He just hadn't expected Paul would be anxious to see him behind bars. Yet, here he stood, a few pounds heavier, but looking a great deal as he did thirteen years ago—tall, fit, handsome, and blocking his avenue of escape.

"Hello, Jamie." Paul breathed heavily from the high altitude and his fast climb. "I wondered if it really was you."

"Hello, Paul." He'd once been closer to this man than any other, more like a brother than a friend. Any last minute thoughts of escape were much more difficult—he could never shoot Paul. He released his fingers from the gun and continued to the front door of his cabin. Somehow he'd have to take down Sweeny who was a good forty pounds heavier than he should have been, and bluff his way past Paul, and he better do it fast before the next wave appeared.

"Hell of a way to be meeting after so many years," Paul said. "With all the racket your dogs have been making for the last fifteen minutes, I thought you'd be long gone."

Maggie opened the cabin door, leaning a shoulder against the frame.

"Hello, Maggie," Paul said. "Glad to see you're safe and sound. Matt here, too?"

When Maggie didn't respond immediately, Paul glanced at Will.

"Dead. He didn't make it." Will was sweating now in his fur-lined jacket. But he thought the sweat was mostly from fear. He heard the drone of another aircraft not far away, and his jaw tightened. In short order more men would begin the climb. Would Hilton be with them? He almost wanted to stay just to confront the man face-to-face. But this wasn't the right time. He couldn't wait any longer to make his move.

"Officer," Maggie said.

Sweeny cut his eyes to Maggie. It was all the distraction Will needed, and Sweeny's fatal mistake. Will knocked the gun from the man's hand, sending his shot wild. And immediately, before the deputy could recover, Will's own gun was in his hand, the butt end coming down hard on the back of Deputy Sweeny's head.

"Sorry, Sweeny, nothing personal," he said and watched the deputy crumple to the ground. "But I'm in a hurry." Then he added, "Move aside, Paul." Will waved his gun in Paul's general direction, and he took a few backward steps toward the sled. But Paul was a big man, almost as tall as Will, and if he decided to fight, it wouldn't be an easy one, and it would take too long.

Maggie put a restraining hand on Paul's arm. "Please . . ."

When Will started to run, Paul lurched after him, grabbed his shoulder, and swung him around. Nose to nose, Paul shouted, "Did you murder my sister?"

"Damn you for asking. I loved her. You know that better than anyone. Now let me pass before you force me to do something I'll regret."

"I had to ask." The anger seemed to empty out of Paul. "Now if you don't mind, I'd like you to turn that gun and aim it at me so I won't have to lie. Then as far as I'm concerned you can get the hell out of here."

Surprised he could do so at such a time, Will laughed. Maybe from relief; he didn't know. But complying, he turned the gun on him. "I'd forgotten you're a lawyer. Thank you, my friend." He clasped Paul's arm, then he ran.

Will released the sled's brake and, bracing himself, shoved hard. "Mush!"

The dogs surged forward in their harnesses. At first the sled balked in the freezing snow, then broke free with a sudden jerk. Will ran behind pushing the sled until they'd passed over the first snow drift. From behind, shots were fired, and he figured Sweeny had revived.

He headed down the opposite side of the mountain, away from where the authorities were climbing. Once again he was on the run.

Though he couldn't honestly say Maggie's laughter and bright conversation were things he'd missed during his years on the run, it was only because he'd never experienced them. He didn't want involvement, gone out of his way to avoid it. As long as Hilton and his minions were out there trying to get to him, he couldn't allow himself to become attached, to care.

"Ha!" he laughed aloud. Too late for that. He'd been a fool to stay so long.

He cursed under his breath. Maggie's arrival had changed everything.

* * * *

Inside the cabin, Maggie looked out the window at the empty kennels. With the dogs' departure, an unnatural silence prevailed. Sixty minutes had passed since Will Connor had driven off and out of her life. Now no dogs would bark out a warning. But Will had taught her what to listen for, the occasional snap of a branch, a cough, or a hissed curse. She heard those sounds now and opened the door to listen. Men were coming. She stood in the doorway with Paul and waited.

The wait wasn't long.

Hilton, the last man to struggle up the hill, stepped forward. He shivered in the bitter cold. "Where is he?"

"He's not here."

"Damn shame we missed him. Where do you think he's headed?"

Maggie shook her head. "Who knows? Whatever he might've been before, he's a man of the mountains now."

"I don't see how he can escape by sled. He's leaving tracks. The planes will see him if he leaves the forest. I won't give up the search."

"I know." Silently, she looked out at the sled marks in the snow, wisps of her hair blowing in the breeze. *Will knows it, too. He's strong and wise. It will be hard to find him if not impossible.*

* * * *

Will ran beside the sled. He whistled to Hilde, his lead dog, heading her along the path toward the bend in the Yukon River and the vast tundra beyond, then hopped on for a ride. The trail he made wasn't of concern for they were searching by plane. Even if they'd dispatched a sled from Circle City, they would have a devil of a time getting to his cabin from that direction. He doubted Deputy Douglas and his men were fit enough physically to follow on foot. No, they'd look for him from above. When he came out of the trees, they'd be waiting for him.

He had to make damn sure they didn't see him.

An hour and a half later, he heard a plane. Hopefully, Maggie was on it headed for the Anchorage hospital to have her injuries checked. Two hours passed, and daylight wasn't gone. Except for that one plane leaving, he'd neither seen nor heard anyone. Certain two planes had flown in, someone was still at his cabin. Near the river, he signaled his dogs to stop in the trees and took shelter under an overhang to wait.

Were they searching his cabin? What would they take for evidence?

He'd grabbed the cribbage board at the last minute, a frivolous thing, extra weight, but it would remind him of Maggie, not that he needed a reminder. Maybe some day they would keep that *date*, and she could teach him to play. Maybe. He'd packed his camera with the photos he'd snapped of her sitting on the hearth in his overlarge plaid shirt and jeans. If he ever got the chance, he would paint her. *I hope Maggie took the wolf painting, or anything she wanted.*

He'd taken his notebook computer, only because he didn't want the authorities to get it. He planned to bury it somewhere.

Am I getting soft, getting too used to modern inventions. God, I'm tired of running.

Just before dark the hum of a plane sounded, headed southwest toward Fairbanks. Was he mistaken? Had they flown in more than two planes? He waited until night settled in. Once he left the woods, there was no place to hide for miles.

To wait, to sleep, knowing they were hunting him, was the hardest thing of all. But hiding for nearly half his life, he'd learned patience. He curled up in a bear-skin blanket, careful to keep his nose and ears protected from frostbite. Up all last night, he needed sleep, but he slept fitfully. The cold kept waking him, and his mind wouldn't rest.

As soon as it was fully dark, he started out again. He had to cross many miles of open tundra where he'd be visible from a plane.

His plan was to sleep during the day and travel by night until he reached John Sugpiaq's village. John would take care of his dogs and sled. He couldn't take his dogs where he was going. He hated to leave them. They were his best friends.

Growing up in the orphanage, he'd been alone. When he ran from Chicago, there'd been no one he could turn to, no one he trusted. Though he liked people, enjoyed the conversations, the interaction, the friendship, when he'd had to act, he'd always done it alone. Throughout the years of running, he'd made friends, some more dear than others. None he wished to put into danger. When all was said and done, he was still alone.

* * * *

"Gene, you got a call," the bartender yelled over the buzz of conversation and the Duke vs. North Carolina basketball game playing on a TV above the bar.

He looked up and saw the bartender point to the phone hanging on the dark paneled wall outside the men's room. "There's a call for you. You can take it over there."

Gene tipped up his beer then set it on the scarred table.

"Probably the wife checking up on you." Evegeny and three others sitting in the booth with him laughed.

Gene shrugged as he hurried over. Was one of his kids sick? Brier wasn't the type to call for no reason. "Yes," he said into the receiver, offering a grin to his friends.

"Gene, that you?"

His heart lurched. His grin fell away and he lowered his voice to a whisper. "Will!" He turned and hunched over the receiver. "Yes, it's me. I'm glad to hear from you, buddy. You all right?"

"I'm fine. Sorry to interrupt you on your night out, but I thought maybe they might have your home phone bugged, and our office, and Jim's phone, too."

"You're probably right, though I couldn't find any on our phones at home or in the office. I looked. They probably got more sophisticated stuff these days that this ol' flyboy can't find."

"I got to thinking it's Friday and that you might be at Papa Bear's."

"Pizza night—like always. Nothing ever changes around here." He became serious. "I hoped you'd call. I've been worried sick about you this past month. Can I do anything for you?"

"Have they gotten my plane?" Will asked.

"I don't think so. They tried. Word around is that it's missing some parts."

Gene imagined Will's smile, a slow burning one, the kind that got the girls' attention.

"A few key parts." Will chuckled. "I took the liberty of removing them same as I always did when I bedded the plane down for the winter. It'll only take about an hour to replace them."

"Don't know as I would have thought of doing that," Gene said.

"You would have. I've had some narrow escapes. You learn to plan ahead. But I didn't plan on Jack's plane going down. I'm really sorry. He was dead when I got there. Both guys were wearing safety harnesses, but a limb came right through the windshield and broke both their necks. I heard Jack working the engine before he crashed."

"Feds will be checking it out come spring. They've already been sniffing around, had us take them out one day. Still too much snow on the ground to see much."

"Look about ten miles down river from where you turn up to my place. How's Nancy getting along?"

"Well as can be expected. The whole business has been hard on her with the new baby and all. Her parents flew out for a while, but they've gone back. I think she's going to move to Michigan to be closer to them."

"Not a bad idea . . ." Will got quiet. Like he was thinking on Jack's wife and kid. "Have you heard anything about Maggie Raine—you remember Hilton's ex daughter-in-law who survived the crash?"

"Of course, who could forget a woman that attractive? She called once, said she'd heard so much about me that she felt like she knew me. Sounded like a nice lady. She asked about you. Anyway she's back in Chicago living at her folks' old house. She said she's fine, that she still hasn't figured out who murdered Hilton's daughter, but she's working on it, and if I ever heard from you she wanted me to tell you that someone sent her a puppy and that the puppy is keeping her bed warm." Will's chuckle made Gene smile. "And she wanted me to tell you she misses you. Am I missing something between you two— something happen up there?"

"Yeah . . . you might say. Anyway, tell her I'm going to try and keep that promise I made to her. I just don't know when. Glad she likes the dog."

"Anything I can do to help?"

"Keep tabs on her for me, will you? Give her a call every once in a while to make sure she's doing all right."

"Glad to, anything else?"

"You remember where my plane went down in '98?"

"That the time when the mama polar bear and her cub came sniffing?"

"Right. Think you can find the place again?"

"Sure. Why?"

"I was wondering if you could pick me up there—take me to my plane. Couple of Fish and Game officials flew into this place last night. Got me to thinking it's more than likely they've seen some photo of me on the internet or some bulletin. Time for me to go. I left my sled and dogs with a friend and said my good-byes. I'm headed out on foot soon as I hang up."

"Damn long walk from anywhere to anywhere out there."

"Yeah. Thought maybe you could pick me up."

"You know I will."

"Don't answer quite so fast. It's a risk for you, Gene. And don't say yes if you think you'll be followed."

"Hilton had some lackeys here for a while, but I guess even a rich senator can't afford to keep paying them forever. Cops are looking, too, but not very hard. You've got a lot of friends here."

"That's nice to hear."

The operator cut in and asked for more money. Gene waited while Will added several more coins. "Tell me when to pick you up. I'll bring some money."

"Thanks, I suppose I should have some." Will laughed. "How soon do you think you can get here?"

"Weather permitting I've got a mail delivery not too far from there next Monday. Can you get there that soon?"

"I'll make sure I do. I'll look for you Monday. But don't take chances. And thanks, Gene."

"Nothing you wouldn't and haven't already done for me. How about parts—can I bring parts for your plane?"

"Got the parts taken care of, but if you got room for a few gallons of gas, that will help. And, Gene, a good topographical map of Canada with the airports indicated will get you a gold star."

"Will do. Take care of yourself."

Chapter Seventeen

Chicago, December 18th

Maggie pulled her red Accord into the driveway of an attractive white stucco house in a Chicago suburb.

Two days earlier Maggie, reading over the files on Ellen Raine's murder case, suddenly stopped. How had she missed this? The hand-drawn sketch of the parlor where the murder was committed showed a pocket door between the dining room and the front parlor. In the months she lived in Rutland Manor she didn't recall a pocket door between the two rooms.

Yesterday she'd paid Celia a short visit. As she thought, the pocket door was no longer there. It had been replaced with a wall and bookshelves. Through a cracked pocket door a maid as attentive as Thea Johnson could easily have witnessed a murder or slipped inside the parlor to commit one.

At first when Maggie identified herself on the telephone, Thea had sounded surprised. Then her voice had flattened, and she'd sounded tired and defensive. The woman had been questioned many times before. Maggie had read the transcripts of each interview several times, seen the photos, and spoken to Thea on the phone more than once, but this was the first time she'd visited her.

At sixty-three, Thea was slightly stooped with gray hair pulled tightly back into a bun. The fourteen years since she'd quit the Raines' employment hadn't been kind to her. The long, gaunt, brown face was heavily lined, her movements arthritic. She stood holding onto the rails of her walker.

Maggie held out her hand, staving off a pang of guilt that she was about to upset the woman. "I got held up at the department, then I missed my exit off the turnpike and had to backtrack."

Thea nodded and gave her a wan smile, then turned. Maggie followed.

"Matt came here the day before he flew to Alaska," Thea said, pointing Maggie to the sofa and maneuvered to an upholstered chair beside it. "Did you know that?" Her voice sounded nervous, high-pitched.

What had prompted Matt's last minute visit? It wasn't mentioned in his notes. "No, I didn't."

Cups and saucers and a plate of store-bought Pecan Sandies sat on the coffee table. Thea reached for the coffeepot, her hand shaking.

"The last time I saw Matt before that visit," Thea reminisced aloud, "he was sitting in the breakfast room eating supper. I fixed him a plate early as he was spending the night out. That was the night of Paul's graduation party, the night Ellen . . ." The cup rattled on the saucer. Alarmed, Maggie reached over to take the coffeepot from her hand. A thin sheen of perspiration beaded on Thea's forehead.

"Mrs. Johnson, are you all right?"

Thea glanced out the window. Outside was overcast and looked like it might snow. "Yes, ma'am. I'm fine." Maggie poured the coffee. Thea lifted her cup, but her hand shook so badly, she put it down.

Maggie sipped her coffee, then looked to the wall over Thea's shoulder. "That must be your daughter Tabatha in the photograph behind you. I've been admiring how stunning she is."

Thea smiled, obviously pleased. "She favors her father."

"I heard she's teaching school."

"In Calumet. She got the *Teacher of the Month* award last May." Maggie heard the pride in her voice.

The phone rang. "Excuse me. My telephone is in the kitchen."

Maggie took the opportunity to look at other photos on a Duncan Fife table behind the sofa. Several were of Thea's husband, the Raines' gardener for many years. When Thea left their employ immediately after the murder, he had quit, too. He died of a heart attack some years later.

Maggie overheard: "No, I can't. No, you don't understand. I've got to go now. I'll call you back later."

When Thea returned, she wore a frown, prompting Maggie to wonder who had called. "I know you're wondering why I'm here."

"Not really. I figure you came to ask me the same questions 'bout the murder like the other cops did, your ex-husband included. I told them the same thing I told you on the phone, but I'll say it again. When I heard gunshots, I ran from that house. I don't know nothin' more 'bout that murder." Thea's words were reeled off like she'd committed them to memory. "Is there anything else you wanted to talk to me about? Tabatha is waiting for me to return her call."

So, her daughter was on the telephone moments ago. Thea was hiding something. Maggie decided to take a chance. "Mrs. Johnson, I believe you know something about the murder. Something you've never told anyone, except maybe your daughter. Is that why Tabatha called you? Did you tell her I was coming, and she urged you to let go of your secret?"

Thea shook her head, her complexion pale. "I-I don't have a secret."

Maggie pushed on, sensing whatever Thea had seen had brought her near to a breaking point. "Here's what I think happened that night, Mrs. Johnson. I think you were setting the dining room table, and you heard Ellen scream. You opened the little pocket door that once connected the parlor to the dining room to see if you could help, and you saw something.

"Fourteen years, Thea, *is* a long time for an innocent man to be on the run. Whatever you saw that night scared you so much, you ran from the house and never returned again. I believe you know Jamie Donovan did not murder Ellen Raine."

"I was in the kitchen. I didn't see anything." Thea wrapped her arms around her waist, tucked her hands under her armpits, and rocked forward, looking down. Maggie waited.

Without lifting her gaze, Thea spoke softly. "The papers said you tried to arrest Jamie Donovan in Alaska, but that he escaped again."

"That's true, but one day someone will catch him. I believe Jamie Donovan is innocent, Thea. I think you *know* he's innocent. Jamie has spent nearly half his life on the run because a politically powerful man accused him of murder. If you saw something and don't speak up, you'll be responsible for the death of an innocent man."

Thea suddenly shoved to her feet and reached for her walker. Tears glazed her eyes, and her voice was just above a whisper. "It's time for you to leave, Mrs. Raine."

Maggie extracted her card from her purse and handed it to Thea. "When you're ready to talk, please call me. Please. If you're afraid, I'll see that the police protect you. It's long past time that the right person is arrested for Ellen's murder."

At the front door, Maggie turned to look at the former maid. "One more question, Mrs. Johnson. Did Hilton Raine buy this house for you? Is he paying you to keep your mouth shut? Before you answer, remember it's something I can check."

"He's not giving me nothin' I didn't earn. I worked for him for nearly thirty years." Thea shut the door.

"And kept his secret for fourteen years after that," Maggie said under her breath. She descended the steps. *Yes, Thea, you earned the house.*

* * * *

O'Hare Airport's new security annoyed Hilton. Since 9/11, cars weren't allowed to park for curb-side pickup. Four days before Christmas, he stood outside in the cold for fifteen minutes before he finally spotted his new Lexus in the line of cars. The chauffer pulled up a few feet from him, popped the trunk, and ran around to open Hilton's door. He tipped the porter and climbed into the back seat.

"Has my son arrived yet?"

"I pick up he and he niña dis morning." Rodriguez swerved around a taxi then darted into traffic.

Hilton flipped open his newspaper and swore under his breath. The corner of the front page headline read, "Woman's Body Found." The subheading asked, "The Work of the Lakeshore Murderer?" The body, found two days ago by a man walking his dog, was the same woman Paul mentioned had disappeared from the fundraiser. Hilton remembered she was an attractive young widow whose husband had left her bundles of money. He'd even had a one night fling with her. Her body had turned up on the Lake Michigan shore, exactly like the other victims of the Lakeshore murderer. His gaze moved restlessly out the window. The gray of the wintry late-afternoon light blended with the slate and concrete of the road and buildings, making the city look cold, inhospitable. The wind blew in fits and starts, rocking the car, and howling like a lost soul. He flipped open his cell phone to check its signal.

Three new messages. He scrolled to one from Celia and listened. "Hi, darling. I'm calling to remind you of the family dinner party here on the 22nd. Father arrived a few days ago. Paul and Tiffany should be flying in on the 21st. I've invited Maggie and my sisters and their families, too. Ruby's planned a special meal. We're counting on you being here with us." The message was dated the evening before. Unfortunately, he'd be there in plenty of time for the dinner.

The notion of spending an evening with Matt's former wife made Hilton grimace. He never had liked her, and the thought of seeing his ex-daughter-in-law didn't warm his heart. Celia didn't seem to care Maggie was an *ex*-daughter-in-law to his now deceased son. She considered Maggie family, and family was of the utmost importance to Celia, to wit, that old bag-of-bones she insisted on inviting to all family affairs—her father. The old man was nearing ninety-three and refused to die and leave his doting daughter all his millions.

Hilton would have preferred stopping by his club to have a bite and a few drinks, but that wasn't what was driving him now.

As soon as he'd read about the latest body finding, he'd decided to attend his wife's annual family dinner. He looked forward to visiting with Paul. But more importantly, he needed to check on something at home.

* * * *

Inside the brick house on Chestnut Street that had once belonged to her parents, Maggie looped the last garland around the tree's branches and stepped back to admire her handiwork. A small Christmas tree, barely five feet, its limbs were heavily draped with multicolored lights, and ornaments filled with precious memories.

The tree gave Maggie little pleasure. She turned and stared out the frost-etched window. The gray and gloomy day had darkened into an early night, edgy with a fitful wind and cold. Maggie shivered, drawing her sweater tighter over her breasts.

As if on cue, the old steam-heated radiator she'd never got around to updating hissed and clacked.

Although Maggie had pored over the files on Ellen's murder hundreds of times, she'd stayed late at the station to study them again, keeping in mind the pocket door that connected the parlor to the dining room. In the current floor plan of Rutland Manor, the dining room was adjacent to a large butler's pantry that led through a short hallway to the kitchen. In that hallway to the right was a servants' stairway, to the left a door to the cellar.

The cellar had a rarely used outside door that was well screened behind a brick wall. So the pocket door opened up a whole line of new possibilities. Sadly, if any traces of blood showed the murderer's trail, they were long gone. How thoroughly had the police investigated the scene to disprove Jamie Donovan had committed the murder?

Maggie had scoured interview transcripts she'd transferred to her computer, matching the written words with what Will had told her, racking her brain to find something everyone had missed. She'd studied until her eyes blurred and doubts that she'd ever be able to solve the case knotted her stomach. She'd sent the file to her home computer and driven home.

Since her visit to Thea Johnson's house she'd called the woman several times, leaving messages on her answering machine. Maggie hoped Thea would crack and come clean. She'd discovered that Thea had purchased the house shortly after Ellen's murder, that she'd paid in cash, and that Elegant Interior Decorators had been hired by Mary Raine to decorate and furnish the house—a gift to a faithful retired servant. No crime there. No crime even if Hilton had paid for her house, although Maggie couldn't prove he had. But the gifts were beginning to add up.

For income, Thea received disability insurance and her husband's Social Security, both legit. But there was also a nice stipend from another policy that Maggie guessed Hilton funded. Still, nothing illegal. But Maggie suspected Hilton held more than money over Thea's head. Had he threatened her?

There was little joy in Maggie's heart. Her brother Tyler who always made every effort to spend Christmas with her was deployed to the Mediterranean this year and couldn't get leave.

Fears of never seeing Will again and never clearing his name piled up inside of her. Her eyes felt raw, as if tears were stacked up behind the lids.

Maggie sighed and looked down at her five-month-old Golden Retriever playing at her feet. Innocently oblivious to her concerns, the puppy entertained herself by removing tissue paper from one of the Christmas storage boxes. Maggie smiled.

"No, Misty. Eating paper can make you sick." She removed the wad of shredded paper from the puppy's mouth and tossed her one of the many tennis balls scattered around the floor.

The Saturday after her birthday, a cold rain was turning a recent snow to slush. The doorbell chimed and Maggie answered, expecting to find books she'd ordered online. Instead, a UPS man stood with an umbrella in one hand and a crate in the other. Inside the screened gray crate was a bundle of white fur with a black nose and two black eyes peering up at her. It was love at first sight.

"Maggie Raine?" the UPS man queried.

"Yes, but I think there must be some mistake . . ."

"Twenty-seven eleven Chestnut Street?"

Maggie nodded.

"There's a card." He handed her the envelope, but even before she read the card, she knew.

Hello, Maggie,

You said you always wanted a golden, but in case you've changed your mind, the kennel will take her back. She was meant to be a present for your birthday, but the puppy wasn't quite ready to leave her mother then. The puppy's records and the kennel information are attached to the crate. I miss you.

Since returning home, it was the only time she'd heard directly from Will. His friend Gene had phoned. Will wanted her to know he was managing fine and he missed her. That conversation had been short and guarded, as were all Gene's calls. During the last one, she'd confessed she'd made little progress in her investigation. Gene always called from a different cell number. When he didn't call last week, she'd tried his home phone only to learn his number had been changed to a private one. But a day didn't pass without hoping she'd hear from Will. His silence boded nothing good, and she worried about him.

With a deep sigh she sagged to the floor, Misty pouncing in front of her ready to play. Absentmindedly, she grabbed hold of one end of a nearby toy, let the puppy grab the other, and braced herself for Misty's powerful pull.

Her gaze drifted above the mantle where she'd hung a J.W. Wilding painting of a polar bear on the barren Alaska tundra. Wilding was Will's pseudonym. The painting arrived shortly after the puppy, the canvas removed from the stretchers and rolled, the frame Will had made from rough timbers and the stretchers disassembled and packaged with the canvas. No note, but she recognized it. She wondered if wherever Will was he'd been able to continue with his painting.

When Gene phoned, she asked about the gift. "You can be assured the artist specifically requested that you have it," was his response.

She loved the painting—every day it spoke to her about the artist, the nomad of the mountains. But the little lone wolf watercolor he'd given her was her favorite. She'd had it framed and hung it in her bedroom where she could see it first thing each morning. Without exception when she looked at the wolf standing alone and lonely atop the mountain ridge, her heart ached as it ached now for the man who was somewhere out in the cold with no place to call home.

After returning from Alaska, she'd taken a few days of sick leave to heal completely. During that time, she'd attended Matt's funeral service, and endured hours of grilling by the police. She was relieved to get past those events. Once again, Ellen's murder and Jamie Donovan's newest escape ran rampant in the news, right beside the murder of another pretty, young socialite.

Tomorrow evening she was invited for Christmas dinner at Rutland Manor. She grimaced, dreading the thought of spending any time with Hilton. But Celia would be heartbroken if she didn't attend. No matter how she felt about Hilton, Maggie was fond of his wife. The family gathering would be a stilted affair, with grief and the desire for revenge casting a pall over the Christmas cheer Celia tried so hard to generate.

A palpable mistrust and mutual dislike existed between Maggie and the powerful senator. Hilton was aware she was actively researching his daughter's murder. He strongly disapproved and at every opportunity told her so. She believed Hilton had at worse gotten away with murder, at best knew who had killed Ellen and still let the crime be pinned on Will.

Sighing deeply, she clicked on Fox News and unfolded the *Daily News*. Another woman's body found, the second in less than a year.

Four months ago Maggie was assigned to the case. This recent killing was the fifth in a string of unsolved murders that stretched over ten years. All of them women who frequented the upper socioeconomic class, each woman's body was mutilated with a knife before it was dumped into Lake Michigan. But the similarities ended there. Cause of death differed in each case. These differences didn't point to a serial murderer, though Maggie wasn't so sure. All the bodies were washed ashore along Lakeshore Drive.

Years ago the newspaper dubbed the perpetrator the "Lakeshore murderer."

Maggie took another swallow of coffee and pondered the latest murder. Something about the victims eluded her—some piece of evidence that niggled at her brain. Poring over Ellen's murder, it had tickled the edges of her mind, but she just couldn't quite catch it. Deep in thought, her head jerked up when the doorbell unexpectedly chimed.

She glanced at the clock. Eight-thirty, late to be calling. Against her will, her thoughts jumped to Will. She hurried to the front entryway and yanked open the door.

Chapter Eighteen

Nerves on edge, Will walked down the quiet, tree-lined street, checking house numbers. He hadn't planned his return to Chicago like this, in the dark of the night, all his worldly belongings in his knapsack. In his plans, his dreams, he came back in triumph, a free man, all charges against him dropped.

Maggie awaiting him with open arms. Would she welcome him? Or in the reality of the everyday world had their brief affair faded?

Entering the home of a Chicago cop was a risk he was willing to take. The trouble it might cause Maggie concerned him more.

Colored Christmas lights hung along the front portico of the modest two-story house. A Scotch pine wreath, tied with a red bow, adorned the door. The pungent fragrance filled Will with images of the home, wife, and children of his dreams. It also reminded him of his cabin, its cozy warmth where he could settle his bones, and where his dogs welcomed him. God, he was so damn tired of running. He breathed deeply, closing his eyes. Headlights approached and he stepped into the shadows of a pine.

He missed the mountains, the isolation. He missed Alaska. After so many years, the city seemed too busy, noisy, dirty.

The car passed, and Will stepped out from the protection of the tree. Between the front window curtains, a small Christmas tree twinkled with lights and beckoned invitingly.

Soft strains of Christmas music played inside. Did she have company? Someone had cleared the snow off the drive and walkway. Who? Should he just turn around and leave? She was a beautiful woman. What if she'd found someone else?

Doubts assailed him, but he'd come a long and arduous way to fulfill a promise. If he walked away, he'd never know whether the feelings that had ignited between them were still there.

Gene had picked him up and dropped him off at his plane. Will retrieved the hidden parts and the extra gasoline Gene had brought him, then spent the evening working on his engine.

The next morning he'd flown away. He abandoned his plane in Thunder Bay where he'd hired on a cargo ship that sailed the Great Lakes. From there he worked his way to Chicago.

Car headlights brightened as it approached down the street. Will again ducked behind the spruce. To his disappointment, the car slowed then pulled into Maggie's drive and parked. A stunning woman got out, opened the back door, then turned holding a box. Libby Raine, all grown up, carried the package to the front door.

* * * *

Maggie wasn't surprised to see Libby standing outside the door, her face flushed with the cold, but Maggie was disappointed.

"Hi, Maggie, may I come in?"

She kept hold of Misty's collar and stepped back from the door. "Yes, of course."

Not in the mood for Libby's chit-chat, she was tempted to tell her she had a headache, which was true. But good manners dictated otherwise, and she asked, "Do you have time for coffee?"

"I've got a few minutes." Libby held out the gift. "This is from Celia."

"Oh. I thought we'd exchange gifts at Christmas dinner tomorrow night. Have the plans changed?"

"No. This is a Christmas ham, one of those honey-baked ones. Father received several from his constituents, far more than Celia can use. Since I was heading to a party not far from here she asked me to deliver it for her."

Libby handed the package to Maggie and shrugged out of her coat, tossing the mink onto the sofa.

"Thank you. That was thoughtful of Celia. I'll call her in the morning."

Libby was indeed decked out for a party. The short black satiny cocktail dress was low cut, revealing a great deal of cleavage.

"You look great, Libby. Like a movie star." Maggie felt exceptionally plain in her worn jeans, white jersey top, and oversized navy sweater. Pink fuzzy slippers warmed her feet. "Where'd you get that dress?"

"Got it on sale last week in a little shop downtown called 'The Cat's Meow.'" Libby looked pleased with herself.

Maggie led the way into the kitchen.

Libby stopped in front of the newspaper on the table. "Oh, I see you've been reading about the latest Lakeshore murder. I went to the candlelight service for her at First Baptist last night—nice service."

"You knew the victim?" Maggie put the ham in the refrigerator, box and all, and reached for the coffee pot.

"Yes, I knew her. You working on the case?"

"As a matter of fact, I am." Maggie filled a cup and handed it to Libby

"Thanks." Lazily, Libby sipped her coffee, ambled over to the table, and sat. "I love hearing about your cases. Tell me about this one."

Forcing a smile, Maggie added hot coffee and milk to her cup and carried it back to the table. "You know I can't talk about the case, Libby, even if I did know much about it, which I don't. I haven't had the case long."

Libby studied the paper a moment. "Like I said, I knew her. I can tell you she was a bitch, a rich bitch."

"That's a mighty harsh thing to say." Maggie set her cup down. "Why did you go to her service if you disliked her?"

"Reverend asked us to go, show support to her family. I know it sounds ugly, and I would only say such a thing to you. But I said it because it's the truth. God knew the truth about that woman. Sometimes the truth is harsh. I knew her from a couple of parties. She was a first degree snob. I heard she slept around a lot, a regular slut. Good riddance, I say."

Maggie considered who was talking and thought of some pertinent remarks about *not casting stones if you live in a glass house* . . . "But still, she's dead, Libby. She'll never be able to live out her natural life. I think it's terribly sad. You wouldn't wish that on anyone."

"I suppose . . . but I overheard her saying some nasty things about Father. I don't like people saying ugly things about the people I care for." Libby's attention returned to the front page.

171

"It says the Lakeshore murders could be the work of a serial killer. You think that's possible?"

Maggie shuddered. The thought of some maniac murderer out there gave her goosebumps.

What she told Libby about not knowing much wasn't entirely true. She'd read all the files, then researched the MO of serial killers, reading several articles and talking with Lieutenant Ross, the department's reigning expert on the subject. She'd learned it was often the control, the hunt, the heady thrill of power that drove a serial killer. According to Ross, the killer might actually want to be caught. He might even suffer from guilt, but his need to kill outweighed everything else.

"We've just begun the investigation," Maggie said quietly.

The possibility was strong that all the Lakeshore killings were linked. Although there were differences in each of the murders, there were more similarities. What her department hadn't revealed was that before each of the last four murders the police had received a note predicting a future murder. Mailed from different places within fifty miles of Chicago, the notes gave no clues as to where or whom the killer would strike. Maggie hypothesized that the killer might be mailing the notes when the urge to kill began to manifest within him, but he, too, had no idea who his next victim might be. But she hadn't yet voiced that theory.

"This killer has been out there for a long time," Libby said. "I suppose serial killers are hard to detect."

"Not necessarily. If one person did commit all the murders, you're right about this killer. He's already proved hard to catch. These murders go back at least ten years. Anyway, I'm not going to discuss the case, Libby."

Frowning, Libby fingered the little gold cross she wore around her neck. A nervous habit Maggie had observed many times.

"So, you think you're smart enough to catch this killer?"

Something in Libby's tone, a challenge perhaps, jerked Maggie's head up. She looked directly into Libby's eyes. "Me, personally? I don't know about that, but there are others smarter and more experienced than I who are working the case. Eventually the killer will make a mistake. They always do. We'll get him in the end." Maggie lifted her chin a notch. "But until we catch this murderer, you should be particularly careful. He seems to be hitting on people who frequent the circles you move in."

"I know, and I will." Libby pulled a cigarette from a pack in her bag and stuck it in her mouth.

"Libby, please, I'd prefer you didn't smoke here."

"Yes, I forgot." Libby threw the cigarette in her purse and snapped it shut. Abruptly she changed the subject. "Talking about unsolved murders, anything new on Jamie Donovan? You're still working on the case, aren't you?"

Maggie closed her eyes and took a deep breath. Somehow when Libby stopped by for a visit or they ran into each other at Rutland Manor, sooner or later Jamie's name always came up. Officially she was off the Donovan case though on her own time and with the permission of her captain, she spent every spare moment working it.

"The case is old, old and cold." She shook her head. "All the evidence points to Jamie Donovan, so no one's much interested in pursuing it."

"But you don't think Jamie Donovan killed Ellen."

Maggie had to tread carefully. She shrugged and picked up the cups.

"You paid a visit to Thea Johnson's house the other day," Libby said. It wasn't a question.

In the cozy kitchen, Libby's declaration blew between them like a cold draft.

A muscle tightened in Libby's jaw, and her eyes sparked with something hot before she lowered them to examine her crimson nails. Maggie's palms grew moist as she stood and headed for the sink. Some sixth sense warned her not to pick up the gauntlet.

"What do *you* think, Libby? Do you think Donovan killed your sister? You were there that evening."

"I was upstairs in my room getting dressed. I didn't know anything was going on until I heard the sirens out front."

Maggie placed the cups in the sink, turned, and sighed heavily. "I suppose we'll never see Donovan again, so what we think doesn't really matter."

"But you're trying to clear his name. Why is that?" Libby smiled slightly.

Uneasy, Maggie chose her words carefully. "I'd like the police to catch the person who murdered your sister. If it's Donovan, then I hope to see him in cuffs."

"Ellen shouldn't have let him get her pregnant. If Ellen had kept her skirts down, none of this would have happened."

"Matt told me they were in love," Maggie said softly.

"Half the girls in Montgomery Academy were in love with Jamie. The difference is that Ellen thought that getting pregnant was a way to keep him with her. Look where it landed her. It was a selfish thing for her—"

The ring of the telephone cut off her words and shot a bolt of tension through Maggie. She was sorely tempted to just let it go on ringing. Libby was in an expansive mood—perhaps she'd seen more than she let on and would shed light on the true murderer.

"Aren't you going to get that?" Libby asked after the third ring.

"Yes, of course. Excuse me." Maggie crossed the room. "Hello."

"Maggie. I'm glad you're home."

"Oh, hi. Where else did you think I'd be this late after a long day at work?"

"It's Friday night. I figured you'd be out dancing." Pete, her partner and her brother's best friend, laughed. He was sweet and a little shy, not a quality expected in a policeman, but he was smart and could be tough. She'd seen him in action. "At home, I guess, but I'm glad you are. Actually, I just got a message your next-door neighbor phoned the station. Apparently she was emptying her trash and thought she saw someone go around back of your house. Soon as I heard, I drove by your house—saw a black Cadillac out front when I passed. I would have stopped, but I didn't want to interrupt you. You still have company?"

Maggie glanced toward Libby. She was tilting the shiny toaster, using it like a mirror to freshen her lipstick. "Libby Raine's here. You remember her, don't you?"

"I know she's your ex's sister, but I've never met her. I haven't seen the black Caddy at your house before."

"You wouldn't have, unless Celia or Libby drove it. Is that why you called, to check on me?"

He chuckled. "Shortly after Mrs. Newlin phoned to report the prowler, Don Bradley called to say he'd seen a strange man on your street, too. Not often we get a call about *one* prowler in our neighborhood, let alone two. Yeah. I admit I was worried. Right now I'm down the street at Salvatore's."

"Having Sal's max pizza, I hope."

"Susan's here with me and some of the other guys and their wives, but I suppose tonight's not a good time for you to join us for a late pizza." Voices echoed in the background.

Maggie smelled a whiff of the burned casserole she'd eaten for supper and was tempted. "No, Pete, not tonight, but thanks for thinking of me."

A voice called his name. "Hey, hold on a minute, would you please?" Sounds became muffled—his hand was over the mouthpiece—but she could still hear him shout to his companions to go on and he'd catch up with them later. Then he spoke to her again. "Maggie, you still there?"

"I'm here."

"Sorry about that, just Jeff and Billy and some of the other rowdy guys from the department giving me a hard time. You know how they can be."

She knew though for the most part around her they kept their antics to a minimum.

"You read about the robberies in the area, I'm sure," he said.

"I read the same blurb in the papers that the Bradleys and the Newlins probably did. The suspicious walker is probably a high school kid who missed his ride home from basketball practice."

He paused, and she could almost hear his mind turning. "Yeah, but I wanted to give you a heads-up. Keep your doors locked and be careful."

"Yes, sir, Officer, I will." She laughed. "Thanks for keeping an eye out for me."

Maggie signed off and spoke to Libby. "That was my partner Pete Cramer. He's lived down the street since I was a kid. He and his family are like family to me."

"And now he's checking up on you."

"Yes." She smiled. "He followed his father into the police force, and he's appointed himself my protector as well as my partner."

Maggie pushed the button to the radio, turning off the TV, and Roy Orbison came over the airwaves singing *Pretty Woman*.

Singing along with Roy, she happened to glance at Libby and saw in her face a strained, faraway look as though she were reliving something she preferred to forget. Maggie sat back down at the table. "Hey, everything all right? You look upset."

"I'm fine. It's just that song. I never liked it."

"You don't like *Pretty Woman*? I thought everyone liked it—it's got such a catchy beat I feel like dancing whenever I hear it. I loved the movie. The first time I saw it was with a bunch of girlfriends. Back then we thought that movie was pretty hot stuff—pretty risqué."

"That's just it. It's about a prostitute . . . I remember the band was playing that song the night my sister was murdered. It always reminds me of that terrible night."

"I'm sorry. But Julia Roberts and Richard Gere—it was a great love story. If you can get over the association, you'll love the movie."

"I saw it. She sold herself for money. She pulled the wool over Gere's eyes. I didn't think Gere should have fallen in love with a woman like that."

"Well, the song's over now."

"I have to go." Rising, Libby picked up her bag and headed for the front door. "I'm already late for the party."

Chapter Nineteen

Twenty minutes after he watched Libby drive away, Will stood at the bottom of Maggie's front steps with a bad case of nerves. When the front door suddenly opened, he ducked back into the shadows, watching Maggie bend down to unplug the Christmas lights.

The lights went off, silhouetting her and a Golden Retriever against the hallway lights.

She straightened. He stepped forward. Her head jerked up, and their gazes collided. The dog bounded out the door with a burst of enthusiastic energy that had him laughing.

She wore jeans and a sweater with fluffy slippers on her feet. Her red hair was a little longer than he remembered and loosely tied at the base of her neck, leaving several wispy curls to frame her face.

The initial fear on her face softened into a smile that kicked his gut with sheer pleasure. He stood, grinning, unable to say a word.

"I was just unplugging the Christmas lights." She stepped inside the door. "How long have you been standing here?"

"Not too long. You alone?"

"Yes. Libby left about twenty minutes ago. I'm surprised you didn't see her."

"I did. I waited until I was sure she wasn't coming back."

"You must be frozen. Come in." She glanced up and down the street, but it was quiet and still. Most of the Christmas lights had been turned off.

He hesitated. "You sure?" He'd thought about this meeting so many times, never convinced if it would actually take place, wanting to be absolutely certain he wouldn't be putting her in more danger. "I can go right back where I came from. I expect it would be better for you if I did. But I wanted to see you one more time, how you were. And a telephone call didn't seem enough." He lowered his head, then looked at her with a small smile. "Besides, I did promise I'd come."

She focused her green eyes on him, and a spurt of lust joined his pleasure in seeing her.

"Yes, you did, and I've been waiting for you to keep that promise."

His heartbeat leapt to his throat, choking back the thousand things he wanted to say.

"Come in, Will. For goodness sake come in before I grab you out here on the street for all the neighbors to see."

Inside, he pulled off his gloves and stuffed them into his pockets. A silence settled between them. The quiet drip of a faucet that needed fixing, the hiss of the ancient radiator, the radio in the kitchen playing music, a car driving slowly down the road outside, her dog still excited and nuzzling her nose at her legs and his.

A wisp of red hair pulsed at her temple. He raised a hand, lifted the errant lock then let it drift back over her cheek. "I'm having a hard time believing that you're real, that I'm not dreaming." He moved toward her. "You are even more beautiful than the last time I saw you. I wasn't sure I'd ever see you again."

"I've missed you," she whispered and slipped her arms around his waist.

With a low strangled sound he jerked her against his chest, burying his face in her hair. He squeezed his eyes shut. For a long time he held her tightly, needing the feel of her in his arms, needing her warmth, her vitality, needing every bit of her deep down in his weary bones.

"Will." What he heard in the single word squeezed his heart. Her hand came to rest on his chest, and he took a deep breath. "It's so very good to see you."

Her eyes lifted and met his gaze squarely. "I'm so very glad to see you, too."

Inches apart, their lips almost touched. He lowered his head and kissed her softly then pulled away.

She ran her fingers over the muscles in his back and they quaked under her touch.

He wanted her. Desperately wanted her. He kissed her until he felt her legs go wobbly, until he staggered back against the foyer wall, until tears welled in his eyes. At last he lifted his head, his breathing heavy, as was hers, his heart thundering with the ferocity of a freight train.

Still within the circle of his arms, she unbuttoned his heavy jacket and pushed her hand inside to where she could surely feel the rush of his heartbeat through the thickness of his wool shirt. "Why don't you take your coat off and stay awhile?"

Looking at her hard, he saw something in her eyes—a sort of desperate hunger, a burning need that mirrored all his feelings. When he stepped back, it was gone. He shrugged out of his backpack, let it drop to the floor, then removed his jacket and draped it over his pack. Was the need he'd seen in her eyes solely his imagination?

She crossed to the living room windows and pulled the drapes. His gaze followed her and he smiled when she turned. His look roamed all over her, and he thought the flush that rose to her cheeks was from the message in his eyes.

He took a step toward her Christmas tree. "Your tree's beautiful."

"I finished decorating it earlier this evening. Misty helped me. She tried to eat the decorations." She laughed.

He laughed with her, then gave the dog a lusty rub. "Hello, Misty." He lifted his head and gave Maggie a searching look. "She's working out then?"

"She's still teething, so if you don't want something nibbled on, you better put it above eye-level. She's a sweetheart, a great friend."

The shrill ring of the telephone jerked Maggie's head around. For a moment she stared at the offensive instrument, not moving. When she finally lifted the receiver to check the caller ID, she frowned. "The police department." He didn't have to be told to retrieve his pack and jacket. Into the receiver she said, "Kilpatrick here."

Her maiden name. He figured it was probably more comfortable for her after the divorce without the instant name-recognition associated with Senator Hilton Raine.

"Hi, Maggie, it's Pete. Sorry to disturb you again, but remember the prowler I mentioned earlier?" Without pausing for Maggie's response, he went on. "Well, a neighbor just called in that she observed a man cutting through your yard. I'm out front of your place right now, and she's right. Someone was on your yard. Looks like whoever it was didn't want to be seen from the street and hid behind a spruce near your front door. Single set of footprints in the snow, a man's. Looks like a dog's been out here, too. Have you heard anything or seen anyone?"

The blood drained from Maggie's face. "No, I haven't. I've been here all night as you know and haven't heard or seen anything. I think Misty would have barked if anyone were outside. Hold on a minute, and I'll check around the house." Maggie pressed mute. "The cops are outside the house right now. Someone reported a prowler."

Will had his jacket on and was slipping his backpack over his shoulders. "I'll go out the back."

"I've got a better idea. Go upstairs. You can see what's going on from the front window. If you have to run, use the window in my bedroom—it's not much of a jump to the back porch roof. But this is a friend of mine, and I know how to get rid of him."

Upstairs, Will hurried to a front bedroom window and eased it open a crack. Crouched out of sight, he saw the officer standing just beyond the portico, and could hear him clearly.

The front porch light came on and Maggie opened the door. He smiled when Misty barged out, running into the yard, effectively obliterating any tracks that were there. "Good Misty," he whispered.

"Hi Pete, Joe. Thanks for checking on me, but no one's in here. I've been trying to think who the neighbor saw. Maybe Tommy, the kid who shoveled the walkway for me this afternoon. He came back this evening to get paid. No kid will stick to the walkways if he can reach his destination quicker by crossing the yard."

The officer at the door laughed and doused his flashlight.

"You find any tracks returning to the street?" Maggie asked.

The officer shook his head.

"There you go. Tommy stuck to the walkway. You guys can come in and take a look if you want, but you see how Misty is. No way anyone could hide in here or outside without her knowing it."

"I expect you're right. As long as you're satisfied, we'll be on our way. But I'll see that someone keeps a close eye on the neighborhood over the holidays just in case."

"Thanks, I appreciate that. Merry Christmas. Misty, come inside girl."

Will heard the door close.

He stood at the top of the stairs. Maggie's gaze settled on him, and he couldn't conceal his profound sadness. Dreams shattered, he lifted his shoulders, drawing on the strength that had sustained him all these years on the run. God knew it was becoming harder and harder to keep the disappointment and anguish from his soul.

"I'm sorry about that. A neighbor called the police to report a prowler."

"I'm the one who's sorry to put you in jeopardy."

He descended the steps slowly, and stood in front of her. His fingers curled under her chin, his thumb stroked her lower lip. "Keep that chin up, Maggie darlin'. Look at it this way. I'll have to stay at least until the watchful neighbor goes to sleep."

"I don't think she ever sleeps." Maggie smiled, slipping her arms around him. She kissed his mouth. She leaned back, assessing him. "You have the look of a hungry man. Have you eaten?"

He hadn't, but he'd gone without so many times it hardly registered. He grinned, dipping his chin ruefully. "That obvious, huh?"

"No—just a guess. But you're in luck." A giggle bubbled from her mouth. "Libby brought a honey-baked ham, a gift from Celia."

She turned toward the kitchen. Will stopped her. He looked down at her, trying to read her thoughts. "You sure you want this, Maggie? I can leave right now if you'd like. I can disappear out of your life. You're taking a huge risk."

"It's not as much as the risk you're taking by being here. Don't go," she said softly.

He swallowed, breathed.

She gave his arm a little tug. "Let me close the blinds, then please, come into the kitchen and I'll fix something to eat. We'll have ham and I have veggies and biscuits in the freezer that I can cook in a jiffy. While I do, fill me in on where you've been since I last saw you."

He smiled. "You've talked me into it, but after your dire warning about Misty, let me put my backpack and jacket somewhere out of reach."

"Good idea."

* * * *

At her kitchen table he ate ham, warmed-up biscuits, and microwaved beans. She had more coffee as they exchanged stories. They talked of everything except Ellen's murder. She couldn't bear to tell him that despite her best efforts she'd learned nothing of consequence, that her best hope lay in a maid who was reliant on a walker and her former boss's goodwill. The hours slipped away and she sensed dawn wasn't far away. He instinctively glanced at the clock, then placed both hands on the edge of the table and boosted himself to his feet.

Not yet. I'm not ready for him to leave.

"I need to go. But before I leave, I'd like to see the rest of your home so I can visualize you here."

Of course he had to leave—that was inevitable, the only prudent solution—but in the joy of seeing him again, she couldn't bear for him to leave. She recalled the scent of the wood-burning fire and timbered pine of his cabin's walls, the quiet of the snow, the moan of the wind. And suddenly she knew how very much she loved this man.

The kitchen fell into a moment of quiet, and the tick-tick-tick of the clock grew loud. Houses away a dog barked. The refrigerator hummed.

He picked up his plate and, in the easy-going, confident way he had, carried it to the sink. He was taller than she remembered, his shoulders broader. His hair had grown long, and he'd tied it at the nape of his neck. Thrilled to be with him again, she could hardly breathe. She swallowed, forcing a smile.

"Of course. Come on, I'll show you the house." She offered her hand, needing his touch, and her mouth trembled.

"Is there anyone else I should know about, a boyfriend?" He took her hand, standing so close she smelled the spicy soap he used. For a long moment they stared at each other, frustrated desire etching sad lines in their faces.

"No, there's no one else, Will."

Maggie looked away, for it hurt to see so much love for her in him, and the pain that turned down his mouth. She slipped her arm through his, leaning into him, and for a long time they stood gazing at each other.

At length they walked arm-in-arm into the dining room. She flicked on the light and said nothing as he surveyed the room, then she flicked the light off. She led him to the front parlor, up the steps to the three bedrooms on the second floor. In the hallway outside the master bedroom he turned her in his arms, his blue eyes dark and burning with hunger.

Maggie's heart tightened with desire. She wanted him to stay. "I want . . ."

He reached out and put a finger on her lips.

She laid her cheek on his chest and hugged him. He slipped one arm beneath her knees, lifted her and held her close against his heart.

"Time for you to go to bed," he said softly. He lowered her to her feet in front of her bed and gripped her face between his hands. "Go to sleep, Maggie. I need to leave while it's still dark."

It was a terrible thing to say good-bye, more so this time for there was no hope for a future with this man. Her emotions were going round and round like a Ferris wheel, her mind filled only with him. She couldn't let him go, not yet, not with her love for him so great.

She reached up to touch his face with her fingertips. "Stay. We haven't talked about the investigation yet."

He looked at the ceiling then back at her. "I figured you'd tell me if anything came up."

She hated the disappointment in his eyes. "Yes, but Thea knows more than she's letting on. I'm sure of it. I think she opened the pocket door to the dining room and saw something she wishes she hadn't. Trouble is, she's afraid to talk. I can't prove it, but Hilton paid for the house she's living in—I checked the records. She paid cash for the house, and I couldn't find any evidence that Hilton withdrew that amount of money around that time, so there's nothing concrete. But she doesn't know that, and after leaving follow-up messages on her answering machine, she finally phoned today. As soon as I got her message, I returned her call immediately, and she invited me over the day after Christmas. I accepted, of course."

"Why do you think she suddenly developed a conscience after all this time?"

"Her daughter. She called while I was there. The call upset Thea. I think it's because Tabatha is pressuring her mother to talk to me. Also, she didn't look well. My guess is her silence is weighing heavily on her mind. I'm certain she's afraid. Clearly, until she feels safe, she'll keep her mouth shut. I'm hoping I can convince her we'll protect her. She didn't say, but I'm speculating Tabatha will be there when I arrive."

Maggie's gaze dropped to their entwined fingers, then slid down to his boots.

"I want to be there, too. Until then I'll find a place to stay, and I'll meet you there. Thea just might talk to me. You meeting at her house?"

"Yes, but, Will, don't come. That's too dangerous. She might call the police."

"I don't think so. Thea and I always got along. She might not tell either of us anything, but somehow, I doubt she'd turn me in, especially if she knows I didn't kill Ellen."

"Tabatha might. After all, it's aiding and abetting. You can't take the chance. I'm just praying Thea'll let go of what she knows. I keep thinking the murderer will make a mistake, and we'll nab him. But after so many years, I guess he's learned to keep his mouth shut. If he makes a mistake, I'll be there."

"Not too close. I don't want you to get hurt." He offered her a smile, but she heard the concern in his voice.

"I've been trained to take care of myself. Besides, I have this tall, dark, and handsome partner called Pete, my self-appointed guardian angel."

"Ummm, not *too* handsome, I hope." He kissed her cheek and chuckled.

She grinned back. "Darn handsome. I had a crush on him until he married his high school sweetheart. That was Pete outside tonight. He and his wife live down the street in his mom's old house with their two kids. He's been looking after me for as long as I can remember—rather too much in high school." She laughed, but then her laughter died. When she lifted her gaze back to his face, there was hurt in his eyes like he hated it that circumstances didn't allow him to look after her.

His next words confirmed it. "I wish I could be here for you."

She managed a smile. "You're here now." But it wasn't enough, and she knew it.

Suddenly she was wondering if she should voice to him her qualms about Libby. They weren't exactly suspicions, rather an uneasiness, based more on feelings than anything concrete. It felt to her that Libby, like Thea, knew more than she admitted.

"Have you formed any new theories?" he asked as though he'd read her mind.

Wariness came into his eyes as if he expected to hear more bad news, but she plunged on anyway. "Not exactly a theory. Since returning from Alaska I've had an uncomfortable feeling about Libby, and I can't tell you exactly why. I have no knowledge of anything she's done wrong—quite the opposite. She's very religious, attends church several times a week, volunteers to work with children of unwed mothers. On the surface these are good, selfless activities, but I have a difficult time reconciling them, considering the social life she leads."

He raised an eyebrow. "In high school Libby attracted boys like honey attracts bees. Even then, she had two sides; she was forward with the guys, but sensitive to remarks that suggested her behavior was promiscuous. I always figured it was because of the circumstances of her birth, but in reflection I don't believe very many people knew Mary wasn't her mother. And as you say, she has a lot to be thankful for. Maybe she sincerely wants to help those who are less fortunate."

"You're probably right. Anyway, tonight was one of those nights she made me uncomfortable. She was probing about your case. She knew about my visit to Thea's, which shocked me. I only talked about it to Pete, and he's never even met Libby. Possibly Thea mentioned it to Hilton or to Libby. But why would she tell them unless she was worried they were keeping tabs on her and would already know? It was a relief when Pete phoned and Libby left."

"I'm beginning to like handsome Pete more. But maybe you should drop the investigation."

"Never. Not until I can prove your innocence."

"Well, be very careful of what you do or say around Libby and Hilton. One or both of them knows something more about that night. If either is guilty and thinks you're getting close, you'll be in grave danger. It won't be easy to take either of them down. Don't forget that. Keep your gun loaded and with you at all times and watch your step."

"You're beginning to sound like Pete."

In the weak light coming from the hallway, he stood inches from her. Her heart pounded, yearning for him. His face mirrored her fears.

On the floor at the foot of her bed, Misty slept.

His hands came around to both sides of her face. His gaze burned into her with a tortured expression.

Her mouth curved into a smile.

An answering tender smile flashed across his lips suddenly, then disappeared. He pulled her against him so hard the breath rushed out of her with a groan. He lifted her off her feet and let the momentum roll them both onto the bed.

The kiss between them was filled with urgency.

When he ripped his mouth from hers, his breathing was heavy, pouring over her. He rolled to his side and braced himself on his elbow. With his fingertips he touched her cheek, her lips, then his hand slid over her cotton jersey shirt. The love in his touch went through the cotton, beyond her skin, into the very core of her being.

"Take it off," she said, softly. "I want to feel your hands on my skin."

She held up her arms; he pulled the jersey off, tossing it aside. He tugged the straps of her bra down over her shoulders and laid his hands against her naked breasts, caressing them.

She arched up her chin and closed her eyes. *Let him stay, let him stay . . . stay with me forever.* Oh, the sensations his hands evoked in her body. She felt beautiful and wanted, and burned with her yearning.

Her hands found his face and brought his mouth back to hers.

He kissed her, and she was warm and yielding, and his hand moved so softly, gently over her breast then down across her firm, bare skin. How often in his nights alone had he thought to explore just these things, to love her body as he loved her? How many stars were there in the Heavens?

Love me, his heart cried. He needed her . . . needed her to need him.

She reached up and unbuttoned his shirt, and he had no will to leave her. He let her strip the shirt away from him and pulled off his t-shirt, pitching it to join her top and his shirt on the floor.

He cupped the back of her head with his hand and lowered his mouth to hers once more. Her mouth opened wide, welcoming him in, and nothing else mattered—not all the running, the hiding, the endless wandering with no safe place to put down roots—nothing mattered except that he was with her now, tonight.

His hands moved over her, memorizing her beauty, learning her by touch. She was a dream come true, the most precious thing he'd ever known. But he wasn't free to ever have her, and it was painful to know that.

"Let me . . ." She ran her fingers over the hair on his chest, down his belly and unbuckled his belt and undid the button. Then gently she let her hand slide down, down past his waistband inside his pants and down farther . . .

"God, Maggie, don't." He put his hand around her waist and arched back his head. "I'm trying to hold back. I didn't mean to go this far. It'll be daylight in an hour. I have to leave. Damn it." He squeezed his eyes shut. His heart was hammering. The pack of condoms he'd purchased that afternoon was in his back pocket. "Give me a minute . . . I won't take the chance you'll end up carrying my child, not when I can't be with you."

He knew he had to take her, love her, because he could no longer bear his life without her, and so he prepared himself and gathered her into his arms and entered her. She filled his senses as he filled hers, and together they rode the waves of their passion to the highest peak. And afterward while their tremors subsided, he held her hard against his chest, entwined with her on the bed, his face buried in the crook between her neck and shoulders, fighting tears, holding her hard against his body.

But he knew he could never hold her hard enough to make up for all the empty years ahead. Molded within the circle of his arms, his muscles against her softer flesh, everything was right again. They clung that way.

"I love you, Maggie," he whispered close to her temple, bringing an added glow to her already flushed cheeks.

"I love you, too, Jamie William Donovan." Her voice soft, throaty. "With you beside me everything seems right."

"I want to marry you." He grinned slightly. "And have a passel of kids with you."

"I want that, too. I don't want you to go, not today, or the next day, not ever."

But that was impossible.

"We have what's left of the night." His lips rested on her forehead.

He took a chance by staying, but tonight he wanted her to hold him, to feel the comfort of her arms. He needed it. He closed his eyes.

He didn't expect to fall asleep, but he did.

* * * *

The telephone beside Thea Johnson's bed rang, once, twice . . .

"Hello." Thea glanced at the large numbers on the clock—1:06. Without her glasses the numbers were blurred.

She picked up the receiver. "Hello." Someone was there—she heard them breathing.

Click. The caller hung up.

She rolled over and tried to get back to sleep.

A Cry From the Cold

Chapter Twenty

The insistent ringing of the bedside telephone dragged Maggie from a deep sleep. Several seconds passed before she remembered last night and realized the place in the bed beside her where Will should have been was empty and cold. She shot a quick glance at the clock and bolted upright. Ten o'clock! Long past her alarm's normal 6:30 wake-up call.

She flung the covers back and swung her feet off the bed, then recalled it was Saturday. Naked and cold, she reached for her robe, and remembered it was in the bathroom. The phone continued to ring. She frowned . . . *let the answering machine get it.* Only one person did she want to hear from right now, and he wouldn't call.

Memories of Will flush against her during the night, his arms twined around her, made her smile. Now he was gone. She hugged herself and shivered, then hurried to the bathroom for her robe.

The phone rang again. *Would* Will call? Maybe something had happened to him. Her breath caught. Pale blue robe in hand, she ran back and jerked up the phone. "Hello."

"Maggie, oh, thank God you're there."

"Celia, what's wrong?" Maggie shrugged an arm into her robe.

"Something's happened to Thea." Her voice broke on a sob.

Celia wasn't the type of woman who cried over nothing, and Maggie felt her heartbeat lurch. "What do you mean *something* happened to her? Is she hurt?"

After several moments Celia answered. "I'm pretty sure she's dead . . ."

The words, barely whispered, exploded in Maggie's ear. She clutched the receiver, forcing herself to remain calm. She dropped down to the bed's edge. "Have you called 911?"

"Yes. Can you come?"

"Of course I'll come." Maggie stopped tying her robe, crossed to her closet, and grabbed a pair of jeans. "Are you all right?"

"I'm not hurt if that's what you mean."

"That's what I mean. Are you at Thea's house?" She recalled her interview with Thea a few days ago and how upset the woman was. Only yesterday Thea promised to meet with Maggie the day after Christmas. If Celia was right, whatever Thea saw the night of the murder she'd take to her grave. Maggie's heart sank.

"Yes, I brought her . . . some Christmas gifts. A ham . . . and some other things."

It took Maggie a second to register what Celia was saying.

"The door was unlocked," Celia continued, clearly struggling for breath. "I shouldn't have come in, but I didn't want to leave the gifts outside—you know, with all the crime that goes on, especially at Christmastime. I thought I'd just sneak in for a second and put the presents in the foyer, maybe refrigerate the ham. Oh, Maggie, Thea is lying at the foot of the steps. Blood's everywhere. I tried to wake her . . . I checked to see if she was breathing . . ."

"Celia, it sounds like you did everything you could." With the phone tucked under her chin, she pulled on underpants then jeans. "Is anyone with you? Did Hilton or Libby come with you to deliver the gifts?"

"No, just me."

"Did you get hold of Hilton?"

"He didn't answer his cell. He flew in yesterday, but he left the house this morning before I did. I left a message at his office."

Where exactly was the worthy senator last night when Thea died? "Celia, the police will arrive soon. To be on the safe side, go out and get in your car. Lock yourself in and stay there until someone comes to assist you. You know not to touch anything."

"I know that much from TV . . . but I touched Thea . . . I didn't move her, though. And, Maggie, I washed my hands."

"That's fine. Good. Do you think Thea died just recently—is her body warm?"

"No, it's cold, and some of the blood is crusty already. I think she died last night." Celia was beginning to sound more like her efficient self.

"Don't leave, Celia. Stay in your car. I'll be there in about forty minutes."

"Okay, Maggie."

"And you're sure you're all right?"

"Yes," came the whispered reply.

"I'll call you back on your cell in just a few minutes." She disconnected and dialed the department.

After relating her conversation with Celia to Detective Waller, Maggie told him, "I'm heading over there now. Be sure someone calls Mrs. Johnson's daughter, Tabatha. Hang on a minute. I have her telephone number." She conveyed the information. "Yes, that's right. My former mother-in-law found the body. She's pretty upset. I told her not to leave, so she's waiting in her car in Thea's driveway." Maggie hung up and reached for her shoes.

Movement caught her eye. She stopped breathing. At the bedroom door was a sight she'd only seen in her dreams. Will, wearing nothing but his jeans and a grin that broke what was left of her heart, stood with two cups of coffee in his hands, looking like he belonged.

"I figured the telephone awakened you. Good morning, pretty woman."

"Good morning back." She lifted a worried glance to him, drowning in his blue eyes.

She bit her lower lip and her voice cracked. "I was afraid you'd gone."

"No, Maggie. I wouldn't do that, not without telling you. I've gathered my things away from prying eyes, and made coffee."

He entered the bedroom, set the cups on the nightstand, and reached out to her in invitation. "Bad news?"

She happily allowed herself a moment to glory in the security of having his arms around her before she spoke.

"Very bad. Thea is dead. Celia found her lying at the bottom of her steps a few minutes ago. I think Thea was ready to tell me something, but . . . now . . ."

He pulled her hard against him, her breasts against the solid planes of his chest. On tiptoe, she wrapped her arms around him and buried her face in his neck.

His pulse beat double time. He lowered his head and kissed her temple.

"Oh, Will, I was counting on Thea . . ."

"I know, we both were. Thea was a special person and her death is a tragic loss. We'll just have to find another way to solve who killed Ellen."

"It could be she died from an accidental fall down the stairs."

"But you don't think that, do you?"

"No. It seems too convenient for her to slip and fall to her death just when she showed signs of talking to me, but I may change my mind when I see the crime scene. I'm hoping her daughter knows what Thea saw, but I'm only speculating here— she may only know her mother had something on her mind she needed to let go of. I don't know, but I'll have a talk with her."

She slid her fingers over his bare skin, feeling every muscle in his body tighten wherever she touched, loving that it did. Reluctantly, she stepped away. "I better go. Celia's waiting for me."

He jotted a telephone number on a pad beside her bed. "I have a disposable cell phone. If you need me, call."

She stuck the paper in her pocket. "Stay here, at least until dark. I'm not expecting anyone."

"All right . . . I'll stay." He wasn't smiling, and the sadness in his eyes suggested how very much he yearned to be with her. "Mainly because if Thea's death isn't an accident, the killer could come here looking for you. Be safe." She heard the concern in his tone.

"I will. I expect the troops are already there." Not wanting to leave him, she waited a second more, then kissed him on his lips until she felt her heart give a sad twist. Quickly she looked away, before he could see the anguish on her face, and trotted down the steps. She pulled on her jacket, grabbed her purse, and headed for the kitchen and carport. As she walked, she dialed.

The thought popped into her head out of nowhere. She felt the blood drain from her face. Celia picked up at the other end of her phone. "I'll call you right back," Maggie said breathlessly.

Without waiting for Celia's reply, she closed the receiver and walked quickly back to the front foyer.

"Will . . ." He reappeared at the top of the stairs. "I just had this idea."

"What is it? You look as though you've seen a ghost."

"Maybe I have. Maybe not. I could be way off base, grasping for straws, but do you remember what song the band was playing when you first arrived at Ellen's on the night of her murder?"

His eyes narrowed. "Hmmm? You've got to be kidding. What does—"

She shushed him with a wave of her hand. "In a minute. First tell me if you remember the song."

Will braced a hand on the wall.

"Think, Will. It's important. You told me you remembered everything."

"I recall the Kingston Trio song about the MTA—you know the one that says, 'Did he ever return, no he never returned . . .' I remember thinking later that that was ironic, but I'm pretty sure something else was playing when I walked up the steps. I'm trying to remember. I can't think . . ."

"You've got to. Think while I'm gone. If you don't remember, then my connection is no good."

Fifteen seconds later her hand was on the swinging door to the kitchen, when he shouted, "*Pretty Woman*." Abruptly, she stopped.

"Me or the song?" She started breathing again, her legs weak.

"Both."

"Bingo." She ran back through the living room, up the steps, and showered his face with kisses. "Bingo, Bingo, Bingo."

"What's this all about?"

His lips brushed over hers, feather light kisses; his teeth nibbled her lip. "Now tell me what's so important about the song *Pretty Woman*?"

"Libby hates the song."

He fixed her with an incredulous stare. A laugh bubbled up from his chest. "So? She's always preferred Country and Western. Is that it? Is that what all your excitement's about?"

She opened the door. "It's a connection, Will—a connection, that's all. Another tiny piece to the puzzle. The song upsets Libby. When I asked her about it, she expressed strong feelings against prostitutes."

"Lots of people have strong feelings against prostitution. Libby in particular because of her mother. We went over this last night. Hell, Libby was only fourteen when Ellen was murdered."

"She was nearly fifteen and in your own words, a mature girl for her age. I'm not saying Libby killed Ellen, but I'm beginning to believe she knows more than she's let on. The same goes for Hilton. Maybe the song upsets Libby because it reminds her of witnessing Hilton murder her sister. I don't know why it upsets her, but I'm going to find out.

"By the way, the file on Ellen's murder is in my briefcase on the bedroom floor. You might want to take a look. Who knows, something in there might jog a memory. There's more on my computer."

She told him how to access her files, closed the door, and ran for the car.

* * * *

The first wave of officers had arrived at the scene at 10:20. Assured that Celia wasn't in any immediate danger, Maggie ended their call. Forty-five minutes later, Maggie reached Thea's house.

No longer in her car, Celia sat on an outdoor chair someone had thoughtfully set on the front drive for her. She was talking with Detective Ned Waller when Maggie parked. Waller was writing something in a notebook. A middle-aged man, he was tall and skinny and wore horn-rimmed glasses. He was an excellent detective and Maggie was glad to have him on the case.

The morning was cold and gray, but it wasn't snowing yet, which was a blessing. Maggie eyed the trampled mess the police had made of the walkway. Recently shoveled, footprints from an intruder would have been hard to detect in any case. Now it would be impossible.

As she walked from her car through the police barricade Maggie felt the stares of the people lined up outside the house to gawk. Deliberately, she set her face in a half smile and walked up to Celia.

Detective Waller looked up at her approach.

"Morning, Ned." She bypassed him to give Celia a hug. "Sorry it took me so long to get here, Celia. You all right?"

Celia nodded, but she looked pale and shaken, as was to be expected after the morning she'd been through. "If Detective Waller doesn't have any more questions for you, I'm sure he'll get one of his men to drive you home."

"Absolutely. But if you don't mind, Mrs. Raine, I'd appreciate it if you'd come to the station tomorrow. I'd like to go over everything again while it's fresh in your mind. At home, jot down what happened, include every detail you can recall— you never know what little fact might help. Just call in the morning and set up a time that's convenient for you."

"Yes, sir, I'd like to help catch whoever did this to Thea, but I don't know as I can shed much light on anything." Celia dabbed at her eyes and blew her nose.

Maggie watched her. Celia was a strong woman, but what she'd been through this morning would test anyone's mettle.

Waller smiled at Celia. "You've already been a help, ma'am. I'll look forward to seeing you tomorrow. Excuse me; I'll get someone to drive you home."

Maggie leaned closer to Celia and spoke close to her ear. "If you'd prefer, I'll be glad to drive you home myself. It'll take me about half an hour to wrap it up here, if you don't mind waiting."

Celia stood and put her hand on Maggie's arm. "Thank you, dear, but no. I'll be all right—don't worry about me. You've got your work to do here. Kind Detective Waller will find someone to take me home. I'll send Luis back with him for my car."

"Will anyone be at the house when you get there?"

"Yes, dear, several people. Ruby—she won't leave until after our family Christmas dinner tonight. In fact, she's brought in some others to help . . . oh, dear . . ." Celia choked back a sob, her eyes brimmed.

"What is it?"

"I just remembered that Thea and . . ."—she sobbed, running a finger over her eyes to catch the sudden tears—"her family were to join us for dinner tonight—they sometimes did and now . . ."

Maggie embraced Celia's slight body. There was nothing she could say to make the situation better.

Celia straightened and adjusted her scarf around her neck. "Even if Hilton's not back yet, my dad and Libby should be there." She glanced at her watch. "*And* Paul and his daughter came in early yesterday, so I have a house full. Don't worry about me."

Celia's face had brightened, and Maggie thought it was mostly at the prospect of seeing Paul and his seven-year-old daughter, Tiffany, a favorite of Celia's. The woman was a survivor—she'd have to be to live with Hilton.

A policeman joined them. Maggie relented. "Okay, Celia. If you're sure you'll be all right then you go with Officer Clark. I'll try to arrive early this evening to help. But please, if you need me before then, call."

Maggie patted the older woman's shoulder and watched her leave. She turned to Detective Waller. "You guys take any photos of the sidewalk before it got trampled?"

He smiled indulgently. "Yes, Detective." He chuckled. "But the walkway was already contaminated by Mrs. Raine coming and going. We took photos anyway, and made one cast. Never know what might turn up. The footprints all belonged to women, high heels as far as I could tell, so probably not Mrs. Johnson's. The snow wasn't deep enough to get decent prints. Anyway, I think they'll turn out to be Mrs. Raine's. Satisfied?"

Maggie accepted the soft rebuke good naturedly and nodded.

"Okay, then let's take a look inside. I instructed the men not to touch anything. I knew you'd want to examine the place before they started moving out specimens."

"How'd you know?" Maggie glanced up at him with a half smile.

"I've seen the files on Ellen Raine's murder case marching home with you every night. Half the force knows how much you're trying to solve that case—the other half is in a deep sleep.

Thea Johnson's murder may have nothing to do with the Donovan case, you know."

"I know. So you think it's murder and not an accident?"

"I do. But you take a look."

"Any signs of forcible entry?"

"No. Front and back doors were both unlocked. Mrs. Johnson was a very trusting soul."

"Any footprints on the back steps?"

"A few, not very good. They'd been swept, but the men are working on retrieving impressions."

"The broom?" Maggie took sterile latex gloves from her shoulder bag and pulled them on.

"Haven't found one yet, but we're looking." Two policemen were on the front porch, dusting the door, the knocker, and doorbell for prints.

"By the way," Waller said, leading the way into the house. "I called Pete—told him what happened and that you were on your way over. Caught him on the road halfway to Milwaukee to visit his brother's family. He's on his way back."

"He's on vacation time. You shouldn't have asked him to return."

"He offered. He didn't sound too upset." Ned laughed. "He sent his wife, mother, and kids on without him—he should be on a Greyhound about now. Plans to drive his mother's car to rejoin the family in time for Christmas."

Three policemen stood inside the hallway; one with a camera busily taking pictures of Thea's body. Maggie nodded greetings, then stepped closer to examine the body.

Thea lay stomach down, her head positioned at an odd angle like her neck had been broken in the fall. The amount of pooled blood was excessive for a tumble down carpet-covered steps.

"I don't think the fall killed her," Maggie said.

"I agree. I figure she was stabbed, and was dead before someone tossed her down the steps. Nice guy."

Maggie looked up the steps. The Berber carpet, a mixture of light color fibers, had spots of blood. Thea had either been wounded and tried to escape up the steps when she was pulled from behind, or dead and dragged up the steps before being pushed down to give the impression of an accident. Halfway up the steps the blood stains stopped. Forensic tests would determine that.

"Did Thea sleep upstairs?" Maggie hadn't had a tour of the house on her visit.

Ned shook his head. "I think not. There's a downstairs bedroom. This way."

The bedroom, located down a short hall, faced the backyard. As the rest of the house, the room was neat and clean with a few obvious exceptions: a lamp yanked from its socket on the floor beside the bed, its base shattered; Thea's walker on its side close to the broken lamp; the tennis ball Maggie recalled attached to the walker dislodged and resting some six feet from the walker; and blood splatters on the carpet, a section of bedspread, and up a wall.

"Looks like Thea put up a fight." Maggie bent over to examine the ball without touching it. "She might have used the walker to help her fend off the assault. There's blood on the tennis ball, and that walker leg is definitely bent."

"If we're lucky, we might find some tissue belonging to the murderer."

Back in the front foyer Maggie spotted a few wrapped Christmas gifts on the floor. She squatted beside a large one and took a sniff. "Someone better refrigerate this box. They can lift it with rubber gloves, but I think you'll find it's the ham Celia was delivering."

Waller directed one of his men to take care of it. "Maggie, one curious thing. We found an empty pizza box on the kitchen floor. Leaving trash there doesn't seem in keeping with a person who kept her house as clean as Mrs. Johnson did."

"I agree. You're checking it for prints."

"Of course, but I think our murderer wore gloves."

"Any signs of a safe?"

"Not yet. The victim's daughter might be able to help us in that regard. She also can better determine if anything is missing. You thinking of something in particular?"

Maggie nodded. "I believe the night Ellen was murdered Thea saw a great deal more than she let on. Since then I think she has lived in fear for her life. I'm hoping she kept a diary of some sort or filed a document with a confession that might be found upon her death."

"We'll ask her daughter about a safety deposit box, too." He jotted something in his notebook.

They walked through the rest of the downstairs. In the kitchen, a Madonna and child figurine lay in front of a counter, broken into several pieces. "Be sure to get some pictures of this and bag and print this figurine and everything else on this counter."

"We plan to, but why the counter in particular?"

"As you mentioned, Thea was exceptionally neat. She'd have cleaned up the pieces unless prevented from doing so or . . . she didn't break it?" Maggie moved around slowly. Something about the kitchen bothered her.

In the living room, she sat on the sofa where she'd sat on her visit with Thea. She scanned the room: reproductions hung exactly as they had then; photographs in the same places. But something wasn't quite right.

Someone's cell phone rang, and she knew what it was. She jumped up and hurried to the kitchen.

"Ned?" When he entered, she pointed. "When I was questioning Thea a few days ago, the telephone rang. Thea went to the kitchen to answer it, but after she hung up, she carried the portable into the living room with her. So, where's the phone's base? There's an outlet here on the counter where the broken statue is. My guess is that the phone was here and that it had an answering machine. Her daughter will know."

"She and her husband are on their way to the station now," Waller said, jotting down some notes. "Meanwhile, we'll check out trash receptacles in the area, but our killer probably pitched the phone miles from here. The question is: why would the killer want the answering machine?"

"The first thing that comes to my mind is the killer called before coming to be sure Thea was home, and his voice is on the answering tape."

"Certainly possible, and a smart killer knows that a good technician can retrieve the message even after it's erased."

In the foyer, medical technicians were carefully turning the body over and sliding Thea onto a stretcher. Waller tried to block Maggie. "This isn't good. Maybe you should wait until they get her—"

"I'll be all right." Maggie gulped. Thea had been stabbed . . . brutally. She forced herself to study the body for several minutes before she left.

Whatever wrongs Thea had done by keeping secrets that forced Will to remain a fugitive for a crime he didn't commit, she didn't deserve this.

Chapter Twenty-one

The temptation to stick around and read the police files was too great for Will to ignore. He located the briefcase and stretched out on the floor, his back against Maggie's bed. With Misty beside him, he began to read. Everything confirmed what he'd read in the newspapers and what Maggie had told him, down to the details that his blood had been found at the scene and matched the DNA of hair samples found in his room at St. Mary's.

Will squeezed his eyes shut when he flipped over the crime scene photo of Ellen lying bloody on the sofa. He fingered the four-inch scar on his forearm where he'd fended off the lamp Hilton had thrown at him. That gash had bled for days. Afraid to seek medical attention, alone and bitter at the sudden turn his life had taken, he'd been sure his life was over. Fourteen years later, the hard knot of skin remained a vivid reminder of that night's horror.

He drew in a deep breath, mentally berated himself for his melancholy thoughts, and went back to work. As he scanned the material, his mind kept returning to the earlier discussion with Maggie about Libby and the circumstantial case she was trying to build against her ex-sister-in-law. He'd been a fugitive long enough and read enough cases to know that circumstantial evidence could wash away like water down a drain. What it boiled down to was there was no case against Libby or Hilton. All the evidence pointed to him.

And now Thea's death just when Maggie believed she was on the verge of coming clean about what she'd seen. The timing set off warning signals in his mind.

The cell phone in his pocket vibrated and Will froze. Only Maggie and Gene Pryor knew of the existence of the new phone. He studied the number without recognition, and flipped open the cover. "Yes?"

"Will?" The male voice was breathing hard.

"Who is this?"

"Gene."

"Gene! I didn't recognize the number. You all right? You sound like someone's chasing you."

"Nothing chasing me but middle age."

"Wish I could say the same." Will laughed. "Where are you?"

"Chicago—in a park near my sister's home in Evanston—trying to get a run in before the snow arrives. Brier, the kids, and I flew in a couple days ago to spend the holidays with my sister and her family. How are you?"

Will glanced out the window at the lightly falling snow. It was going to make his departure this evening much more miserable. "Doing particularly well right now." He pushed aside thoughts of spending another night in the snow as he ran his fingers through Misty's thick fur. "Actually, I'm not far from you in a fair lady's bedroom. The lady's gone right now, but I have a friendly Golden Retriever with me."

"Where's the fair lady?"

"Called away on an emergency. How's John managing Hilde and Lucy?"

"I flew up to his village last month and saw them. They're doing well so I left them there."

"They're good dogs." He swallowed down a wistful longing. "Any chance you can meet me somewhere? There've been some developments in the case, and I could use your expertise."

"I was hoping you'd ask. How about this afternoon? After lunch Brier is dropping the kids off to go skating with friends, then she and my sister are heading downtown for some last-minute shopping, so I'm free until dinnertime. Name the time and place."

"O'Reilly's Pub, a beer and pizza bar. Ever heard of it?"

"Can't say that I have."

"It's off the beaten path. Hang on. Let me see if it still exists." After a minute he was back on the line. "It does." Will gave Gene the address. "How about 2:30?"

"Great. I'll be there. Oh, Will. I have a new cell number."

"I noticed that when you called. Why'd you change cell numbers again?"

"Libby and Hilton called in the past few months. They have some crazy idea that I know how to reach you." He laughed.

"I thought that last number was private."

"It was."

"Curious how they got it."

"All I can think is that maybe one of the guys at the office gave it out without thinking. Anyway, this one is for you only. I'll check messages at least once a day."

Will leaned back against the bed and sighed. "Last night Thea Johnson died. I don't know if you remember her, but Thea was the maid who worked at the Raine's household when Ellen was murdered. They haven't determined whether she died of natural causes or not. Maggie's at the scene now."

"Why would anyone want to kill the Raines' maid?"

"I've got a few thoughts on that, but they'll hold until this afternoon."

Suddenly, Misty cocked her head and sprung to her feet. She made a beeline for the steps and trotted down. Quickly, Will gathered up the papers and shoved to his feet.

"Will, you still there?"

"Yeah, I'm here. Something's aroused Maggie's dog. I better check it out. I'll see you at 2:30." He closed the receiver.

He stuffed his gun in his back pocket. In the hallway he glanced downstairs. Tail wagging, Misty paced back and forth eagerly at the front door. At a front bedroom window he tipped back the curtain's edge. A UPS truck pulled away from the curb. Moments later, Misty bounded up the steps.

"Good dog, Misty." Without barking she'd let him know someone was at the door. She looked very pleased with herself, and as he rubbed her, he couldn't help smiling.

In Maggie's bedroom a few papers had fallen to the floor. One caught his eye. The large, unusual bold print stood out. He picked it up. A wave of apprehension made his breath come faster.

The Ellen Raine murder has already been solved. If you value your life, you'll get off the case.

Maggie had received a threatening note. Why hadn't she mentioned it? When did she get it? Where? Were there others? Had she reported the note to the Department? Did she have reason to believe the note was a hoax? Will was accustomed to working and planning alone, but now he had to think about defending and protecting Maggie. The more he thought about her out there trying to solve the case virtually alone, the more uneasy he got. A murderer was still at large. The police department and the Feds were concentrating on finding him, all except Maggie. She was looking for the real killer.

Obviously, whoever killed Ellen was threatened by Maggie's dogged pursuit. He doubted the note a hoax. Since leaving her at his cabin, this had worried him. It was why he'd had Gene keep tabs on her as much as he could without arousing suspicion. It was a strong part of why he'd returned to Chicago, and why he'd risk leaving her house in daylight to talk the situation over with Gene. Holed up in her bedroom or miles away on the run, how could he protect her? After meeting with Gene, he was going to check out a few things. Unfortunately, one of the people he hoped to talk to was dead.

Worry for Maggie gnawed his insides. Last night Libby made it clear that she knew Maggie had been to Thea's house, although Maggie had told no one except her partner, Pete. A few days later, less than twenty-four hours after Thea telephoned to agree to a second meeting with Maggie—presumably to reveal whatever she'd seen the night Ellen was murdered—she's found dead. A coincidence? Not likely.

Maggie said Libby often made her feel uncomfortable and last night she felt as though Libby had become hostile toward her. Was Libby hiding something, too? Was she protecting her father or could it be the other way around? Either way, Maggie was in danger. But from what?

* * * *

Maggie's head ached, a dull throbbing. She'd forgotten to eat lunch after only coffee for breakfast—now it was 2:00 p.m. She glanced at her half-written report, and considered venturing across the street to the cafeteria. No . . . she'd continue writing. Fingertips against her temples, she rubbed as she analyzed what she'd seen and what she knew about Thea's murder and the Ellen Raine case. How to connect the dots? Some salient point was missing, and no matter how hard she studied the facts, it remained just out of her cognizant thoughts. It was driving her nuts.

She uploaded the photos taken that morning at the murder scene, then opened the Ellen Raine murder file on her computer and scanned the all-too-familiar photos of that case, comparing the details of both cases.

A cold draft seeped through the window, and Maggie tugged her sweater over her shoulders, her concentration pinned on the screen. In the photos of Ellen and Thea, the majority of the multiple jabs dissected the abdomen. Were both murders committed by the same hand?

Head still pounding, she needed food. About to turn away, she gasped. Suddenly, what had been bothering her since she'd been assigned to the Lakeshore murders became clear. On the surface the circumstances of Ellen's murder and those of the Lakeshore murder victims were different—the only similarities: the victims were women and had been stabbed. Until this moment Ellen's murder had remained an isolated incident in her mind, but now . . . On an impulse she pulled up a photo of the most recent Lakeshore murder victim. Her heart pounded. Not exactly the same, but if her assumption were right, Ellen's killing was the first and probably unplanned; Thea's the latest, was only to protect the murderer.

Were all the murders connected? Was that what she'd been missing? Did the Lakeshore murders actually begin with Ellen and continue right on up to Thea? The notion astounded her. But the similarities were too strong to ignore.

For several long minutes she stared blankly at her computer screen. Out of the corner of her eye she saw Pete Cramer conversing with a colleague at the far end of the room. He carried a big red Christmas cactus in full bloom. No doubt the cactus was meant for her, and he would be at her desk in moments. If she hurried, there was time to email the pictures to Will. She reached into her jeans' pocket and pulled out a crumpled piece of paper. Before Will left this morning he'd written his email address on the corner of an envelope along with his telephone number. She typed as fast as she could, then stuffed the paper back into her pocket. Barely did she have time to attach the photos before Pete arrived at her desk.

She pushed *send* mid sentence and closed the screen. She rocked back in her chair and sat motionless in front of her computer.

"Merry Christmas from Mom." Pete set the cactus on her desk with a thud. "I forgot to give it to you yesterday, and the first thing Mom asked when I picked her up this morning was whether I'd delivered it. I almost lied, but she gave me that knowing look. Now, as fate would have it, I've been given a second chance." Pete stopped talking and waved his hand in front of her face. "Hello-oo, Maggie. You all right?"

She swung her chair around to face him with a smile. "Oh, sorry, Pete, I'm fine. What were saying?"

"Forget it. I was trying to cheer you up—you look so glum."

"Sometimes this business can get pretty glum. Just trying to make sense out of the Johnson murder, that's all. I'm sorry you had to come back from your vacation."

"Not a problem. I didn't feel good leaving you to face it alone. Anyway, this is from Mom."

"My goodness, what a beautiful cactus." She opened the card attached to the bow. "How sweet of your mother. Be sure to thank her for me."

"Mom said to say you'll have a hard time killing it—just water now and then and give it some partial shade in the summer."

"Thanks, I'll do my best. You should be on your way to join your family before the roads get too bad."

"I'm heading out shortly. You have any theories on the murder?"

Maggie remembered the frightened woman she'd interviewed the week before. Something had definitely upset Thea.

Earlier that morning, Thea's daughter informed the department that the empty pizza box found in her mother's kitchen had contained a large sum of money, though she didn't know exactly how much. That made robbery a motive for the break-in but was a little too neat for Maggie to buy into that theory.

If she hadn't been so close to Ellen Raine's unsolved case, she might have been willing to accept the robbery theory and not connected Ellen's murder to Thea Johnson's fourteen years later, and surely she wouldn't have linked either with the Lakeshore murders. Maggie considered sharing her new hypothesis about the murders being connected to the

Lakeshore murders with Pete, but didn't feel any particular urgency to do so.

Whoever killed these women had been at large for almost fourteen years, depending on whether Ellen's murder was the first. She wanted to run her thoughts by Will before she mentioned them to anyone in the Department. Besides, Pete was heading out of town, and she didn't want to delay him any longer or spoil his Christmas break. More importantly, she wanted to keep her thoughts to herself a little longer because she was concerned that if someone discovered Will was in town on the same day that Hilton Raine's former maid was murdered, fingers would again point to him as the prime suspect. So with some guilt she held her suspicions to herself.

She swallowed, and her tone lowered. "Well, I don't think her murder was random. And I don't think the murderer was after the money her daughter says Thea kept in her freezer."

Pete pulled a chair up to her desk and straddled it, folding his arms around the hollow-metal chair back. "What makes you think that?"

"I know the cash is gone, but I think it was taken to throw us off track. Last week I paid a visit to Thea to ask her a few questions about the night Ellen was murdered. She seemed particularly nervous, more so than in our previous telephone conversations."

"You think she was afraid?"

"Exactly what I suspected, but I didn't act on my suspicions. Now I'm certain she was scared, and I'm kicking myself. Could I have done something different and prevented her murder?"

"Don't second guess yourself, Maggie. I'm sure you did all you could. She was probably just upset about being questioned again."

"That probably played into it, but I've no doubt she was holding something back."

"Are you suggesting Thea might have been murdered because she knew something that would confirm Jamie Donovan's guilt?"

Maggie shook her head emphatically. "Listen to me, Pete. While in Alaska I spent a lot of time with Jamie Donovan. Despite the popular belief, I do *not* believe Donovan murdered Ellen Raine. But I think Thea knew who *did*, and it's a theory

I'm going to work on during the holidays." She turned off the computer, then pulled her purse from the bottom drawer and stood. "I've got to go. I'm due at the Raines' this evening for Celia's annual family Christmas shindig. I promised I'd try to get there a little early.

"Have a wonderful Christmas, Pete, and give your mom a special hug from me. The cactus is beautiful."

He pulled her into his arms and squeezed. "I will, and Merry Christmas to you, too. Please don't hesitate to call me if something else develops."

Moments later she walked out of the office, Christmas cactus in tow, her cell phone in hand. The battery low indicator flashed. She punched in Will's cell number. She was taking a huge chance, for the call would be recorded and could be used as evidence if he were ever put on trial. But the point was moot. He was already staying at her house.

He answered. "Yes . . ."

Then the phone went dead.

* * * *

Seated in the last booth at O'Reilly's pub, his backpack beside him, the file open in front of him, Will relaxed against the cracked vinyl, waiting for Maggie to call back. He sensed someone's approach and glanced up, everything about him suddenly controlled and alert. Then he grinned.

Gene Pryor, his jacket unzipped and a knit cap pulled over his head, walked toward him, two longneck beers in hand. "Hello, buddy," Gene said quietly.

"Hello." Will, throat tight with emotion, rose slowly to hug his friend. "It's so damn good to see you again."

He felt the tension in his friend's embrace, the same that churned in him. Will clasped Gene's biceps. Close as any brother, the emotion on Gene's face mirrored his own. Several long seconds passed in tight silence before he released Gene, then took his seat. His friend slid in across from him.

"I've missed you." Gene shrugged out of his jacket. "No one up there to watch my backside like you've always done. These last weeks with no word from you . . . damn it, Will, I got to wondering if I'd ever hear from you again, so I decided to try this number you gave me . . . see if it would reach you. So how have you *really* been doing?"

Will's gaze locked onto Gene's. Finally he heaved in a breath. "Truthfully? Up and down—some days aren't so bad, others not so good. But I'm still alive and that's more than I expected when the cops started to close in around my cabin." He sighed. "Maggie called a few minutes ago, but her phone cut off before we could talk. Hopefully, she'll get back to me." Will brought Gene up to date on the case, then handed him the threatening note Maggie had received.

"This was sent to Maggie?"

"I assume so. I found it in her files."

"When did she get it?"

"A notation on the file copy said she found it tucked in her newspaper on November 20th—two days after she phone interviewed the Raines' former maid, the woman murdered last night. Four days ago she visited the maid's home to conduct a second interview in person."

"I assume it's been checked for prints."

"According to Maggie's notes none were found. This note"—Will pointed to the paper Gene held—"was computer generated, paper Walmart brand. I'm definitely worried about her safety."

"You have every right to be. If your assumptions are correct, Maggie could have stumbled onto some incriminating information against Ellen's killer without knowing it. Her life could be in grave danger."

Ann Merritt

Chapter Twenty-two

The car radio's weather forecaster predicted eight-inches of new snow, the season's first major storm. Maggie changed the station to Christmas music.

After promising Celia she'd come to the annual family Christmas dinner, despite her desire to do so, she couldn't beg off—especially considering what had happened to Thea last night. Besides, it would give her a chance to observe her prime suspects together and under somewhat relaxed circumstances.

Just after 4:00, Misty welcomed Maggie home with a happy whine and an enthusiastic circle dance. Otherwise the house was silent. Will hadn't returned. Had he been here and not picked up when she phoned earlier?

Leaving her boots at the door, she checked to see if he'd left a message on her answering machine, then ran upstairs to check the rooms. Certain she was alone, she opened the back door to take Misty outside and paused in confusion. The door was unlocked. *I know I locked this last night and Will wouldn't have left it unlocked. I gave him a key.* She glanced back inside the kitchen. Everything appeared normal. She resisted the urge to check the house. If an intruder were inside, Misty would have alerted her.

With a shrug she slipped into the boots she kept at the back door and walked out into the yard. Footprints were over the pup's earlier tracks, both now lightly covered by fresh snow. She scuffed up the yard and the tracks, then returned inside and plugged her cell phone into the charger. Impatient to hear from Will, she dialed his cell from her land line. After six rings a generic voice asked her to leave a message.

"It's me." She ended the call and headed upstairs to shower and dress. She chose a Kelly-green dress with three-quarter sleeves and empire waist.

Before leaving, she tried twice more to reach Will, only to get the same generic message. It irritated her that she had to leave the house when Will might return at any time.

She slipped on boots and left at 5:00. Even though snowplows were hard at work, road conditions promised to make her return trip miserable.

On the spur of the moment she drove to the park where Will had described having picnics with Ellen—not far from where a couple of the bodies had washed ashore—and pulled into the nearly empty parking lot. The place was only a few blocks from Rutland Manor, and she was still early. Exiting her car, she walked along the Lake Michigan shore.

At 5:15, darkness was complete, and the lights of the city circled the lake's distant shores like a Christmas wreath. Veiled by the falling snow, the normally harsh security lights were softened, and their warm glow bathed the park. Snow along the lake and clinging to trees transformed the attractive waterfront area to Christmas-card beauty.

She gazed out at the ice forming on the water's edge, thinking of the young woman's body recently found floating in the lake. As long as the real killer remained unidentified, she and Will couldn't be together. That knowledge stole much of the beauty from the evening. Until she found a way to prove his innocence, he couldn't safely walk the streets in the daylight or sit at the water's edge and capture the beauty of the snow on the boats and trees along Lake Michigan with his paints. Her steps slowed. If only she were smart enough to think of a way to prove Will's innocence.

If her hypothesis was correct that the murders started with Ellen's and were all committed by the same person, someone had a lot to hide. That someone had been worried enough about her last visit with Thea to silence her. Did the killer have the same fate in mind for her?

Maggie followed the journey of a distant ship as it made its way across the horizon, away from the icy coast, and wondered if a boat could have been used to transport the bodies from the scene of the murders? At the time of Ellen's murder, whether Hilton owned a boat or didn't own one hadn't been relevant to the case. Now it had significance. When she was married to Matt, Hilton owned a twenty-seven foot Bayliner. She'd check to see if he still owned the boat and if so try to get a warrant to have forensics go over it.

Maggie's thrill upon learning that the song that was playing right after Ellen's death upset Libby had waned. In hindsight, it was normal to dislike things associated with bad experiences. She was grasping at straws, yet straws were all she had, and few of those at that. But that was the nature of her job—squeeze something out of nothing. Some crimes never were solved. The "good guy" didn't always win.

Look at the young women, by all accounts innocent of any wrongdoing, who were murdered and thrown into Lake Michigan for no apparent reason. Why was each woman picked to die? Was it simply a matter of being in the wrong place at the wrong time? Probably not. Something more than their place in society connected them. She had to find out what the connection was.

Maggie could no longer deny she was in danger. Someone was watching her. The threatening note she'd received took on more significance. The Lakeshore murderer had sent notes to the police department before each of the murders. The direct threat to her came to her house. Was it the same thing? How much more time did she have to solve the crime before she ended up like poor Thea? A sense of isolation descended; a sadness that went beyond the deaths of so many innocents. In the end, *she* had to solve Ellen's murder. As far as anyone else was concerned, Will was the guilty party, and since he was on the Most Wanted list and on the run, he couldn't prove his own innocence.

Maggie got back in her car and drove the few blocks to Rutland Manor. As expected, the old mansion and grounds were a Christmas symphony beneath the dusting of snow—trees wrapped in strings of tiny white lights, a solitary white light aglow in every window, pine garlands draped from the wrought-iron banister rails and secured with red bows. A wreath of fresh spruce, nuts, and holly berries hung on the front door.

Maggie pushed the doorbell, edgy with worry. Welcomed into the candle-lit front hall by Ruby, she was unable to banish the image of Thea, white-haired and bent with age as she had ushered her into her home; unable to dispel the feeling that

Thea had seen something on that fateful night and as a consequence lost her life.

In the foyer, Maggie couldn't stop herself from glancing to her left to the front parlor where the murder had taken place. Though the room like the house had been completely redecorated since the murder and Maggie hadn't known any of it before, her nerves jumped uneasily at the evil that had taken place in that room.

In front of her and slightly to the right a gracefully winding staircase curved left over the foyer. She envisioned Hilton standing at its foot, his face contorted with anger and grief as he'd confronted Jamie Donovan. And Jamie, just inside the door, unaware that his life was about to change forever.

She blinked and turned away, but the apprehension remained.

"It's good to see you again, Miss Maggie." Ruby's early childhood in Virginia had left a trace of a Southern drawl in her voice, and Maggie enjoyed hearing it.

"You, too, Ruby. Is your family well? I expect your grandkids are getting excited about Santa coming."

"They sure is, and everyone's doin' jes fine. Let me take that coat for you."

"Is the nativity set up this year?" Maggie uncoiled her Christmas-red scarf from her neck and stuffed it in the coat pocket before releasing the coat to Ruby.

"Why, yes, ma'am, in the back garden jes like always. Can I get you anything—coffee, tea, cider, wine?—we have a nice Merlot like you like."

She thought about having something strong to help calm her uneasiness but decided she needed to have all her faculties working tonight. "Coffee would be lovely."

Ruby nodded. "Well, make yourself at home. You know where everything is. I'll let Miss Celia know you've arrived. She shouldn't be but a moment or two. I believe Miss Celia's father and some of her nieces and nephews are already in the sunroom. I'll bring the coffee in there."

"Thank you, Ruby."

Pausing to admire the huge Christmas tree in the foyer, Maggie made her way slowly past the dining room, with its oversized table and magnificent chandelier, to the back of the house, noting the exquisite holiday decorations in all the rooms. But even with all the beauty surrounding her, Maggie couldn't rid herself of the prickly feeling that the man she loved had been framed for murder in this house.

As its name implied, the sunroom was a cheerful, sunny room in daylight, but tonight it was the security lights from the backyard that streamed through the double French doors. Admonishing herself for her foolish discomfort in Hilton's home, she glanced about the room. A fireplace dominated the wall to her left, and a second tree decorated for the children's benefit occupied the corner beside it, reminding her that Paul and his daughter had come in from California to join the household for Christmas. She liked Paul and was looking forward to seeing him and his daughter. With them in the house, the uncomfortable feeling diminished some.

A toy box familiar from years past was prominently placed on an oriental rug in the middle of the room. A handsome rocking horse, several dolls, and some building blocks sat beside it. The rocking horse was new, beautifully carved of wood and attractively painted. The blocks were old, but had been well cared for. Two young boys and a girl were at play, laying out a maze of block tracks and running Matchbox cars over them. How like Celia to make this a fun occasion for the children.

Beside the tree, in a wingback chair, Celia's father sat, an open newspaper in his hands. When Maggie entered the room, he looked up from his reading and smiled. Observing his well-fitting suit, Christmas tie, and meticulously groomed hair, she crossed the room, took the hand he held out, and kissed his cheek.

After a few words with him she grabbed a blanket from the back of the sofa, tented it over her head, and stepped outside to where snow had turned the garden and the crèche into something magical. Carved from wood and meticulously painted, the crèche was exquisite, her favorite of all Celia's Christmas decorations.

Musical strains of an old Hank Williams tune drifted from Libby's garage apartment. Illuminated in the apartment window, Libby held a cell phone to her ear.

The heavy crunch of shoe leather on ice drew Maggie's attention. A suited Hilton, without overcoat or hat, trudged up the apartment steps, tightly clutching the railing. He frowned in concentration and didn't appear to notice Maggie standing beside the Nativity scene.

Maggie turned to go inside, but stopped. Hilton and Libby stood in the apartment doorway, their voices raised in argument. Although she suspected they couldn't see her through the snow, she stepped behind a fountain and listened shamelessly.

Father and daughter faced each other in anger. Maggie held her breath, not knowing exactly what she expected to hear, but here in the quiet of the snow-covered garden, her two prime suspects in Ellen's murder were exchanging strong words.

Hilton's voice carried to her ears. "I've been trying to talk to you since I arrived. Where the hell do you go all the time?"

Libby looked ready to answer, but he cut her off and swept a glance behind him. "Never mind. I don't want to know. Just give me the damn knife."

Suddenly Maggie couldn't breathe.

"I know you took it from my closet."

"You shouldn't have hidden it from me, Daddy."

"Libby, please—"

"Don't ask me to give it to you, because I can't. And keep your voice down or, better yet, come inside."

Hilton stepped into the doorway. Maggie strained to hear.

"I haven't time to come in. As you damn well know, Celia's having the family gathering tonight. So stop arguing with me and hand it over. I'll feel better with it in my care. Then you need to dress in something appropriate and come to the house."

"I'm sorry, but I won't let you have the knife."

"You must, Libby. I'm telling you, you damn well better give it to me. I don't understand any of this business. I don't understand why it's happening. It's eating me up, just tearing me up. I can't sleep."

"Maybe a doctor can give you something to help."

"That's not the point. I'm telling you that it's got to stop. I have a position to uphold."

"I know, Daddy. You're an important man. That's why you've got to trust me to take care of the knife. You can depend on me."

"Yes, but . . . Libby, that last girl . . ."

The patio doors suddenly swung open. "Maggie! There you are!"

Maggie spun around to see Celia coming toward her, carefully tiptoeing across the snow-covered patio, blissfully unaware of the angry words her arrival had brought to a screeching halt. Exposed, Maggie stood mute.

With effort Maggie pushed back her emotions and called on her training to collect herself. By the time she moved through the sliding doors with Celia's arm around her, she'd found her voice.

"I was looking at the crèche. You know how much I love it. And the way you've lit it this year is beautiful, especially with the snow falling on it. I couldn't resist taking a closer look." She was babbling. She hoped Celia was too preoccupied to notice.

"In weather like this it's meant to be viewed through the windows," Celia scolded mildly.

"I borrowed this lap robe of yours to help keep the snow off. I hope it isn't some precious antique."

Celia laughed. "Not at all. Come over here and sit by the fire." She bustled Maggie across the room to where a gas fire was burning an invitation.

"I'm fine, Celia, really I am. I wasn't outside more than a couple of minutes."

"All right, dear, but humor me and sit here for a minute." Celia indicated one of the two pink brocade chairs that flanked the white marble fireplace. "I've a few things to attend to, but I'll be right back to visit with you. Meanwhile I'll have Ruby bring you some hot tea."

Maggie caught Sherman's amused glance and despite her anxiety, she couldn't help smiling. Celia was at her best when she could mother you to death. "Celia, I don't need a thing. I'm already warming up, and I believe that's my coffee over there on the table by the patio door."

"Well, then I'll have Ruby warm it up."

Maggie put both her hands on Celia's arms and held her still. "Celia, stop fussing, please. I'm fine. I came early so I could help, so tell me what to do."

Celia had the grace to look duly contrite. "All right, dear. If you won't let me coddle you, grab that coffee and come with me. There seems to be a little crisis in the kitchen. One of the cooks sliced her finger rather badly, so I've dispatched my sister's husband to take her to the hospital. That leaves us shorthanded." Leading Maggie from the room, Celia turned her head and spoke over her shoulder. "Thank you, dear, for braving this miserable weather to come."

"I wouldn't miss it. Besides, it's perfect Christmas weather."

"True, but I know it would've been easier for you to stay home. If the roads get too bad, dear, we can make room for you to stay here tonight, so don't fret."

Staying the night at Rutland Manor was the last thing Maggie intended to do. What she desperately wanted was to discuss what she'd just overheard. She considered phoning the department, but what could she say—that the senator and his daughter were having a disagreement about a knife? She pictured black and whites racing through the gates of Rutland Manor, sirens blaring, and had to smile. Now *that* would really be just the perfect ending to Celia's day. But it would serve no purpose. Even if the police arrived in unmarked cars and knocked on the door, the only result would be to frighten everyone and alert Hilton she was onto him.

Truthfully, the conversation she just overheard scared the heck out of her. What were Hilton's unfinished words to ". . . that last girl was . . ."?

As soon as she could she'd phone Will. Where was he?

She followed Celia through the dining room where the table was set for nineteen. American Atelier China, a winter green pattern with embossed holly leaves and red berries, a red damask tablecloth, green napkins with embroidered holly and red berries, and an elegant centerpiece of spruce, holly, and red roses in a low crystal bowl, very Christmasy and very chic.

The aroma of spicy apple cider and hazelnut coffee greeted Maggie even before Celia swung open the kitchen door and led her through the butler's pantry to the kitchen. Along one counter of the pantry she noted an assortment of cheesecakes and pies—pecan, minced meat, apple, coconut cream, chocolate, lemon meringue, and pumpkin for starters—waiting to be the dinner's finale. Maggie wouldn't have been surprised if Celia, an excellent cook in her own right, had made most of them herself.

"I had the kitchen remodeled last year. What do you think?"

"Wow! It looks like you doubled the size." Several weeks ago, when Maggie stopped by, she'd been preoccupied with finding any traces of a pocket door and hadn't actually stepped into the kitchen. Now she saw that the room was large enough to accommodate a fireplace and a table and chairs with seating for ten. The overall effect was not only of grandeur but of richness and warmth.

"You must love working in here," Maggie said.

"I do, and I love this utility/workroom we added, too. It can be converted into an extra kitchen for nights like tonight. Come, let me show you."

Maggie followed.

On a large island in the center of the kitchen Maggie noticed several racks of lamb were being seasoned by a woman Maggie had never before seen. At the six-burner stove Ruby stirred something that smelled like hollandaise sauce. They exchanged smiles, and Maggie found the kitchen bustle reassuring.

"Earlier a neighbor was having some repairs done," Celia said as she moved briskly through the kitchen checking briefly on each food item being prepared, "and our electric line was inadvertently cut. It all happened while all that sad business with Thea was going on this morning." She stopped abruptly and looked up at the ceiling, visibly trying to control her emotions. "Oh poor, dear Thea," she said softly. "I'm going to miss her . . ." Celia's voice hitched. She wiped a finger to her eye and made a nervous laugh. "I mustn't cry or I'll mess my mascara. I just can't let myself think of Thea right now. I've got nineteen hungry people to feed. Anyway, the meal is going to be a little later than planned."

Out of the mouth of a woman who was used to her schedules being adhered to, Maggie thought. "To fill the delay we'll just have to dig into some of the smorgasbord of cheeses and hors d'oeuvres I saw in the butler's pantry and drink lots of your good wine," Maggie said and shot Celia a smile.

"Yes, dear, that's precisely my plan." In the new utility room an oversized refrigerator stood beside a counter with a large sink. "I have about seven pounds of asparagus in here. Would you be a dear and snap them for me? I thought you could work right in here at this sink. I'll get you the steamer basket. There are so many I'm afraid we'll have to cook them in batches."

Maggie went to work snapping off the tough stems from the asparagus, and her mind wandered back to Hilton and Libby's conversation. She didn't want to forget a word of it. Was it Hilton all along, like Will thought? It sure sounded like it to her. So neat and tidy when the pieces fell into place. Hilton found Jamie's knife in Ellen's car and confronted her about a forbidden rendezvous with Donovan, a man he had prohibited her to see. Under his interrogation, Ellen confessed her love for Jamie and that she carried his child. Hilton snapped.

At the impressionable age of fourteen, Libby had seen it. How horrible it must have been for her, how horrible it must still be. No wonder she spent so much time in church. All these years she'd kept her mouth shut while in return Hilton turned a blind eye to her indiscretions and gave her whatever money she needed.

And Thea. She'd seen the murder as well. Ellen probably cried out, Thea went to her aid, and consequently, through no fault of her own, became a witness. For fourteen years she'd kept quiet about it in exchange for a comfortable retirement on Hilton's dime.

Maggie opened a fresh bunch of asparagus into the sink. As soon as she finished, she'd call the station.

Deep in thought, she didn't hear anyone approach. When a hand touched her shoulder, she jumped.

"Sorry. Didn't mean to startle you."

She took a deep breath and turned. "Paul, how lovely to see you. Celia putting you to work, too?"

"Not yet, but I heard you were in here helping so thought I'd come say hello. Need a hand?" Before she could answer he picked up a handful of asparagus and began to snap. "Back in this house again I can't get away from thoughts of Jamie. I often wonder if he's still alive and if so, how he's doing. I don't suppose anyone's heard from him."

She paused. She could trust him, but how much did she dare divulge? After all, it was Paul's father she suspected. "A couple of months ago Gene called. He said Jamie was surviving the best he can. It can't be easy."

"No . . . I really thought the department would've found the killer by now."

She nodded. "They're not looking. They think they've found Ellen's killer—the evidence all points to Jamie. I'm doing all I can, but so far nothing good enough to remove the suspicion from him. My feeling is that Thea knew something. We were going to get together right after Christmas, but now . . ." She shrugged and grabbed a handful of asparagus, snapping them in quick succession. *It had taken almost fourteen years, but Hilton had finally made his first mistake. Soon, she hoped, she'd have enough evidence to bring him in.*

Paul left. She dried her hands and slipped from the kitchen. Retrieving her purse, she entered the powder room and reached for her cell phone. It was missing from the side pocket. She dumped the contents of the purse onto the counter. No phone. Had Hilton taken it from her purse when she left it unattended in the sunroom? Not very likely. Too many people would have noticed him doing so. Then it dawned on her. When she'd switched to a smaller purse for the evening, she must have left it charging in the kitchen. Great! She didn't want to use the Raines's phone. She'd wait until she got home.

Finally dinner was announced. Her companions were Libby on her left, Celia's brother on her right, and across from her Celia's father, Sherman, who turned out to be an active conversationalist. Throughout the evening she managed to avoid conversing with Hilton. At the end of the dinner he rose and proposed a toast. His gaze swept each of his extended family. For an instant his glance touched hers, and Maggie saw Hilton's eyes narrow.

Chapter Twenty-three

The drone of television voices, punctuated by childish giggles, came from the front parlor where Ellen Raine had been murdered. Maggie poked her head inside to say good-bye. The children were draped over a sofa and sprawled on the floor watching a Christmas video on a large screen TV.

Paul came up beside her. "It's *Elf*," he said, "a perennial favorite with them. You ever watched it?"

"Of course." She remembered that she'd laughed at least as hard as the kids were.

"I've asked Luis to bring your car around for you. You sure you won't reconsider and spend the night?"

"Positive, but thanks. I've got a dog who's counting on me coming back tonight."

Hilton joined his wife and son at the front door. Maggie's smile vanished.

"I just checked the weather conditions. The report says the snow will continue throughout the night and into tomorrow with a possible accumulation of between six to eight inches. The main roads have been plowed, but even so, the roads won't be good. Be careful on your way home." Hilton's face was grim.

Was there more meaning to his warning? She shrugged away her sense of uneasiness. "I will." She quickly turned and peered through the side glass panels, impatient for the chauffeur to bring her car around.

Celia put her arm around Maggie's back. "Our invitation to spend the night here is still open. We'd love to have you, you know."

Before Maggie could respond, the chauffeur opened the front door. Hilton caught up with her before Paul and placed a hand beneath her elbow. Maggie wanted to protest, but for Celia's sake she allowed Hilton to guide her down the icy steps.

At the bottom, he put his hand at the small of her back and gently led her to the car. When she was seated inside, he leaned on the door and said quietly, "Whatever you may have thought you heard out there in the garden was nothing—just an argument with my daughter, nothing serious. The knife I use when I go hunting has gone missing. It'll show up. None of it should be of concern to you."

He made it all sound so reasonable. She stared at the hand he had latched on her door and turned the key in the ignition. "Of course, Senator, what else could it be? Where's Libby, by the way? I wanted to wish her Merry Christmas before I left, and I haven't seen her for the past half hour."

"I believe Libby retired to her rooms for the evening, but I'll tell her tomorrow. Be careful, Maggie."

Again the warning.

* * * *

Patches of roadway ice and rapidly falling snow made driving treacherous. The roads were nearly deserted, but stalled cars that hadn't quite gotten off the road were downright liabilities. Whoever declared the roads clear hadn't been outside recently to check.

Shortly after leaving Rutland Manor, headlights came up behind her—the driver following her too closely. When the car hadn't turned off after ten minutes, she pulled to the side to let it pass. She didn't recognize the vehicle as it drove by and thought nothing of it until a few minutes later when headlights reappeared in her rearview mirror, again following her too closely. She couldn't tell if it was the same car. She slowed. The car made no attempt to pass. Was she paranoid? She laughed at herself, ignored the car, and turned on the radio, rotating the dial until she found Christmas music.

Sharp wind blew snow against the windshield, the defroster only clearing a small half circle. Hunched forward, she squinted to see out of the allotted space and turned up the heat and the fan, then ran her sleeve on the inside of the windshield. If only she hadn't forgotten her cell phone . . .

She turned into her neighborhood, the car still behind her. She made some unexpected turns, made a circle around a block, and the car followed. *I could circle back. Go to the police department, but that was a good twenty minutes in the wrong direction. Conditions as they were, even longer.* She'd stop at her neighbor's house—but they were away for the holidays.

Chestnut Street was completely dark; not even a Christmas light burning. Were the streetlights out before tonight? She'd never noticed. A glance at the dashboard clock—11:09. Everyone had retired for the night.

She checked the rearview mirror. The headlights behind her were gone. So far as she could see no dark shadow of a car lurked with the headlights turned off. The car must have turned off somewhere in her neighborhood. She breathed a sigh of relief and drove her Honda into her carport. She waited a full minute inside the car with the ignition still on, studying the rear and side view mirrors, before she turned the ignition off and stepped out into the cold.

She hurried through the back door and immediately engaged the deadbolt. The house was so quiet she had the sinking certainty Will hadn't returned. Removing her gloves and hat, she hung them along with her coat and scarf on the coat tree. Misty wagged up a storm of welcome in front of her. Only when she gave her dog a hug did Maggie begin to relax.

Her cell was right where she'd left it, plugged into the charger. The house was warm and cozy, but she couldn't entirely shake a feeling of discomfort. She checked for messages on her cell and found several from Will.

She punched in his number.

"Damn it, Maggie, where've you been?"

He sounded pissed, and for some reason that pleased her. "Rutland Manor—you remember that family Christmas party I mentioned Celia has every year?"

"I know, but it's after eleven, and I was beginning to worry. I've been trying to reach you for hours. You home yet?"

"Just got in a minute ago." Too many years had gone by since anyone had cared. She liked the feeling. "I tried to call you before I left, but I didn't get through. I was already at Celia's, when I realized I'd left my cell plugged into the charger. I've wanted to call you all evening, but I didn't want to use Hilton's phones."

"No. Everything secure at the house?"

"Seems to be. I'm checking right now, but everything appears fine." She walked around the house, turning on lights, pulling shutters and curtains closed, checking to see all doors and windows were still securely locked. "Where are you?"

"About five miles west of downtown at a coffee house on my third cup."

She pictured him sitting at the table lingering over his coffee with several newspapers, probably his computer. "Tell me where the coffee house is, and I'll pick you up."

"Thanks, but forget it. The weather's too bad for you to be going out on the road again tonight. I'll catch a bus. I was just about to go to your house anyway to see if you were all right. I spent the afternoon with Gene, going over all the information you gave me. He has some interesting thoughts. Build a fire, Maggie, and I'll share everything with you soon as I can get there."

"Hurry. I've got a story to tell you, too—I overheard Hilton and Libby talking about a knife. I think you're right. I think Hilton killed Ellen."

After a long pause, Will spoke. "What did he say that makes you think that?"

"It's what Libby said. She was trying to keep the knife from him, trying to prevent him from killing any others."

Another pause. "I'm not so sure . . . Gene thinks Libby's our killer. And I believe he's right. I know I've judged Hilton to be the guilty party for fourteen years, but I think I was wrong. I think when Hilton saw me in the front foyer that night he assumed I'd killed Ellen the same way I assumed he'd killed her. I figured he was covering up his own deed by accusing me, but now I don't think so. I was going to wait until I saw you, but let me give you the scenario as Gene and I speculated on it this afternoon.

"Moments before I showed up, Libby must have run from the front parlor, and Hilton happened to see her. She may have been crying or even have shouted something to her father as she ran past him. Hilton went into the room to determine what had upset his daughter. After Hilton determined Ellen was dead and covered her body, he returned to the foyer, saw me and dismissed any thoughts that his young daughter had committed such a heinous crime. I was the more *likely* person. If he noticed any blood on Libby's dress, he dismissed it as having gotten on her when she got too close to the body, same as it had gotten on him."

As Will spoke Maggie walked through the kitchen to the living room and sat heavily on the sofa. *Libby.* She sighed. "It makes perfect sense. But I always considered Libby too young to have committed such a monstrous crime, and I suppose Hilton did, too. In all the interrogations, he never mentioned his brief encounter with his daughter in the hallway, therefore misleading the police that he'd been the one to find Ellen's body. All these years he's been protecting Libby."

"*. . . give me the damn knife.*"

Maggie sat forward. "Somewhere along the line he must have learned of her misdeed."

"Probably sooner rather than later. My guess is he helped her get rid of her bloody clothes."

"Yet he continued to lie for her," she said.

"Because his career and reputation were at stake."

With Libby's conversation with her father running through her head, Maggie paid little attention to Misty getting up and trotting back to the kitchen.

"*. . . I'm sorry, but I won't let you have the knife . . .*"

"*. . . it has got to stop . . .*"

"*I know, Daddy. You can depend on me.*"

"*Yes but . . . Libby, that last girl . . .*"

"Maggie? You still there?"

"Yes. Just mulling over Libby and Hilton's conversation. I thought Hilton was trying to get the knife back from Libby because it could be used as evidence against him. But after listening to you, I'm pretty sure he was trying to keep her from using the knife again. My God, Will, it was Libby all along. And it's worse than even you know. I think Ellen's murder and the murders of those other women who were knifed and thrown into Lake Michigan—the Lakeshore Murders—were all done by the same hand . . ." She rubbed her mouth.

"What? Maggie? You're fading out on me again."

She drew in a deep breath. "Will, I was followed home tonight—I'm pretty sure of that. Whoever it was made no pretense of following me, but then when I pulled into the driveway, the car was gone. It might be someone harassing me."

"Maggie. Listen to me. You're in grave danger. Call the police right now."

"That was my next call, right after you, but if you're coming here, I don't know . . ."

"Don't worry about that. I'll take care of myself. Check the doors and windows again. Be sure they're all secured."

"Already done." She closed her eyes and drew in a breath. "Will, somebody may have a key."

"What?"

"When I got home this afternoon, there were signs that someone had been in the house. The back door was unlocked—did you leave it unlocked?"

"Of course not. Damn it, Maggie, do you have your gun with you?"

"It's in my purse in the kitchen."

"Get it right now while we're talking, and keep it on you at all times. I'm on the street now, heading for the cab stand in the next block." He sounded breathless, worried, and running. "I'll get there a lot faster in a cab. Have you got your purse?"

"I'm on my way . . ." At the kitchen entrance, she froze. Misty wagged her tail at someone standing inside the back door. "Libby . . . you scared me for a moment. What are you doing here? How'd you get in?"

Libby held up a key and stepped forward. "Hang up."

Fired by instinct, Maggie dropped the phone. In the split-second Libby's attention darted downward, Maggie lunged for her purse on the counter and the police-issued Glock. She grabbed the purse, but before she found her weapon, she was brought to an abrupt stop by a .40 Smith and Wesson that suddenly materialized in Libby's hand. It was pointed at Maggie's head.

"Put the purse back on the counter."

The gun was so close, inches from Maggie's fingers. She debated her chances of pulling out the gun, releasing the safety, and getting off a shot before Libby pulled the trigger—slim to none. She swallowed hard and forced herself to be calm. Slowly, she slid the purse onto the countertop. Between them the phone lay on the white vinyl floor. Will shouted her name. Libby took a few steps and stomped on it with her high-heeled boot. The line went silent.

* * * *

Cold terror plunged into Will's chest. Suddenly he was trembling, running. He jerked open the door of the first cab he came to and threw his pack into the back seat, hurling himself in beside it.

"I'm in a hurry. You Silas?" he asked, reading the name on the registration.

"Yes." The driver turned to look at him.

"You speak English, Silas?"

"Yes, I was born in New York. You got a problem?"

Will gave him Maggie's address. "You know where that is?"

"I have a GPS," Silas said, "but I know that neighborhood because I got a friend who lives in the area."

"All right. Now put your foot on the gas and listen up. Right now I'm holding a gun at your head." He lifted the Glock so Silas could see it in his rearview mirror and resisted the urge to smile when Silas swore. "Don't try any foolish business, Silas, like reaching for a silent alarm. You want to survive the night, you'll do exactly what I tell you. Use that phone of yours to call the police."

"Huh? The police?" The cabbie turned around again. He was big, forty or fifty pounds overweight, and he looked scared and confused.

"That's right. Call the police, 911 will do. Tell them that Detective Maggie Raine is about to be murdered at 2711 Chestnut Street and that they better get over there quick. Got that?"

"You planning on murdering this cop?"

"No questions, Silas, just concentrate on the driving."

When Silas had duly contacted the police department, Will said. "So far so good, Silas, but at the rate you're driving we won't be there for an hour. I want you to move this bucket of yours."

"Hell, Mister, I can't see twenty feet ahead of me."

"Then you'll have to make some good guesses."

The cab slowed for a red light, and Will shouted, "Through the lights, damn you. Drive like hell. Drive like the cops are after you and you got to beat them to Chestnut Street or die. Red lights, stop signs, ice on the roads. None of it exists. Got that? We don't stop unless we hit something."

"Whatever you say. You're the one with the gun."

"Yes I am, and just so there's no misunderstanding between us, I'm already wanted for murder so I have nothing to lose by knocking you off."

* * * *

The chatty, smiling woman who had shared coffee with her the day before bore little resemblance to the cold one staring at her now. In the florescent lighting of the kitchen Libby's face appeared pale as the frost and just as hard. Maggie stared at her. Sometimes she forgot how good-looking Libby really was. But tonight Libby was different; something burning in her heavily made-up eyes, an intense and hollow look that wasn't rational, a look Maggie had never before seen.

Even as chills of fear slithered up Maggie's spine, it was imperative to keep her composure, and her wits. But when she opened her mouth to speak, her throat constricted tightly and it took every ounce of self-discipline to keep her voice calm.

"Put the gun away, Libby. There's no need for that."

"Who were you talking to?" Libby picked up the receiver to assure the line was dead before tossing it onto the counter.

"My brother." She said the first person who came to mind. "He's on a Mediterranean cruise. What's wrong, Libby? Why the gun?"

Libby's eyes burned, burned with an eerie fire that had Maggie backing up until the counter brought her to a stop. "As if you didn't know. You were on the patio when Daddy and I were arguing before dinner. I don't know what you heard, but I want you to stay out of our business. Stop the investigation."

Maggie told herself not to be afraid, not yet. "*Please* put away the gun, Libby. I'll fix coffee and we can sit and talk like we did yesterday."

"Not tonight. All this delving into our family history is tearing our family apart, and it isn't going to help Ellen. Are you going to stop the investigation?"

"You know I can't."

"Yes you can." Libby snorted a sound that couldn't be mistaken for mirth. "You're a smart person, Maggie, a dedicated cop, but in some ways you're as dumb as that counter you're hanging onto. You think you know something, but you've got it all wrong."

"What have I got wrong, Libby? Tell me what you and your father were talking about this evening, if it wasn't the knife used to kill Thea Johnson in order to cover up the murder of your sister?"

Libby stepped closer, stopping a few feet from Maggie, her lips curved into a frightening smile. "No one but you remembers Ellen's murder anymore."

"Someone remembers," Maggie said softly. "Jamie Donovan remembers, and he's lived under the shadow of that crime for nearly half his life. Don't you think he deserves a chance to be free?"

If possible, Libby's face grew paler behind the blush of her rouge. "Daddy would never have allowed Ellen to marry Jamie, you know. Ellen was his precious daughter, the one he loved the best. All Daddy ever wanted was to protect the family from scandal, and Ellen let him down. When Mary told him Ellen was pregnant earlier that afternoon, he was furious. I was outside on the swing, and I heard everything; he was going to keep her from attending the party and send her to Europe to be with some cousin. But Mary convinced him to wait until after the party to confront Ellen."

With one hand still holding the gun, Libby plopped her purse on the counter and began to rummage inside. The purse was an oversized affair that looked more like a shopping bag and was out-of-place beside her full-length mink coat. Was her knife in there? Maggie stilled, bracing herself.

Libby withdrew her hand, her fingers wrapped around a pack of cigarettes and a lighter. She stuck one between her lips. "Mary wasn't my real mother, you know?"

Maggie nodded. "Matt told me."

She expected further comment, but Libby lit the cigarette and inhaled deeply. With the cigarette clenched between her lips, she stuffed the pack and lighter in her purse. Then she removed the cigarette, blew smoke into the air, and went on as if Maggie hadn't spoken. "Ellen confided in me, too. She was going to tell Jamie about the baby at the party. She planned to run off with him. Having Jamie's baby was the only way she could hold him. Her bag was packed and hidden under her bed. You didn't know that, did you, Maggie? It would have broken Daddy's heart if Ellen ran away. He's an important man, and the scandal would have ruined him. I begged Ellen to get the baby problem taken care of, that no one outside the family need know. But her mind was made up. She wanted Jamie, and she wanted his baby. Someone had to protect the family's reputation."

"So you did."

"I couldn't trust Daddy to do it." A dreamy look came into Libby's eyes. "But at first I didn't know how to stop Ellen. I was lost. Then God found me. He reminded me about the knife I'd discovered on the floor of Ellen's car the previous afternoon; He suggested the latex gloves in the laundry room; then He told me what to do." Sweat beaded on Libby's temples, and when she brushed her hair back, her hand shook as though she were reliving a bad dream.

The pain and sadness in her former sister-in-law's words moved Maggie. Somewhere along life's trail, Libby had indeed lost her way. Suddenly, Libby's tone became cold, hard.

"You think I'm crazy, don't you? You think you can lock me away in some kind of nut house to spend the rest of my days and everything will be all right?"

Maggie sighed deeply. "I'm thinking about a hospital, Libby, where you'd be under the care of good doctors. Over the years you took the lives of other young women who were bright and pretty and privileged just like you. The killing needs to stop."

Libby's voice turned cold. "They were sluts, all of them. They deserved to die."

From the corner of her eye Maggie saw the edge of the Glock in her purse. She leaned against the counter, her hands clasped on the edge not far from her purse. Cautiously, she inched sideways until her body was a screen in front of the purse.

"No, Maggie, don't move."

She stopped. Behind her back she walked her fingers slowly toward the purse. When she felt the black leather, she eased it closer. It wasn't in Libby's M.O. to shoot her victim—she cut them up—and Maggie had to gamble that tonight wouldn't be any different from the other times she'd killed.

When Libby cut her eyes toward the sink to pitch her cigarette butt there, Maggie didn't hesitate. In one motion she snatched the weapon from her purse and swung around as she released the safety, ducked, and fired.

Click.

Maggie didn't pause, but aimed and squeezed the trigger a second time.

Libby's chortle reeked of sly amusement. "You can forget about that little handgun. It isn't going to do you any good. You don't think I would have let you inch over toward it if it were loaded, do you? When you were working in Celia's kitchen I removed the bullets."

"That was clever of you, Libby, to think ahead and empty my gun."

The grandfather clock chimed once, then stopped, 11:30. Maggie's nerves were running wild over her skin. Libby was toying with her. *Why haven't the police arrived? What's keeping Will?*

Libby skewered her with a gaze as cold as the icicles hanging from the eaves outside the kitchen window. "My gun *is* loaded, Maggie, so drop your gun to the floor and kick it into the corner. And don't make any more foolish moves."

Suddenly Libby's hand was back in her purse. This time, when it came out again, it wielded a long knife.

Fear shot up Maggie's spine. "Libby, for God's Sake, please . . . put the knife away."

"I'm sorry, but it's gone too far for that. You know too much."

I need to keep her talking. Surely the police will be here any minute. "I don't leave a hide-a-key outside. How did you get one?"

Libby snorted. "I had it made years ago, when you and Matt were living at Rutland Manor. For being cops, you and Matt didn't pay much attention to your own security. You left your keys on your dresser, the key to this house clearly labeled 'house.' Since it didn't fit Rutland Manor I figured it was this house. I simply borrowed it when you were away at work, had a copy made, and returned it to the key ring before you returned. Just in case. I spent lots of time in here when you were in Alaska, and you didn't have a clue, did you?"

"No, I didn't. Tell me, why did you kill your sister?"

"I already told you. I had no choice. Ellen asked for it, and I had to do it. I loved Ellen. When I was young, I tried to be like her in every way. But she betrayed me. Everyone thought Ellen was perfect. Daddy and Mary doted on her. But Ellen was no better than my mother—the mother who birthed me. She was no better than a prostitute. Ellen was going to break Daddy's heart. I told you someone had to protect him. Someone had to protect the family's good name."

"It doesn't have to be this way, Libby."

"I'm sorry, Maggie, I didn't want it to end like this. It would have been so much easier if you had died with Matt in that plane crash."

The terrible light of madness was bright in Libby's eyes. Seeing it so clearly now Maggie wondered how she could have overlooked it before. She braced herself. "I intend to fight, Libby. I won't submit easily."

Brave words, mighty brave words.

The gun, and the nasty length of steel she held, put the odds all on Libby's side.

Chapter Twenty-four

The taxi plowed through the snow onto La Salle Boulevard, spinning into the intersection and barely missing a streetlight. Silas went with the slide until the treads grabbed the pavement, then he pressed on the gas, lurching forward. Along the sides of the road, a curb, hidden beneath the snow, acted like a guardrail, bouncing the Chevy from side to side like a puck in arcade hockey. Without regard to storm and speed limits the taxi skidded through the streets.

Pedestrians were few, cars weren't crowding the streets, but whenever vehicle or people came into sight, Silas honked his horn wildly. Several drivers didn't see him coming, and he floored the brake pedal to avoid a collision. Will had to hand it to Silas. Every time he thought their wild ride would end up in a ditch, Silas had the cab going again with only seconds lost.

When they got to the recently plowed I-94, Silas ran his engine up to 91 mph and looked like he was enjoying it.

Will glanced at his watch. They'd been on the road ten minutes, an awfully long time to keep a killer at bay.

"You're not going to kill that cop, are you?" Silas whizzed past a Ford Taurus, weaving in and out of the slow-moving traffic.

"Nope."

"And you're not really wanted for murder either?"

"You should've quit while you were ahead."

* * * *

"You made a mistake, Libby. You might have gotten away with killing the other ladies, but when you killed Thea, you made a mistake."

"She should have kept her mouth shut," Libby snarled, her eyes bright with madness.

It was futile to reason with someone incapable of understanding the nature and impact of her actions, but Maggie was fighting for time.

"You're not as bright as you think, Libby. Thea *did* keep your secret. She didn't tell me anything. And *I* didn't figure out that you killed the other girls. I thought Hilton was the killer. Jamie Donovan is in town, and I gave him your file and the files on the Lakeshore murders to study. He and his friend Gene Pryor figured it was you. So you see, by killing me you won't solve a thing. Everything I know about those murders is on the computer and in hardcopy files that are available to any of the officers in the department."

"I don't believe you. You're bluffing. I've read enough detective stories to know that's what cops do when they're in a jam." Libby looked confused, nervous. "And I fooled you about the gun. You never suspected when I took those bullets out. And I fooled everyone about Ellen's murder."

"Except your father. He figured it out right away, didn't he?"

Libby's mouth turned down, and her lips trembled. "Daddy loves me. He knows I didn't mean to hurt Ellen. I was trying to save her, keep her from putting a stain on Daddy' career. Ellen wouldn't listen to me. And you, Maggie, you were always the wise-ass girl detective, so proud of yourself. Well, it doesn't matter anymore what you know. It'll go to the grave with you."

"If I turn up dead, the Department will know you did it. Hilton will know. He won't protect you forever. Eventually you'll be caught."

Libby frowned and her mouth twisted with disdain. "Not necessarily. They're looking for a man. And I can handle my daddy."

"Put the gun and knife down, Libby, and I promise I'll do all I can to see you get proper care."

Libby threw back her head and cackled. "You're talking about doctors again, sanitariums, living with a bunch of crazies. I think I'd have a hard time adjusting to a life like that. Thanks, but no thanks. The Lakeshore murderer is about to strike again. I like that name, by the way. The Lakeshore murders. The papers came up with it, and after that I made sure all the bodies ended up in the lake." She pressed a hand to her temple as though her head were aching. "Enough talk."

Maggie tried one more tack. "When you arrived, that was Jamie not my brother I was talking to on the phone. He'll be here any minute now. Put the weapons away."

"Shut up. I'm tired of talking." Libby lifted the blade and lunged.

Maggie screamed and recoiled, but not fast enough. The knife ripped through her dress and into her side. Even before she registered the sting, she kicked out a foot with all her might. Her heel hit Libby square in the stomach. With a surprised look, Libby staggered backward, giving Maggie a valuable second to run for the living room and the fireplace poker.

Libby laughed wildly and took up the chase. "Good, that's good, Maggie. I love a good fight."

Poker clutched with both hands, Maggie whipped it in front of her in an effort to knock the weapons from Libby's hands. Why Libby hadn't already pulled the trigger and shot Maggie dead only Libby could answer. All Maggie knew for certain was that to date Libby had never shot one of her victims. With that in mind Maggie had no intention of letting Libby get close enough to tie her up or choke her or worse, stab her. With her poker weaving and jabbing to keep Libby at bay, Maggie concentrated on knocking the knife out of her hand while she worked herself closer to the front door and escape. But if she was wrong about Libby and Libby did fire the gun, from the distance that separated them she couldn't miss.

At the sound of slamming car doors and pounding feet running up the front walkway, hope surged through Maggie.

The front door knocker banged as the doorbell chimed. "Police. You all right in there?"

For the first time alarm flared in Libby's eyes.

"No, I'm not! Hurry! She's got a knife and a gun." Maggie barely dodged Libby's next thrust. She struck the poker against Libby's arm and thought she heard a bone crack, but Libby still wielded the knife.

"Give up, Libby. It's all over." Sirens wailed as more squad cars arrived.

The wildness in Libby's eyes blazed. "Not a chance, policewoman. I'm not going to spend the rest of my days in a nut house!"

The front door splintered and for a second Libby hesitated. Then, what Maggie feared most, happened.

Libby whirled and shot.

* * * *

Silas skidded the cab around the corner and came to a jarring stop behind a police car with flashing lights. The street was crowded with squad cars and neighbors stood in their doorways in nightclothes.

Will was out of the car and running. He skirted through the trees to avoid the officers in front of the house and headed for the back. He vaulted over the chain-link fence. A gunshot from inside the house froze him in his tracks.

Moments later the back door flew open, and a swath of light spilled onto the patio seconds before Libby appeared. Will stood in the dark, looking for signs of Maggie. His gaze swept beyond the doorway to where a table had been knocked over. But no sign of the woman he loved nor of the police.

"Hello, Libby," he said, when she passed within fifteen feet of him. "It's me, Jamie. Let's go inside where it's warm."

He stepped from the trees and slowly began to walk toward her. The gun and knife were clearly visible. If she shot, he would be an easy target.

"Jamie. Maggie said you were here. I thought she was lying. I'm glad you're okay. I never wanted to hurt you."

"Once we were friends, Libby."

Moments later a police officer came out the back door, his gun drawn and aimed at Libby. Two other officers were close on his heels.

"Drop your gun and the knife, lady," the first officer said.

Libby kept moving away but slowed as she approached the fence. She turned, tossed her head brazenly and aimed her gun at the officer. "Then shoot, damn you, but I'll take you with me. I'll never give in to you willingly."

"Back off, officer," Will said. "For a moment. Please. I'm Jamie Donovan, and I'd like a moment to talk with her."

"I don't care who the hell you are." Will's name evidently didn't ring a bell with the officer. "Back off yourself, before I put you in my sights. I'm the cop here."

"Just give me a couple of minutes to talk with her. Libby and I have always been friends. There's no need for any more killing."

"I know this man." Maggie stepped outside.

Maggie, alive. She was partially concealed behind a police officer and holding Misty by the collar. Will had never felt so glad to see anyone in his life.

"Give him a few minutes to talk with her." Maggie's voice carried police authority. "Like he says, maybe we can avoid any further bloodshed."

With obvious reluctance the officer nodded at his superior officer, but his gun was still aimed at Libby. "All right, you've got a couple of minutes. But by God, if she tries to make a run for it, I'll be forced to shoot her."

Cautiously, Will walked toward Libby.

"That's close enough." Libby lowered the handgun and studied it as if seeing it for the first time. "Daddy gave this pretty little gun to me years ago." Her mouth twisted into a grotesque attempt at a smile. "He thought I needed protection."

For a long time she was quiet, studying her gun, and Will scoured his brain for the right thing to say or do that would reach down into the rational part of her mind and get her to give herself up.

Then Libby surprised him. She sagged into the snow at the base of an oak tree and looked at him. "Jamie?"

A bad feeling churned in the pit of his stomach.

"Tell Daddy I'm sorry for everything, for all of it . . . but I'm afraid I can't come in."

"Don't do anything hasty, Libby. It doesn't have to end like this. There are places where you can get help." Will quickened his steps toward her.

She looked at him, then at the gun in her hand as if considering her options and giggled a high-pitched hysterical sound. "You're suggesting I go to an institution just like Maggie did. I thought you of all people knew me better than that. I would never survive in a place like that. But anyway, don't worry, the gun's not meant for you. I've always figured it might come to this one day, and it's my solution. I'm sorry, but I don't think we can have that talk . . . I'd have liked to . . ."

Will watched in horror as she lifted the gun to her head. "No, Libby!"

She pulled the trigger.

It was over.

* * * *

One of the officers pushed Maggie behind him. It was Detective Ned Waller—he'd been at Thea Johnson's murder scene—was that only this morning? "Come on, Maggie, you need to get back inside."

Maggie heard the talking that was going on around her. She heard the wail of a siren in her front yard and saw the policemen walking through her living room and kitchen with guns in their hands and snow on their feet. But she was shaky inside and out.

Afraid if she let Misty go she would bolt into the yard and interfere with police business, Maggie kept hold of her collar. On unsteady legs she stepped back through the doorway into the kitchen as Ned requested.

"You've got a hell of a lot of explaining to do, Detective, but it'll wait. Right now you need to sit down and wait for medical help. That cut of yours is bleeding pretty badly." He led her to one of the chairs Libby had overturned in her rush to escape and set it on its legs. "Help should be along—"

The gunshot blast had shaken her to the core. She laid her head against the soft fur of Misty's back and waited.

Moments later she felt steadying hands on her shoulders, those strong hands that had protected her before, and she lifted her head to face Will.

Anguish was clear in his face, the same anguish she felt.

"I'm fine. Maggie, you're bleeding. Did she shoot you?"

"No, and she was so close to me that there was no way she could miss me, and yet somehow she did . . ." Her voice broke on a wrenching sob. "Oh, Will, I'm glad she didn't shoot you . . ."

Chapter Twenty-Five

Nationwide, reporters ran carte blanche with theory after theory of Libby's motivations—her past examined under a microscope. The byproduct of an affair between a drug-using prostitute mother and the promiscuous Congressman Hilton Raine, she was jealous, easily roused, and had killed her half-sister in a rage over Jamie Donovan, the man they both loved. Her two marriages had failed. A couple of her so-called friends came forward to say she had been known to use Ecstasy.

A few astute reporters brought out the fact that Libby was acquainted with many of the women who had been murdered over the past fourteen years, but when no formal charges were ever made against her for the Lakeshore Murders, the stories faded.

After three weeks of being headline news, Libby's crime and subsequent suicide ran out of steam. The country was in the midst of a contentious presidential race. With unrest still raging in the Middle East, the housing market down, the country turned its attention to other matters.

But the suspicion that Hilton was aware of his daughter's crime and covered up for her, continued to capture the back pages. Hilton buckled under pressure from Capitol Hill and resigned the Senate.

All charges against Jamie Donovan were dropped.

Ellen Raine's case file was officially closed.

With the death of Libby Raine, the Lakeshore Murders ceased.

* * * *

Early on New Year's Eve, as frigid winds blew across frozen Lake Michigan, fanning Chicago with several more inches of snow, Jamie 'Will' Donovan and Maggie Kilpatrick were married in the simple white church that Maggie had attended since childhood.

Celia Raine, thrilled to be asked to stand up beside Maggie, left her husband home and braved the media circus to be present. When Paul's daughter Tiffany and Gene's son Billy jointly delivered the ring to Will on a satin cushion, Celia and Maggie's neighbor, Jenny, walked behind.

Standing beside Will in rented tuxedos were Paul Raine, Gene Pryor, and Maggie's brother Tyler who'd been given special leave from the Navy.

At the end of the day the small and intimate wedding had burgeoned. With so many friends and colleagues anxious to wish the couple well, every pew of the little church was filled.

* * * *

An old farmhouse on the outskirts of Fairbanks had been recently vacated when the owners moved back to South Carolina to live closer to their kids. It was perfect. With its two bedrooms, two baths, a living room with a huge stone fireplace, and a quaint kitchen with a second fireplace, it was all Maggie and Will had hoped for and more. When Gene's wife wrote them about it a few months after the wedding, Maggie and Will jumped at the opportunity.

In their new home, sitting on their new bed, Will hugged his wife's naked body against his and ran his fingers down her back then around to the slight swelling in her abdomen. "When are you going to start showing? I can't wait to tell everyone I know."

She kissed his chin and cheek, then punched him lightly in the chest. "All too soon, I'll be big as a house."

"I can't wait."

"Well, I can. There's a lot of work I need to do around here before I can't move. And you've got a room to build on." She swung her legs over the mattress to the bare hardwood floor. The room was empty of furniture except for the mattress and box springs drawn up against a wall and a crate set beside it with a lamp and a clock.

He sat beside her and looked at her tousled red hair and cheeks still flushed from their lovemaking. He kissed the smudge of ivory paint she missed on her right ear in last night's shower, and pulled her back into his arms.

Leaning against the wall across from the mattress and attractively framed was the wolf painting he'd given her. She was looking at it now, a half smile softening her mouth, and as he lifted his gaze to his work, he was flooded with memories of the only home he'd ever called his own.

"I wonder what's happened to your cabin?" she asked, as if privy to his thoughts. "I was thinking we should go see it soon as weather permits. I'd like to stay there again and bring more of your paintings back here if the police didn't impound everything or burn the place to the ground."

"I'd like that too. Gene told me he flew over it recently, and it's still there. He doesn't see that there should be any problems landing on the river while it's still frozen. How would you like to go next week?"

"If the weather's good." She laughed. "I don't want to get caught in any more of Alaska's winter storms . . . or then again, maybe I do."

He pulled on his pajama bottoms and grabbed a quilt from the bed, the floral one that had been on her bed in Chicago, wrapped it around her, and lifted her into his arms. He carried her past the bucket of paint and the ladder to the row of windows in the empty living room. It was one of his favorite things about the house, the windows that melded the outside with the inside.

Hilde, Lucy, and Misty got up from the spots they'd claimed for the night, stretched, and followed behind them. Will smiled at them. He had missed his dogs, and he was pleased that neither showed any signs of jealousy or temper when Misty was brought into the fold or when Gene's kids pulled their hair or tried to climb on them.

On this morning after their second night together in their new home, the sun shone brightly over the blanket of newly fallen snow. Outside the wind puffed in little fits that lifted the snow into dancing dervishes. It sent a dead branch rolling into the creek. Near an old barn, Will's sled dogs slept in their houses, and at the edge of the trees a moose foraged.

He let Maggie slide down the length of him until her feet touched the floor, then pulled her back against his chest and buried his face in the crook of her neck.

Will lifted his head. "Look!" He pointed. "Just in front of that tumbling fence, can you see the tiny sprig of green peeking through the snow?"

Maggie nodded. "Maybe it's a hyacinth. A promise of spring."

He looked at her, into her eyes. She had beautiful eyes.

"Yes." He smiled with more happiness inside him than he'd ever known. His head dipped so his forehead touched hers, and a solitary tear welled and rolled down his cheek. "Thank you, my love. For my life, for a place to call home, for the promise that each sunrise brings . . . thank you. I love you, Maggie."

"I love you back."

A Cry From the Cold

Praise for
Highland Press Books!

I enjoyed the wide vistas of Canadian scenery and the strong role of animals in the plot, especially the dogs and horses. **Passion and Prejudice** by Gail MacMillan is a thoroughly enjoyable read.
~ *Sunflower, Long and Short Reviews*
* * * *

Camelot's Enchantment is a highly original and captivating tale!
~ *Joy Nash, USA Today Best Seller*
* * * *

An anthology by amazing women with character and grace—incredible writers, wonderful stories! ***For Your Heart Only*** is not to be missed!
~ *Heather Graham, NYT Best Seller*
* * * *

Through its collection of descriptive phrases, **The Millennium Phrase Book** offers writers concrete examples of rich and evocative descriptions. Browsing through its pages offers a jumpstart to the imagination, helping authors deepen the intensity of scenes and enhance their own writing.
~ *Tami Cowden, Author of The Complete Guide to Heroes & Heroines, Sixteen Master Archetypes*
* * * *

Brynn Chapman makes you question how far science should take humanity. **Project Mendel** blurs the distinction between genetics and horror and merges them in a reality all too plausible. A gripping read.
~*Jennifer Linforth, Author, Historical Fiction and Romance*
* * * *

Kemberlee Shortland's ***A Piece of My Heart*** is terrific romantic/suspense fiction to savor and share with family and friends.
~*Viviane Crystal, Crystal Reviews*
* * * *

From betrayal, to broken hearts, to finding love again, ***Second Time Around*** has a story for just about anyone. these fine ladies created stories that will always stay fresh in my heart; ones I will treasure forever.
~ *Cherokee , Coffee Time Romance & More*
* * * *

The Mosquito Tapes - Nobody tells a bio-terror story better than Chris Holmes. Just nobody. And like all of Chris Holmes' books, this one begins well—when San Diego County Chief Medical Examiner Jack Youngblood discovers a strange mosquito in the pocket of a murder victim. Taut, tingly, and downright scary, *The Mosquito Tapes* will keep you reading well into the night. But best be wary: Spray yourself with Deet and have a

243

fly swatter nearby.
~ *Ben F. Small, author of Alibi On Ice and The Olive Horseshoe, a Preditors & Editors Top Ten Pick*
* * * *

Cynthia Breeding's **Prelude to Camelot** is a lovely and fascinating read, a book worthy of being shelved with my Arthurania fiction and non-fiction.
~ *Brenda Thatcher, Mystique Books*
* * * *

Romance on Route 66 by Judith Leigh and Cheryl Norman – Norman and Leigh break the romance speed limit on America's historic roadway.
~ *Anne Krist, Ecataromance, Reviewers' Choice Award Winner*
* * * *

Ah, the memories that **Operation: L.O.V.E.** brings to mind. As an Air Force nurse who married an Air Force fighter pilot, I relived the days of glory through each and every story. While covering all the military branches, each story holds a special spark of its own that readers will love!
~ *Lori Avocato, Best Selling Author*
* * * *

In **Fate of Camelot**, Cynthia Breeding develops the Arthur-Lancelot-Gwenhwyfar relationship. In many Arthurian tales, Guinevere is a rather flat character. Cynthia Breeding gives her a depth of character as the reader sees her love for Lancelot and her devotion to the realm as its queen. The reader feels the pull she experiences between both men. In addition, the reader feels more of the deep friendship between Arthur and Lancelot seen in Malory's Arthurian tales. In this area, Cynthia Breeding is more faithful to the medieval Arthurian tradition than a glamorized Hollywood version. She does not gloss over the difficulties of Gwenhwyfar's role as queen and as woman, but rather develops them to give the reader a vision of a woman who lives her role as queen and lover with all that she is.
~ *Merri, Merrimon Books*
* * * *

Rape of the Soul - Ms. Thompson's characters are unforgettable. Deep, promising and suspenseful this story was. I couldn't put it down. Around every corner was something that you didn't know was going to happen. If you love a sense of history in a book, then I suggest reading this book!
~ *Ruth Schaller, Paranormal Romance Reviews*
* * * *

Static Resistance and Rose – An enticing, fresh voice. Lee Roland knows how to capture your heart.
~ *Kelley St. John, National Readers Choice Award Winner*
* * * *

Southern Fried Trouble - Katherine Deauxville is at the top of her form with mayhem, sizzle and murder.
~ *Nan Ryan, NY Times Best-Selling Author*
* * * *

Madrigal: A Novel of Gaston Leroux's Phantom of the Opera takes place four years after the events of the original novel. The classic novel aside, this book is a wonderful historical tale of life, love, and choices. However, the most impressive aspect that stands out to me is the writing. Ms. Linforth's prose is phenomenally beautiful and hauntingly breathtaking.

~ *Bonnie-Lass, Coffee Time Romance*

* * * *

Cave of Terror by Amber Dawn Bell - Highly entertaining and fun, **Cave of Terror** was impossible to put down. Though at times dark and evil, Ms. Bell never failed to inject some light-hearted humor into the story. Delightfully funny with a true sense of teenagers, Cheyenne is believable and her emotional struggles are on par with most teens. The author gave just enough background to understand the workings of her vampires. I truly enjoyed Ryan and Constantine. Ryan was adorable and a teenager's dream. Constantine was deliciously dark. Ms. Bell has done an admirable job of telling a story suitable for young adults.

~ *Dawnie, Fallen Angel Reviews*

* * * *

The Sense of Honor - Ashley Kath-Bilsky has written a historical romance of the highest caliber. This reviewer fell in love with the hero and was cheering for the heroine all the way through. The plot is exciting, characters are multi-dimensional, and the secondary characters bring life to the story. Sexual tension rages through this story and Ms. Kath-Bilsky gives her readers a breathtaking romance. The love scenes are sensual and very romantic. This reviewer was very pleased with how the author handled all the secrets and both characters reacted very maturely when the secrets finally came to light.

~ *Valerie, Love Romances and More*

* * * *

Highland Wishes by Leanne Burroughs. The storyline, set in a time when tension was high between England and Scotland, is a fast-paced tale. The reader can feel this author's love for Scotland and its many wonderful heroes. This reviewer was easily captivated by the story and was enthralled by it until the end. The reader will laugh and cry as you read this wonderful story. The reader feels all the pain, torment and disillusionment felt by both main characters, but also the joy and love they felt. Ms. Burroughs has crafted a well-researched story that gives a glimpse into Scotland during a time when there was upheaval and war for independence. This reviewer commends her for a wonderful job done.

~*Dawn Roberto, Love Romances*

* * * *

I adore this Scottish historical romance! **Blood on the Tartan** has more history than some historical romances—but never dry history! Readers will find themselves completely immersed in the scene, the history and the characters. Chris Holmes creates a multi-dimensional theme of justice in his depiction of all the nuances and forces at work from the laird down to the land tenants. This intricate historical detail emanates from the story itself, heightening the suspense and the reader's understanding of the history in a vivid manner as if it were current and present. The extra historical detail just makes their life stories more memorable and lasting because the emotions were grounded in events. **Blood On The Tartan** is a must read for romance and historical fiction lovers of Scottish heritage.

~*Merri, Merrimon Reviews*

* * * *

Chasing Byron by Molly Zenk is a page turner of a book not only because of the engaging characters, but also by the lovely prose. Reading this book was a jolly fun time all through the eyes of Miss Woodhouse, yet also one that touches the heart. It was an experience I would definitely repeat. Ms. Zenk must have had a glorious time penning this story.

~Orange Blossom, Long and Short Reviews
* * * *

Moon of the Falling Leaves is an incredible read. The characters are not only believable, but the blending in of how Swift Eagle shows Jessica and her children the acts of survival is remarkably done. Diane Davis White pens a poignant tale that really grabbed this reader. She tells a descriptive story of discipline, trust and love in a time where hatred and prejudice abounded among many. This rich tale offers vivid imagery of the beautiful scenery and landscape, and brings in the tribal customs of each person, as Jessica and Swift Eagle search their heart.

~Cherokee, Coffee Time Romance
* * * *

Jean Harrington's ***The Barefoot Queen*** is a superb historical with a lushly painted setting. I adored Grace for her courage and the cleverness with which she sets out to make Owen see her love for him. The bond between Grace and Owen is tenderly portrayed and their love had me rooting for them right up until the last page. Ms. Harrington's ***The Barefoot Queen*** is a treasure in the historical romance genre you'll want to read for yourself!
Five Star Pick of the Week!!!

~ Crave More Romance
* * * *

Almost Taken by Isabel Mere takes the reader on an exciting adventure. The compelling characters of Deran Morissey, the Earl of Atherton, and Ava Fychon, a young woman from Wales, find themselves drawn together as they search for her missing siblings.
Readers will watch in interest as they fall in love and overcome obstacles. This is a sensual romance, and a creative and fast moving storyline that will enthrall readers. Ava, who is highly spirited and stubborn, will win the respect of the readers for her courage and determination. Deran, who is rumored in the beginning to be an ice king, not caring about anyone, will prove how wrong people's perceptions can be. ***Almost Taken*** is an emotionally moving historical romance that I highly recommend.

~ Anita, The Romance Studio
* * * *

Leanne Burroughs easily will captivate the reader with intricate details, a mystery that ensnares the reader and characters that will touch their hearts.
By the end of the first chapter, this reviewer was enthralled with ***Her Highland Rogue*** and was rooting for Duncan and Catherine to admit their love. Laughter, tears and love shine through this wonderful novel. This reviewer was amazed at Ms. Burroughs' depth and perception in this storyline. Her wonderful way with words plays itself through each page like a lyrical note and will captivate the reader till the very end.
Read ***Her Highland Rogue*** and be transported to a time full of mystery and promise of a future. This reviewer is highly recommending this book for those who enjoy an engrossing Scottish tale full of humor, love and laughter.

A Cry From the Cold

~Dawn Roberto, Love Romances

* * * *

Bride of Blackbeard by Brynn Chapman is a compelling tale of sorrow, pain, love, and hate. From the moment I started reading about Constanza and her upbringing, I was torn. Each of the people she encounters on her journey has an experience to share, drawing in the reader more. Ms. Chapman sketches a story that tugs at the heartstrings. I believe many will be touched in some way by this extraordinary book that leaves much thought.

~ *Cherokee, Coffee Time Romance*

* * * *

Isabel Mere's skill with words and the turn of a phrase makes **Almost Guilty** a joy to read. Her characters reach out and pull the reader into the trials, tribulations, simple pleasures, and sensual joy that they enjoy. Ms. Mere unravels the tangled web of murder, smuggling, kidnapping, hatred and faithless friends, while weaving a web of caring, sensual love that leaves a special joy and hope in the reader's heart.

~ *Camellia, Long and Short Reviews*

* * * *

Beats A Wild Heart - In the ancient, Celtic land of Cornwall, Emma Hayward searched for a myth and found truth. The legend of the black cat of Bodmin Moor is a well known Cornish legend. Jean Adams has merged the essence of myth and romance into a fascinating story which catches the imagination. I enjoyed the way the story unfolded at a smooth and steady pace with Emma and Seth appearing as real people who feel an instant attraction for one another. At first the story appears to be straightforward, but as it evolves mystery, love and intrigue intervene to make a vibrant story with hidden depths. Once you start reading you won't be able to put this book down.

~ *Orchid, Long and Short Reviews*

* * * *

Down Home Ever Lovin' Mule Blues by Jacquie Rogers - How can true love fail when everyone and their mule, cat, and skunk know that Brody and Rita belong together, even if Rita is engaged to another man? Needless to say, this is a fabulous roll on the floor while laughing out loud story. I am so thrilled to discover this book, and the author who wrote it. Rarely do I locate a story with as much humor, joy, and downright lust spread so thickly on the pages that I am surprised I could turn the pages. A treasure not to be missed.

~Suziq2, Single Titles.com

* * * *

Saving Tampa - What if you knew something horrible was going to happen but you could prevent it? Would you tell someone? What if you saw it in a vision and had no proof? Would you risk your credibility to come forward? These are the questions at the heart of **Saving Tampa**, an on-the-edge-of-your-seat thriller from Jo Webnar, who has written a wonderful suspense that is as timely as it is entertaining.

~ *Mairead Walpole, Reviews by Crystal*

* * * *

When the Vow Breaks by Judith Leigh - This book is about a woman who fights breast cancer. I assumed it would be extremely emotional and hard to read, but it was not. The storyline dealt more with the commitment between a man and a woman, with a true belief of God.

The intrigue was that of finding a rock to lean upon through faith in God. Not only did she learn to lean on her relationship with Him, but she also learned how to forgive her husband. This is a great look at not only a breast cancer survivor, but also a couple whose commitment to each other through their faith grew stronger. It is an easy read and one I highly recommend.

~ Brenda Talley, The Romance Studio

* * * *

A Heated Romance by Candace Gold - A fascinating romantic suspense tells the story of Marcie O'Dwyer, a female firefighter who has had to struggle to prove herself. While the first part of the book seems to focus on the romance and Marcie's daily life, the second part transitions into a suspense novel as Marcie witnesses something suspicious at one of the fires. Her life is endangered by what she possibly knows and I found myself anticipating the outcome almost as much as Marcie.

~ Lilac, Long and Short Reviews

* * * *

Into the Woods by R.R. Smythe - This Young Adult Fantasy will send chills down your spine. I, as the reader, followed Callum and witnessed everything he and his friends went through as they attempted to decipher the messages. At the same time, I watched Callum's mother, Ellsbeth, as she walked through the Netherwood. Each time Callum deciphered one of the four messages, some villagers awakened. Through the eyes of Ellsbeth, I saw the other sleepers wander, make mistakes, and be released from the Netherwood, leaving Ellsbeth alone. Excellent reading for any age of fantasy fans!

~ Detra Fitch, Huntress Reviews

* * * *

Like the Lion, the Witch, and the Wardrobe, ***Dark Well of Decision*** is a grand adventure with a likable girl who is a little like all of us. Zoe's insecurities are realistically drawn and her struggle with both her faith and the new direction her life will take is poignant. The references to the Bible and the teachings presented are appropriately captured. Author Anne Kimberly is an author to watch; her gift for penning a grand childhood adventure is a great one. This one is well worth the time and money spent.

~Lettetia, Coffee Time Romance

* * * *

The Crystal Heart by Katherine Deauxville brims with ribald humor and authentic historical detail. Enjoy!

~ Virginia Henley, NY Times bestselling author

* * * *

In Sunshine or In Shadow by Cynthia Owens - If you adore the stormy heroes of 'Wuthering Heights' and 'Jane Eyre' (and who doesn't?) you'll be entranced by Owens' passionate story of Ireland after the Great Famine, and David Burke - a man from America with a hidden past and a secret name. Only one woman, the fiery, luscious Siobhan, can unlock the bonds that imprison him. Highly recommended for those who love classic romance and an action-packed story.

~ Best Selling Author, Maggie Davis,
AKA Katherine Deauxville

A Cry From the Cold

* * * *

Rebel Heart - Jannine Corti Petska used a myriad of emotions to tell this story and the reader quickly becomes entranced in the ways Courtney's stubborn attitude works to her advantage in surviving this disastrous beginning to her new life. This is a wonderful rendition of a different type which is a welcome addition to the historical romance genre. I believe that you will enjoy this story; I know I did!

~ *Brenda Talley, The Romance Studio*

* * * *

Cat O' Nine Tales by Deborah MacGillivray. Enchanting tales from the most wicked, award-winning author today. Spellbinding! A treat for all.

~ *Detra Fitch, Huntress Reviews*

* * * *

Brides of the West by Michèle Ann Young, Kimberly Ivey, and Billie Warren Chai - All three of the stories in this wonderful anthology are based on women who gambled their future in blindly accepting complete strangers for husbands. It was a different era when a woman must have a husband to survive and all three of these phenomenal authors wrote exceptional stories featuring fascinating and gutsy heroines and the men who loved them. For an engrossing read with splendid original stories I highly encourage readers to pick up a copy of this marvelous anthology.

~ *Marilyn Rondeau, Reviewers International Organization*

* * * *

Faery Special Romances - Brilliantly magical! Jacquie Rogers' special brand of humor and imagination will have you believing in faeries from page one. Absolutely enchanting!

~ *Dawn Thompson, Award Winning Author*

* * * *

Flames of Gold (Anthology) - Within every heart lies a flame of hope, a dream of true love, a glimmering thought that the goodness of life is far, far larger than the challenges and adversities arriving in every life. In **Flames of Gold** lie five short stories wrapping credible characters into that mysterious, poignant mixture of pain and pleasure, sorrow and joy, stony apathy and resurrected hope.
Deftly plotted, paced precisely to hold interest and delightfully unfolding, **Flames of Gold** deserves to be enjoyed in any season, guaranteeing that real holiday spirit endures within the gifts of faith, hope and love personified in these engaging, spirited stories!

~ *Viviane Crystal, Crystal Reviews*

* * * *

Romance Upon A Midnight Clear (Anthology) - Each of these stories is well-written; when grouped together, they pack a powerful punch. Each author shares exceptional characters and a multitude of emotions ranging from grief to elation. You cannot help being able to relate to these stories that touch your heart and will entertain you at any time of year, not just the holidays. I feel honored to have been able to sample the works of such talented authors.

~*Matilda, Coffee Time Romance*

* * * *

Ann Merritt

Christmas is a magical time and twelve talented authors answer the question of what happens when **Christmas Wishes** come true in this incredible anthology. Each of these highly skilled authors brings a slightly different perspective to the Christmas theme to create a book that is sure to leave readers satisfied. What a joy to read such splendid stories! This reviewer looks forward to more anthologies by Highland Press as the quality is simply astonishing.

~ *Debbie, CK2S Kwips and Kritiques*
* * * *

Recipe for Love *(Anthology)* - I don't think the reader will find a better compilation of mouth watering short romantic love stories than in **Recipe for Love**! This is a highly recommended volume–perfect for beaches, doctor's offices, or anywhere you've a few minutes to read.

~ *Marilyn Rondeau, Reviewers International Organization*
* * * *

Holiday in the Heart *(Anthology)* - Twelve stories that would put even Scrooge into the Christmas spirit. It does not matter what *type* of romance genre you prefer. This book has a little bit of everything. The stories are set in the U.S.A. and Europe. Some take place in the past, some in the present, and one story takes place in both! I strongly suggest you put on something comfortable, brew up something hot (tea, coffee or cocoa will do), light up a fire, settle down somewhere quiet and begin reading this anthology.

~ *Detra Fitch, Huntress Reviews*
* * * *

Blue Moon Magic is an enchanting collection of short stories. It offers historicals, contemporaries, time travel, paranormal, and futuristic narratives to tempt your heart.
Legend says that if you wish with all your heart upon the rare blue moon, your wishes were sure to come true. In some of the stories, love happens in the most unusual ways. Angels may help, ancient spells may be broken. Even vampires will find their perfect mate with the power of the blue moon.
Blue Moon Magic is a perfect read for late at night or during your commute to work. The short yet sweet stories are a wonderful way to spend a few minutes. If you do not have the time to finish a full-length novel, and hate stopping in the middle of a loving tale, I highly recommend grabbing this book.

~ *Kim Swiderski, Writers Unlimited Reviewer*
* * * *

Legend has it that a blue moon is enchanted. What happens when fifteen talented authors utilize this theme to create enthralling stories of love? Readers will find a wide variety of time periods and styles showcased in this superb anthology. **Blue Moon Enchantment** is sure to offer a little bit of something for everyone!

~ *Debbie, CK²S Kwips and Kritiques*
* * * *

Love Under the Mistletoe is a fun anthology that infuses the beauty of the season with fun characters and unforgettable situations. This is one of those books you can read year round and still derive great pleasure from each of the charming stories. A wonderful compilation of holiday stories.

~ *Chrissy Dionne, Romance Junkies*

* * * *

Love and Silver Bells - I really enjoyed this heart-warming anthology. The characters are heart-wrenchingly human and hurting and simply looking for a little bit of peace on earth. Luckily they all eventually find it, although not without some strife. But we always appreciate the gifts we receive when we have to work a little harder to keep them. I recommend these warm holiday tales be read by the light of a well-lit tree, with a lovely fire in the fireplace and a nice cup of hot cocoa. All will warm you through and through.

~ *Angi, Night Owl Romance*

* * * *

Love on a Harley is an amazing romantic anthology featuring six amazing stories. Each story was heartwarming, tear jerking, and so perfect. I got tied to each one wanting them to continue on forever. Lost love, rekindling love, and learning to love are all expressed within these pages beautifully. I couldn't ask for a better romance anthology; each author brings that sensual, longing sort of love that every woman dreams of.

Great job ladies!

~ *Crystal, Crystal Book Reviews*

* * * *

No Law Against Love (Anthology) - If you have ever found yourself rolling your eyes at some of the more stupid laws, then you are going to adore this novel. Twenty-four stories fill this anthology, each dealing with at least one stupid or outdated law. Let me give you an example: In Florida, USA, there is a law that states 'If an elephant is left tied to a parking meter, the parking fee has to be paid just as it would for a vehicle.' Yes, you read that correctly. No matter how many times you go back and reread them, the words will remain the same. The tales take place in the present, in the past, in the USA, in England . . . in other words, there is something for everyone! Best yet, profits from the sales of this novel will go to breast cancer prevention.

A stellar anthology that had me laughing, sighing in pleasure, believing in magic, and left me begging for more! This is one novel that will go directly to my 'Keeper' shelf, to be read over and over again. Very highly recommended!

~ *Detra Fitch, Huntress Reviews*

* * * *

No Law Against Love 2 - I'm sure you've heard about some of those silly laws, right? Well, this anthology shows us that sometimes those silly laws can bring just the right people together.

I highly recommend this anthology. Each story is a gem and each author has certainly given their readers value for money.

~ *Valerie, Love Romances and More*

Be sure to check our website often

http://highlandpress.org

Ann Merritt

CPSIA information can be obtained at www.ICGtesting.com
224840LV00003B/55/P